The Landmark Library
No. 36
THE MERCY OF ALLAH

The Landmark Library

OLIVER ONIONS
The Story of Louie
In Accordance with the Evidence · The Debit Account
The Story of Ragged Robyn · Widdershins

GEORGE MOORE
Celibate Lives · Conversations in Ebury Street

ARNOLD BENNETT
Mr Prohack · The Grand Babylon Hotel

C. H. B. KITCHIN
The Auction Sale · Streamers Waving

MARGARET IRWIN
Still She Wished for Company

ANN BRIDGE
The Ginger Griffin

CHARLES MORGAN
The Gunroom

C. E. MONTAGUE
Rough Justice

FR. ROLFE
Don Tarquinio

T. H. WHITE
They Winter Abroad

S. BARING-GOULD
Mehalah

SHANE LESLIE
The Oppidan

JOHN COLLIER
His Monkey Wife

HERBERT READ
The Green Child

COMPTON MACKENZIE
Extremes Meet

WILLIAM PLOMER
The Case is Altered

ENID BAGNOLD
The Loved and Envied

L. A. G. STRONG
The Brothers

ERIC LINKLATER
Mr Byculla

JAMES HANLEY
The Closed Harbour

AUBREY MENEN
The Prevalence of Witches

T. F. POWYS
The Left Leg

SUSAN ERTZ
Julian Probert

MARK RUTHERFORD
The Revolution in
Tanner's Lane

WINSTON CLEWES
The Violent Friends

W. E. HORNUNG
Raffles:
The Amateur Cracksman

DAVID GARNETT
The Grasshoppers Come and
Beany-Eye

HILAIRE BELLOC
The Mercy of Allah

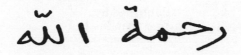

THAT IS:

THE MERCY OF ALLAH

HILAIRE BELLOC

CHATTO & WINDUS
LONDON

Published by
Chatto & Windus Ltd
London

*

Clarke, Irwin & Co. Ltd
Toronto

First published in 1922
This edition first published in 1973

ISBN 0 7011 2001 0

Printed in Great Britain by
Redwood Press Limited,
Trowbridge, Wiltshire

TO

ORIANA HUXLEY HAYNES

CONTENTS

CHAP.   PAGE

    I "*AL-RAFSAT*," OR THE KICK   3

   II *AL-DURAR*, OR THE PEARLS   25

  III *AL-TAWAJIN*, OR THE PIPKINS   41

  IV *AL-KANTARA*, OR THE BRIDGE   57

   V '*MILH*,' OR "SALT"   83

  VI *AL-WUKALÁ*, OR "THE LAWYERS"   109

 VII *GHANAMAT*, OR THE SHEEP   143

VIII *AL-BUSTÁN*, OR THE ORCHARD   161

  IX CAMELS AND DATES   191

   X *AL-HISÁN*, OR THE HORSE   209

  XI *AL-WALI*, OR THE HOLY ONE   227

 XII THE NEW QUARTER OF THE CITY   243

XIII THE MONEY MADE OF PAPER   273

 XIV THE PEACE OF THE SOUL   299

الرّفسة

AL-RAFSAT

That is:

"The Kick"

CHAPTER I

I

IN the days of Abd-er-Rahman, who was among the wisest and most glorious of the Commanders of the Faithful, there resided in the City of Bagdad an elderly merchant of such enormous wealth that his lightest expressions of opinion caused the markets of the Euphrates to fluctuate in the most alarming manner.

This merchant, whose name was Mahmoud, had a brother in the middle ranks of Society, a surgeon by profession, and by name El-Hakim. To this brother he had frequently expressed a fixed determination to leave him no wealth of any kind. " It is my opinion," he would say, " that a man's first duty is to his own children, and though I have no children myself, I must observe the general rule." He was fond of dilating upon this subject whenever he came across his relative, and would discover from time to time new and still better reasons for the resolution he had arrived at. His brother received with great courtesy the prospect held out to him by the wealthy merchant ; but one day, finding tedious the hundredth repetition of that person's pious but somewhat wearisome resolve, said to him :

" Mahmoud, though it would be a mean and even

3

an impious thing to expect an inheritance from you to any of my seven sons, yet perhaps you will allow these boys to receive from your lips some hint as to the manner in which you have accumulated that great wealth which you now so deservedly enjoy."

" By all means," said Mahmoud, who was ever ready to describe his own talents and success. " Send the little fellows round to me to-morrow about the hour the public executions take place before the Palace, for by that time I shall have breakfasted, and shall be ready to receive them."

The Surgeon, with profuse thanks, left his brother and conveyed the good news to the seven lads, who stood in order before him with the respect for parents customary in the Orient, each placed according to his size and running in gradation from eight to sixteen years of age.

Upon the morrow, therefore, the Surgeon's seven sons, seated gravely upon crossed legs, formed a semi-circle at the feet of their revered relative, who, when he had watched them humorously and in silence for some moments, puffing at his great pipe, opened his lips and spoke as follows :

" Your father has wondered, my dear nephews, in what way the fortune I enjoy has been acquired ; for in his own honourable but far from lucrative walk of life, sums which are to me but daily trifles appear like the ransoms of kings. To you, his numerous family, it seems of especial advantage that the road to riches should be discovered. Now I will confess to you, my dear lads, that I am quite ignorant of any rule or plan whereby the perishable goods of this world may be rapidly accumulated in the hands of the Faithful. Nay, did any such rule exist, I am persuaded that by

this time the knowledge of it would be so widely diffused
as to embrace the whole human race. In which case,"
he added, puffing meditatively at his pipe, " all would
cancel out and no result would be achieved ; since a
great fortune, as I need not inform young people of
your sagacity, is hardly to be acquired save at the
expense of others.

" But though I cannot give you those rules for which
your father was seeking when he sent you hither, I
can detail you the steps by which my present affluence
was achieved ; and each of you, according to his
intelligence, will appreciate what sort of accidents may
make for the increase of fortune. When you are
possessed of this knowledge it will serve you through
life for recreation and amusement, though I very much
doubt its making you any richer. For it is not the
method nor even the opportunity of intelligent acqui-
sition which lead to great riches, but two other things
combined : one, the unceasing appetite to snatch and
hold from all and at every season ; the other, that
profound mystery, the Mercy of God.

" For Allah, in his inscrutable choice, frowns on
some and smiles on others. The first he condemns to
contempt, anxiety, duns, bills, Courts of law, sudden
changes of residence and even dungeons ; the second
he gratifies with luxurious vehicles, delicious sherbet
and enormous houses, such as mine. His will be
done.

" A dear friend of mine, one Moshé, was a receiver
of stolen goods in Bosra, until God took him, now
twenty years ago. He left two sons of equal intelligence and rapacity. The one, after numerous degrada-
tions, died of starvation in Armenia ; the other, of
no greater skill, is to-day governor of all Algeirah and

rings the changes at will upon the public purse. *Mektub.*"

For a moment the ancient Captain of Industry paused with bent head in solemn meditation upon the designs of Heaven, then raising his features protested that he had too long delayed the story of his life, with which he would at once proceed.

*   *   *   *   *

" As a boy, my dear nephews," began the kindly uncle, while his dutiful nephews regarded him with round eyes, " I was shy, dirty, ignorant, lazy, and wilful. My parents and teachers had but to give me an order for me to conceive at once some plan of disobeying it. All forms of activity save those connected with dissipation were abhorrent to me. So far from reciting with other boys of my age in chorus and without fault the verses of the Koran, I grew up completely ignorant of that work, the most Solemn Name in which I to this day pronounce with an aspirate from an unfamiliarity with its aspect upon the written page. Yet I am glad to say that I never neglected my religious duties, that I prayed with fervour and regularity, and that I had a singular faith in the loving kindness of my God.

" I had already reached my seventeenth year when my father, who had carefully watched the trend of my nature and the use to which I had put my faculties, addressed me as follows :

" ' Mahmoud, I wish you no ill. I have so far fed and clothed you because the Caliph (whom Allah preserve !) has caused those who neglect their younger offspring to be severely beaten upon the soles of their feet. It is now my intention to send you about your business. I propose '—and here my dear father pulled

out a small purse—' to give you the smallest sum com-
patible with my own interests, so that if any harm
befall you, the vigilant officers of the Crown cannot
ascribe your disaster to my neglect. I request that
you will walk in any direction you choose so only
that it be in a straight line away from my doors. If,
when this your patrimony is spent, you make away with
yourself I shall hold you to blame; I shall be better
pleased to hear that you have sold yourself into slavery
or in some other way provided for your continued
sustenance. But what I should like best would be
never to hear of you again.' With those words my
father (your grandfather, dear boys), seizing me by
the shoulders, turned my back to his doors and thrust
me forth with a hearty kick the better to emphasize
his meaning.

" Thus was I launched out in the dawn of manhood
to try my adventures with the world.

" I discovered in my pouch as I set out along the
streets of the city the sum of 100 dinars, with which
my thoughtful parent had provided me under the
legal compulsion which he so feelingly described.
' With so large a capital,' said I to myself, ' I can exist
for several days, indulge my favourite forms of dissipation, and when they are well spent it will be time
enough to think of some experiment whereby to replace
them.' "

Here the eldest nephew said respectfully and with an
inclination of the head : " Pray, uncle, what is a
dinar ? "

" My dear lad," replied the merchant with a merry
laugh, " I confess that to a man of my position a reply
to your question is impossible. I could only tell you
that it is a coin of considerable value to the impover-

ished, but to men like myself a denomination so inferior as to be indistinguishable from all other coins."

Having so expressed himself the worthy merchant resumed the thread of his tale :

" I had, I say, started forward in high spirits to the sound of the coins jingling in my pouch, when my steps happened to take me to the water-side, where I found a ship about to sail for the Persian Gulf. ' Here,' said I to myself, ' is an excellent opportunity for travelling and for seeing the world.'

" The heat of the day was rising. No one was about but two watermen, who lay dozing upon the bank. I nimbly stepped aboard and hid myself behind one of the bales of goods with which the deck was packed. When the sun declined and work was resumed, the sailors tramped aboard, the sail was hoisted, and we started upon our journey.

" Befriended by the darkness of night I crept out quietly from my hiding-place and found a man watching over the prow, where he was deputed to try the depth of the water from time to time with a long pole. I affected an air of authority, and told him that the Captain had sent me forward to deliver his commands, which were that he should give me a flask of wine, some fruit, and a cake (for I guessed that like all sailors he had in his possession things both lawful and unlawful). These I told him I would take to my relative the Captain. He left me with the pole for a moment and soon returned with the provisions, with which I crept back to my hiding-place, and there heartily consumed them.

" During the whole of the next day I lay sleeping behind the bales of goods. With the fall of the second night I needed a second meal. I dared not

repeat my first experiment, and lay musing till, hunger
having sharpened my wits, I hit upon a plan with
which surely Providence itself must have inspired a
poor lonely lad thrown in his unaided weakness upon
a cruel world.

" I bethought me that the watchman of either
board would have some provision for the night. I
remembered a sort of gangway between the high bales
upon the main deck, which corridor led back far under
the poop into the stern sheets. It had been so
designed for the convenience of stowing and unloading,
affording a passage for the workmen as they handled
the cargo. I put these two things together in my
mind (but to God be the glory) and formed of them
a plan for immediate execution.

" I crept from my hiding-place and sauntered along
the dark deck until I came upon the watchman,
squatting by the rail, and contemplating the stars in
the moonless sky. He had, as I had suspected, a platter
the white of which I could just see glimmering against
the deck beside him. I thought I also discerned a
gourd of wine. I approached him as one of the crew
(for they were chance strangers taken on at the wharf).
We talked in low tones of the girls of Bagdad, of the
police, of opportunities for theft, and of such other
topics as are common to the poor, till, naturally, we
came to wine. He cursed the poor quality of his own,
in the gourd beside him. I, after some mystery,
confided to him that I had a stock of excellent wine,
and, as my friendship for him increased, I made a
clean breast of it and told him it was in the stern
sheets, far under the poop deck along the narrow passage
between the high bales. I offered to go with him and
fetch it, allowing him, in his eagerness, to go first.

When he was well engaged in groping aft I turned, crept forward again silently and rapidly, picked up the loaf and cheese which I found on his platter, as also the gourd, and vanished into my hiding-hole.

" I ate my fill—though somewhat too hurriedly, and remarked how long a time my shipmate was spending at searching that empty place. As I heard him creeping back at last cursing violently in whispers, I was aware of faint dawn in the East, and determined that my cruise must end.

" We were already in the neighbourhood of the sea, as I discovered by tasting the water over the side in the darkness and discovering it to be brackish. I bethought me that my poor comrade had now an excellent reason for ferretting me out, that the Captain also would soon hear of me and that, with daylight, I should certainly be visited with a bastinado or put into chains and sold. I therefore slipped over the side (for I was an excellent swimmer) and made for the shore. There I lay on a warm beach and watched through the reeds the great sail of the ship as it slipped down-stream further and further away in the growing light.

" When the sun rose the vessel was out of sight, and looking about me I discovered a little village not far from the shore inhabited by simple fishermen, but containing several houses of some pretension, the residences of wealthy merchants who came here from Bosra in their moments of leisure to relax themselves from the catch-as-catch-can of commerce in that neighbouring city.

" My first action at the opening of the new day was to fall upon my knees and add to the ritual prayer a humble outpouring of thanks for the benefits I

had already received and a fervent appeal for guidance.
That appeal was heard. I rose from my knees full
of a new-found plan.

"To one of those wealthier houses which stood
near the village I at once proceeded and sent in a
message by a slave to its owner saying that my master,
a wealthy dealer in carpets, solicited the custom of
his lordship, and that if the great man would but
accompany me to the quay I would there show
him wares well worthy of his attention.

"It so happened (and here was Providence again
at work) that this merchant had a passion for a particular sort of carpet which is solely made by the
inhabitants of El Kzar, for they alone possess the secret,
which they very zealously guard. The slave, therefore, brought me back the message that his master
would not be at the pains of accompanying me unless
such wares were present for his inspection. If my
carpets were those of El Kzar he would willingly inspect
them, but if they were of any other brand he was
indifferent.

"And let this teach you, my dear nephews, how
simple are the minds of the rich.

"I was willing enough that the carpets should be
carpets of El Kzar, or, indeed, of any other place under
heaven, for all were at my choice.

"I hastened, therefore, to send back a further
message that by a curious coincidence we had upon
this occasion nothing else in stock but Kzaran carpets,
and begged the slave to emphasize this important
point to his master.

"His reply was to twist his right hand, palm upwards,
with a strange smile. I pulled out my purse, showed
him the shining dinars, and asked him whether he

would rather have *one* now for his fee or *five* on the completion of the transaction ? With glistening eyes—and even (as I thought) a pathetic gratitude—the slave leapt at the latter offer.

" And let this teach you, my dear nephews, how simple are the minds of the poor.

" He hastened off to deliver my message.

" Within a few moments the master of the house appeared in great haste, and all of a fever bade me lead him to the appointed spot."

At this moment the merchant paused and with reverie and reminiscence in his eye remained silent for at least that space of time in which a dexterous pick-pocket may gingerly withdraw a purse from the sleeve of a Holy Man. The second nephew thought the opportunity arrived to suggest a doubt which had been vexing his young mind. He said with an obeisance :

" Venerable uncle, we have listened to the beginnings of your career with admiration and respect, but we are more perplexed than ever to discover how such beginnings could have led to such an end. For you appear to us as yet only to have followed that path which leads to the torturers and the bow-strings."

" Such," replied his uncle, with a look of singular affection, " is the general opinion entertained of all very wealthy men in the first step of their careers; but I hope that the sequel will teach you and your clever little brothers how wrongly informed are the vulgar."

As the Merchant Mahmoud pronounced these words the Call to Prayer was heard from a neighbouring tower, and he hurriedly concluded :

" My dear nephews, we are called to prayer. I

will cease here to speak and will continue to-morrow the story of Myself and Providence."

Upon hearing these words his seven nephews rose together, and crossed their arms ; following which gesture, with three deep bows performed as they walked backwards toward the curtains of the magnificent apartment, they left their uncle's presence.

*   *   *   *   *

" You will remember, my dear nephews," said the Merchant Mahmoud when the lads were once more assembled in a half-circle before him with crossed legs and attentive countenances, " that you left me hurrying with the collector of Kzaran carpets towards the quay where he should enjoy the sight of the merchandise. This merchant was reputed among the people of the place to be of a singularly cunning and secretive temperament, a character which (you may think it strange !) they admired as though it were the summit of human wisdom. I confess that I found him, in the matter of Kzaran carpets at least, very different from his reputation. A more garrulous old gentleman never trod this earth. He was in a perpetual stammer of excitement, and though I was careful to lead him by the most roundabout roads that he might have time to cool his ardour, the delay did but seem to increase it.

" ' I implore you, sir,' he said at last, as one who could no longer restrain some violent passion, ' I implore you, pay no attention to others in this place who may have attempted to forestall me in the matter of your very valuable cargo. Your honour is, I know, sufficient in the matter. . . . I am confident you will give me a free market. Also, they know nothing of Kzaran carpets in these parts : they are mere buyers and sellers . . . and on what a margin ! Let me tell

you in your ear that while many men in this place
carry on the appearance of riches, most are indebted
to Parsees in the capital.   I alone am in an independent position and ' (here he whispered) ' I can well
reward you *privately* and *in your own pocket* for any
favour you may show me.'

" Seeing him so eager, I affected a certain hesitation and embarrassment, and at last confessed that
I had been approached by a local merchant whose
name I was forbidden to mention and who had very
kindly sent me as a present by a slave the sum of 1,000
dinars.   To this he had attached no conditions, but
he had also, quite independently, sent word that he
had himself orders for carpets which he was bound to
fulfil.   His profit (he had said), if I would give him
a first choice, would be so considerable that he would
be very ready to offer me a handsome commission on
the completion of the bargain ; quite apart from the
1,000 dinars which were but a little present from one
man to another.   ' This thousand dinars,' I added,
' now in my possession, I have accepted.   A present
is a graceful act and can be taken with a clean con-
science.   But the *commission* is another matter.   I
must consider beyond everything the interests of my
master.   I shall not mention the offer made to me (for
with all his confidence in me he is himself a business
man and might misunderstand my position), but I
shall think it my duty to give him no advice save to
sell to the highest bidder.'

" ' It is I ! ' shouted the aged connoisseur eagerly,
' it is I who will prove the highest bidder !   Nay, my
dear fellow, since such bargains are often concluded in
private, would it not be better to tell your master
forthwith that no possible competitor can stand against

me in this place ? Let him first discover the sum
offered by my rival and I give you leave to suggest
a sum larger by one-tenth, which shall decide his
judgment. Meanwhile,' he added, ' two thousand
dinars are but a small present for one in your position,
and I shall willingly—joyfully—propose to give you
that sum, not for a moment on account of the service
which I am certain you design to do me, but purely
as an expression of my esteem.'

" His excitement had now so risen that I fear his
judgment was lost. Already he saw before him in
his mind's eye a pile of the noblest Kzaran carpets, all
ready for the caravan. Already he saw a rival calmly
acquiring them on the distant wharf, the witnesses
placing their seals, the words of completion.

" He trembled as again he urged on me the little
gift, the little personal gift, the trifling gift of 2,000
dinars.

" ' Sir,' said I in reply, a little stiffly, ' I am not
accustomed to take secret commissions under any
disguise. My duty is clear : if I cannot receive a firm
offer superior to that already made me, and that
backed with proof that you are indeed, as you say, the
most solid man in the place—then I must close with
my first client. If indeed I were certain of an immediate
payment in a larger sum I would accept your proposal.
But how can I know anything of this place ? The
thousand dinars of which I spoke are coined and in a
wallet ; I have them safe. With all the respect due
to your age, I have no information upon your credit
in this town. And I confess,' I added in another tone,
' that I *am* acquainted with your rival's position, which
is perhaps more solid than you think. I confess I
think it would be simpler and to the better interest

of our house if I were to go straight to him now and have done with it.'

" As I spoke thus the old man lost all reason. It was piteous to see one of his age and venerable hairs dancing and spluttering with excitement. He shook his fists in the air, he called to Heaven in shrill tones, he betrayed all the frenzy of the collector. He contrasted the mercantile motives of the unknown competitor with his own passion for Pure Art. He called Heaven to witness to the reality of his wealth, and at last in a sort of fury tore from his garments the jewels which ornamented them, thrust into my hand all the cash upon his person (it was in a leather bag, and amounted altogether to no more than 500 dinars), added to this a brooch of gold, which he dragged from his scarf, and said that if this instalment were not a sufficient proof of his good faith and credit he knew not how to move' me.

" I shrugged my shoulders and suggested that instead of making so violent a protestation and at such risk to his fortune he should go back soberly to his house and return with an instrument of credit and two witnesses (as the law demands), while I awaited him patiently at that spot. I, at least, was in no haste and would honourably abide his return. He was off at a speed which I should never have thought possible at his age.

" I waited until he had turned the corner of a distant hedge of prickly pears, and not until he was quite out of sight did I gather the jewels, the coins, and the precious ornaments which in his haste he had thrown at my feet, and very rapidly betake myself in the opposite direction.

" Never was the Mercy of Allah more evidently

extended. The plain was naked outside the town, the
river perhaps a mile distant ; my plight, as it might
appear, desperate. I pinned the gold brooch to my
cloak, I distributed the jewels openly upon various
parts of my person, and I proceeded at a smart pace
over the open plain towards the river. It was with
the greatest joy that I found upon its bank two fishermen about to set sail and proceed down-stream to
sea. Their presence inspired me with a plan for escape.

" I chatted negligently with them (still keeping
one eye upon the distant house of my aged but
excitable friend). At last with a light laugh I offered
one of them a piece of gold, saying that I should be
pleased to try the novel experience of a little cruise.
The fisherman, who was quite unacquainted with so
much wealth, and seemed somewhat awestruck, gave
me some grand title or other, and promised me very
good sport with the fish and a novel entertainment.
But even as he and his companion pushed out from
shore I turned in my seat on the deck and perceived in
the plain a rising dust which betrayed the approach
of the merchant with his witnesses and a company of his
slaves.

" Suddenly changing my expression from one of
pleased though wearied expectancy to one of acute
alarm, I shouted to my new companions : ' Push away
for your lives and stretch your sail to its utmost !
These are the Commissioners sent by the Caliph to
re-assess and tax all fishing-boats upon a new valuation ! Already had they seized three upon the beach
when I left and found you here ! '

" At these words the worthy fellows were inspired
by a fear even greater than my own. They manfully
pushed into the swiftest part of the current, and,

though a smart breeze was blowing, hoisted every inch of the sail, so that the boat ran with her gunwale upon the very edge of the water and was indeed dangerously pressed. But I had the satisfaction of seeing the merchant and his retinue vainly descending the river-bank, at perhaps one-half our speed, calling down curses upon us, threatening with their fists, shouting their public titles of authority, their menaces of the law, and in every way confirming my excellent pair of fishermen in the story I had told them.

" It was a pleasant thing to loll on deck under the heat of the day, toying with the valuable ornaments I had so recently acquired and lazily watching my companions as they sweated at the halyards, or alternatively glancing along towards the shore at the little group of disappointed people which fell so rapidly behind us as we bowled down the tide. Soon their features were no longer plain, then their figures could scarcely be distinguished. The last impression conveyed to me was of some little very distant thing, stamping with impotent rage and shaking wild arms against the sky. I could not but deplore so grievous a lapse in dignity in one so venerable.

" When we were well away from the neighbourhood of the city I asked the fishermen whither they were bound ; to which they answered that their business was only to cruise about outside and fish during the night, returning at dawn with their catch. ' Would it not be better,' I suggested, ' seeing that these rapacious fellows will hang about for a day or so, to carry me to some town of your acquaintance along the coast where the reigning powers do not suffer from the tyranny of Bagdad ? For my part I am free to travel where I will, and the prospect of a change pleases me

I shall be happy,' said I, ' to reward the sacrifice of your catch with fifty dinars.'

" At the prospect of much further wealth the fishermen were at once convinced : they sang in the lightness of their hearts, and for three days and three nights we sped down the Gulf, passing bleak mountains and deserted rocky promontories, until upon the fourth day we came to a town the like of which I had never seen.

" ' Shall we land here ? ' said I.

" ' No,' said the fishermen, ' for it is in a manner within the Caliph's dominions, and perhaps that accursed tax of which you spoke will be levied here also.'

" ' You know better than I,' replied I thoughtfully standing for a moment in affected perplexity. ' Let me, however, land in your little boat. I have a passion for new places. I will come out to you again after the hour of the mid-day prayers, while you stand in the offing.'

" To this arrangement they readily consented. I rowed to the land, and when I had reached the shore I was pleased to see my fearful hosts quite three miles out upon the hot and shimmering sea. Gazing at them, I hope with charity, and certainly with interest, I pushed the little boat adrift (for I had no reason to return to those poor people) and made my way inland. I disposed of my jewellery at prices neither low nor high with local merchants. I preserved the old fellow's golden brooch, which I imagined (for I am a trifle weak and superstitious) might bring me good fortune, and when all my transactions were accomplished I counted my total capital, and found myself in possession of no less than 1,500 dinars. The cold of the

evening had come by the time my accounts were
settled and the strings of my pouch were drawn. I set
myself under an arbour where a delicious fountain
played in the light of the setting sun, which shone over
the waters of the sea, and drinking some local beverage
the name of which I knew not, but the taste and effect
of which were equally pleasing, I reflected upon my
increase of fortune.

" ' You left home, Mahmoud,' said I to myself,
' with one hundred dinars, of which your excellent and
careful father deprived himself rather than see you
face the world unarmed, or himself receive the bastinado.
You have been gone from home a week ; you are
perhaps some 800 miles from your native city ; your
capital has been multiplied fifteen-fold, and so far you
may look with an eager courage towards the further
adventures of your life, for very clearly the Mercy of
Allah is upon you.' "

At this moment a nasal hooting from the neighbouring turret warned the company to turn their thoughts
to heaven. The boys, who had sat fascinated by their
uncle's recital, knew that the end of their entertainment had come. The third son of the Surgeon was
therefore impatient to exclaim (as he hurriedly did) :
" But, dear uncle, though we see that a certain chance
favoured you, and not only your native talents, yet
we do not perceive how all this led to any main road
to fortune."

" My boy," said the Merchant Mahmoud, pensively
stroking his beard and gazing vacuously over the heads
of the youngsters, " I do not pretend to unfold you
any such plan. Have I not told you that did such a
plan exist all would be in possession of it ? I am but
retailing you in my humble fashion the steps by which

one merchant in this city has been raised by the Infinite Goodness of the Merciful (His name be adored !) from poverty to riches. . . . But the call for prayer has already been heard and we must part.   Upon this same day of next week, shortly after the last of the public executions has been bungled, you shall again come and hear me recite the next chapter of my varied career."

الدَّرَر

AL-DURAR

That is:
"THE PEARLS"

CHAPTER II

ENTITLED *AL-DURAR*, OR THE PEARLS

A WEEK later, at the hour of Public Executions and Beheadings, the seven boys were again assembled cross-legged at the feet of their revered uncle, who, when he had refreshed them with cold water, and himself with a curious concoction of fermented barley, addressed them as follows :

" You will remember, my lads, how I was left cut off from my dear home and from all companions, in a strange country, and with no more than 1,500 dinars with which to face the world. This sum may seem to you large, but I can assure you that to the operations of commerce " (and here the merchant yawned) " it is but a drop in the ocean ; and I had already so far advanced during one brief week in my character of Financier that I gloomily considered how small a sum that 1,500 was wherewith to meet the cunning, the gluttony, and the avarice of this great world. But a brief sleep (which I took under a Baobab tree to save the cost of lodging) refreshed at once my body and my intelligence, and with the next morning I was ready to meet the world."

Here the merchant coughed slightly, and addressing his nephews said : " You have doubtless been instructed at school upon the nature of the Baobab ? "

" We have," replied his nephews, and they recited

25

in chorus the description which they had been taught
by heart from the text-books of their Academy.

" I am pleased," replied their uncle, smiling, " to discover you thus informed. You will appreciate how
ample a roof this singular vegetable affords.

" Well, I proceeded under the morning sun through
a pleasantly wooded and rising country, considering
by what contrivance of usury or deceit I might next
increase my capital, when I saw in the distance the
groves and white buildings of an unwalled town, to
which (since large places, especially if they are not war-
like, furnish the best field for the enterprise of a Captain
of Industry) I proceeded ; . . . and there, by the Mercy
of Allah, there befell me as singular an adventure as
perhaps ever has fallen to the lot of man.

" I had not taken up my place in the local caravan-
serai for more than an hour—I had met no likely fool,
and my plans for the future were still vague in my
head—when an old gentleman of great dignity, followed
by an obsequious officer and no less than six Ethiopian
slaves, approached me with deep reverence, and prof-
fering me a leathern pouch, of a foreign kind, the like
of which I had never seen before, asked me whether
I were not the young man who had inadvertently left
it upon a prayer-stone at a shrine outside the city.

" I seized the pouch with an eager air, held it up
in transports of joy, and kissing it again and again
said, ' Oh ! my benefactor ! How can I sufficiently
thank you ! It is my father's last gift to me and is
all my viaticum as well ! ' with which I fell to kissing
and fondling it again, pressing it to my heart and so
discovered it to be filled with coins—as indeed I had
suspected it to be.

" Into so active an emotion had I roused myself

that my eyes filled with tears, and the good old man himself was greatly affected. ' I must warn you, young stranger,' he said paternally, ' against this thoughtlessness so common in youth ! A great loss indeed had it been for you, if we had not had the good fortune to recover your property.'

" You may imagine my confusion, my dear nephews, at finding that I had been guilty of so intolerable a fault. I blushed with confusion ; I most heartily thanked the old gentleman, not for his integrity (which it would have been insulting to mention to one of his great wealth) but for the pains he had taken to seek out a careless young man and to prevent his suffering loss.

" ' Nay,' said that aged gentleman to me with a low and pleasant laugh, ' you must not thank me. Perhaps had I myself come upon the treasure I might have thought it too insignificant to restore. But you must know that I am the Chief Magistrate of this city and that last evening my officer noticed from some distance a young man, apparently a stranger to this city, whom he describes as of your height and features, rise from the prayer-stone, but leave behind him some object which, in the gathering dusk, he could not distinguish. On his approach he found it was this purse of yours which some boys had already found and were quarrelling over, when he took it from them. He brought it to me with some description of your person : I thought you might well be at this caravan-serai and brought it with me : I had the pleasure of hearing my officer, who now accompanies me, recognize you as we approached.' That functionary bowed to me and I to him most ceremoniously, and as I did so I was rapidly revolving in my head what I had better do if the real owner should appear. I was torn between two plans : whether to denounce him as a thief before he could speak, or to run off at top speed.

" This preoccupation I dismissed lest the anxiety of it should appear upon my face.

" I again thanked this good old man most warmly, and we entered into a familiar conversation. What was my delight at the close of it when he bade me without ceremony accept of his hospitality and come home to take a meal with him in his palace. I was eager for further adventures, and accompanied him with the greatest joy.

" Reclining at table, where there was served (as I need hardly inform my dear nephews) lamb stuffed with pistachio nuts, the old man asked me whence I had come, what was my trade, and whither I was proceeding.

" I answered (as I thought, prudently) that I had come from Aleppo, that I had been entrusted by my father with the sum in the purse he had so kindly restored to me, in order to purchase pearls, and that when the purchase was completed I had instructions to sell them in India in a market where my father was assured that pearls were rare and fetched the highest prices.

" ' This is indeed well found ! ' exclaimed the old man, with enthusiasm. ' I am myself seeking for some one to whom I may sell a magnificent collection of pearls inherited from my great-grandmother, an Indian Begum. The old woman,' he added nonchalantly enough, ' was a miser ; she kept the drops higgledy-piggledy in an old cedarwood box, and I confess myself quite ignorant of their value. Moreover, as I have taken a liking to you, I shall let you fix your own price, for I should much like to remember when my time comes that I had helped a friendless man in his first step to fortune; only, I am a little ashamed to appear to be making money out of an heirloom!'

" While the old gentleman so spoke I was rapidly revolving in my mind what motive he could have for such an affectation of indifference to wealth, when I recollected that he was the Chief Magistrate of the city, and immediately concluded that these pearls, being the property of local people, and obtained by him for nothing by way of bribes and other legal channels, he would both desire to have them sold at a distance and would let them go cheap.

" ' Nay,' continued he, seeing that I hesitated as these thoughts occurred to me, ' I will take no denial. For me it is but a mere riddance, and for you a most excellent bargain. Come, I trust your honest face and youthful candour. You shall take them at your own price! And I will even advise you of the city of India where you will find your best market.'

" Put thus, the offer, I will confess, attracted me; but I had already learned the wickedness of mankind (though not as yet, I am glad to say, my dear nephews, at my own expense), and I said that I would at least so far meet him as to take the jewels to a local merchant, invent some tale, as though they were my own, and see what sum might be offered for them. Only when I thus had some measure of their value could I honourably make an offer. I continued at some length in this strain, expressing a humble inability to judge, and the fear lest my capital might not be sufficient (which he pooh-poohed). I stipulated, for a reason you will soon perceive, that a slave of his should accompany me—if only as a matter of routine

—for (said I) I was very jealous of my honour. He agreed, though he was good enough to call it a pure formality.

" I left the aged magistrate with many thanks and, accompanied by the slave, proceeded with the pearls to the jewel merchants' quarter in the Bazaar. I stopped before one of the richest and most reputed booths, and spreading the pearls before the merchant told him that I was compelled to sell these under order from authority as the end of a family dispute, to pay the dowry of my sister ; that I therefore was in haste to settle and would take the least price he might choose to mention within reason. I was, said I, wholly in his hands. It was urgent for me that the bargain should be quickly completed, but before I could receive his cash I must hear the lowest figure he would name.

" While I thus spoke the slave stood respectfully behind me and listened to our conversation. The jewel merchant said that no class of merchandise was more distasteful to him than pearls ; there was at this moment no market for them. It was impossible to purchase them save properly set and in regular sizes ; and finally it was well known that pearls were the most unlucky of gems. It was quite impossible for him to offer more than 10,000 dinars, and even so he would doubtless be the loser by the transaction.

" When I heard this I rapidly wrote upon a slip of paper the following words :

" ' MY LORD,—The chief merchant in this city estimates your jewels at 10,000 dinars. I cannot, alas, provide that sum, and therefore I cannot honestly make an offer myself as I had hoped ; if you desire to have them sold here I will faithfully execute your commission, but if you prefer that I should return them to you send me word. Meanwhile, I will still bargain here awaiting your reply.'

" I sent this note by the slave and begged him to give it to his master and to bring me an answer. The slave went off, and when I judged him to be well out of hearing I turned and said to the merchant, sighing : ' Well, since you offer no more I must take what you offer ; the slave whom you saw me despatch carried the news to my family ; I burn when I think of how their scorn will mock my humiliation. I therefore said nothing true of the price. Indeed, I have set it down in that note as something much higher. But I submit, for, as I told you, I am pressed. Come, count me the money, and I will away.'

" The merchant, after I had handed over the pearls, counted me the money into yet another large leathern bag, which I shouldered, and with rapid steps bore out of the Bazaar and soon out of the town itself, by a gate called the Bab-el-Jaffur, that is, the gate of innocence.

" Beyond the town walls was a long roll of dusty sloping land set here and there with dusty stunted bushes and having beyond it a high range of desert hills. A track led roughly rising across it, away from the town.

" I followed this track for one hour and then sat down (for my new fortune was heavy) and rested.

" As I thought it probable that my good old friend himself would return speedily with his slave to the Bazaar, and as the complication of the affair might embroil me, I hid during the remainder of the day squeezed in a jackal's earth beneath a bank. Before nightfall I ventured out and gazed about me, leaving my original pouch, my windfall and my big leathern bag of 10,000 dinars in the jackal's earth while I surveyed the track.

" It was the hour I love above all others.

" The sun had just set beyond the distant ocean towards which my face was turned, and between me and which, upon the plain below—for I had come to the rise of the mountain side—lay the beautiful city I had just left. The fragrant smoke of cedar wood rose from some of its roofs as the evening fell. There was still hanging in the air the coloured dust of evening above the roads of entry, and there came faintly through the distance the cry of the muezzin.

" I was not so entranced by the natural beauty of the scene as to neglect the duty which this sound recalled. I fell immediately upon my knees and was careful to add to the accustomed prayers of that hour my heart-felt thanks for the Guidance and the Grace which had so singularly increased my fortunes in the last few hours.

" As I rose from these devotions I heard upon my right a low wailing sound and was astonished to discover there, seated hopelessly beneath a small shrub and waving his hands in grief, a young man of much my own height and appearance : but I flatter myself that not even in my most careful assumptions of innocence have I ever worn such a booby face.

" He was swaying slowly from side to side, and as he did so moaning a ceaseless plaint, the words of which I caught and which touched me to the heart. Over and over again he recited his irreparable loss. He had but that small sum ! It was his patrimony ! His sole security ! How should he answer for it ?

who should now support him ? or what should he do ?

" So he wailed to himself in miserable monotone till I could bear it no longer, for I saw that I had by a singular coincidence come upon that poor young man whose pouch I had been given in error by the magistrate of the city.

" I bowed before him. He noticed me listlessly enough and asked me what I would. I told him I thought I could give him comfort. Was it not he, said I, who had left a certain pouch (I carefully described it) containing sundry coins upon a prayer-stone outside the city at this very same sunset hour of the day before ? His despair was succeeded by a startling eagerness. He leapt to his feet, seized my arm, rose feverishly and implored me to tell him further.

" ' Alas,' I said, ' what I have to tell you is but little ! I fear to raise your hopes too high—but at any rate I can put you upon the track of your property.'

" ' Sir,' said he, resuming his hopeless tone for a moment, ' I have already done my best. I went to the Chief Magistrate of the city to claim it and was met by an officer of his who told me that the purse had already been delivered to its owner, suspected my claim and bade me return. But how shall I prove that it is mine, or how, indeed, receive it, since the abominable thief who took possession of it must by now be already far away ? '

" ' You do him an injustice,' said I. ' It is precisely of him whom you uncharitably call a thief that I would speak to you. You think that he is far away, whereas he is really at your hand whenever you choose to act, for this is the message that I bring you. He awaits you even now, and if you will present yourself to him he will restore your property.'

" ' How can you know this ? ' said the young man, gazing at me doubtfully. ' By what coincidence have you any knowledge of the affair ? '

" ' It is simple enough,' said I. ' This person to whom your purse was given, and I, were in the same inn. We fell to talking of our adventures along the road, for he also was a stranger, and he told me the singular tale how he had recovered from the authorities a purse which he honestly thought his own, for it was very like one which he himself possessed ; but that on finding his own purse later on in his wallet he was overwhelmed with regret at the thought of the loss he had occasioned ; at the same time he made me his confidant, telling me that he intended to restore it this very evening at sunset to the authorities and that any one claiming it after that hour and proving it was his could recover it at the public offices. But he warned me of one thing : the officers (he told me) were convinced (from what indication I know not, perhaps from the presence of something in the purse, or per- haps from something they had heard) that the owner dealt in *pearls.*'

" Here the young man interrupted me, and assured me he had never bought or sold pearls in his life, nor thought of doing so.

" I answered that no doubt this was so. But that when the authorities had a whim it was well to humour them. He would therefore do well to approach the officer who guarded the gate of the Chief Magistrate's house, with the simple words, ' I am the Seller of Pearls,' on hearing which his path would be made smooth for him, and he would receive his belongings.

" The young man thanked me heartily; he even warmly embraced me for the good news I had given him, and felt, I fear, that his purse and his small fortune were already restored to him. It was a gallant sight to see him in the last of the light swinging down the mountain side with a new life in him, and I sincerely regretted from my heart the necessity under which I was to imperil his liberty and life. But you will agree with me, my dear nephews, that I could not possibly afford to have him at large.

" When he had gone and when it was fully night, there being no moon and only the stars in the warm dark sky, I rapidly took my burdens from their hiding-place and proceeded, though with some difficulty, up the mountain side, staggering under such a weight, and deviating from the track so that there should be less chance of finding myself interrupted.

" I slept for a few hours. I awoke at dawn. I counted my total fortune, and found that it was just about 12,000 dinars, the most of it in silver.

" Carefully concealing it again, I left its hiding-place and glided round the mountain until I came to a place where a new track began to appear, which led to a neighbouring village. Here I bought an ass, and returning with it to my hiding-place and setting my treasure upon it I went off at random to spend the day in travelling as rapidly as I might away from the neighbourhood by the most deserted regions.

" I came, a little before sunset, upon a hermit's cave, where I was hospitably entertained and the tenant of which refused all reward, asking me only to pray for him, as he was certain that the prayers of youth and innocence would merit him a high place in Heaven.

" With this holy man I remained for some four or

five days, passing my time at leisure in his retreat among the mountains, and feeding my donkey upon the dried grasses which I brought in by armfuls at dusk from the woodlands. Upon the fifth day of this concealment the hermit came in pensive and sad, and said to me :

" ' My son, with every day the wickedness of this world increases, and the judgment of God will surely fall upon it in a devastating fire ! I have but just heard that the Chief Magistrate of our capital city, using as a dupe an innocent stranger, sold to one of the great jewellers of the place for no less than 10,000 dinars a quantity of pearls, every one of which now turns out to be false and valueless ! Nay, I am told that the largest are made of nothing but wax ! And, what is worse, not content with this first wickedness, the magistrate under the plea that the young stranger had disappeared confiscated the gems again and had the poor merchant most severely beaten ! But— worse and worse ! the poor youth having innocently returned that very night to the city, was seized by the guard and beheaded. Ya, ya,' said the good old man, throwing up his hands, ' the days increase, and their evil increases with them ! ' "

At this moment the hoarse and discordant voice of the Public Crier croaked its first note from the neighbouring turret, and the nephews, who had sat enraptured at their uncle's tale, knew that it was time to disperse. The eldest brother therefore said :

" O uncle ; before we go let me express the thanks of all of us for your enrapturing story. But let me also express our bewilderment at the absence of all plan in your singular adventures. For though we have listened minutely to all you have said, we cannot dis-

cover what art you showed in the achievement of any
purpose.   For instance, how could you know that the
pearls were false ? "

" I did not know it, my dear nephew," replied the
great Merchant with beautiful simplicity, " and the
whole was the Mercy of Allah ! . . . But come, the
hour of prayer is announced, and we must, following
the invariable custom of the Faithful, make yet another
joint in my singular tale.   Come, therefore, on this day
week, shortly after the last of the public executions of
the vulgar, and I will tell you of my further fortunes :
for you must understand that the 12,000 dinars of
which my story now leaves me possessed are "—and
here the honest old man yawned again and waved
his hand—" but a flea-bite to a man like me."

His seven little nephews bowed repeatedly, and,
walking backwards without a trip, disappeared through
the costly tapestries of their uncle's apartments.

الطواجن

AL-TAWAJIN

That is:

"THE PIPKINS"

CHAPTER III

ON the appointed day of the next week, when, with the hour of public executions, the noonday amusements of the city come to an end, and the citizens betake themselves to the early afternoon's repose, the seven boys were once more seated in the presence of their uncle, whom they discovered in a radiant humour.

He welcomed them so warmly that they imagined for a moment he might be upon the point of offering them sherbet, sweetmeats, or even money ; they were undeceived, however, when the excellent but extremely wealthy old man, drawing his purse lovingly through his fingers, ordered to have poured out for each of them by a slave a further draught of delicious cold water, put himself at his ease for a long story, and resumed his tale :

" You will remember, my delightful nephews," he said, " how I found myself in the hermit's hut without a friend in the world, and with a capital of no more than twelve thousand dinars which I had carried thither in a sack upon donkey-back. Indeed, it was entirely due to the Mercy of Allah that my small capital was even as large as it was: for had the merchant in the bazaar discovered the pearls to be false he would not only have offered me far less but might possibly, after having disposed of the pearls, have given me over

41

to the police. As it was, Heaven had been kind to me, though not bountiful, and I still had to bethink me what to do next if I desired to increase my little treasure.

"Taking leave, therefore, of the good hermit, I pressed into his hand a small brass coin the superscription of which was unknown to me and which I therefore feared I might have some difficulty in passing. I assured my kind host that it was a coin of the second Caliph Omar and of value very far superior to any modern gold piece of a similar size. As the hermit like many other saintly men, was ignorant of letters his gratitude knew no bounds. He dismissed me with a blessing so long and complicated that I cannot but ascribe to it some part of the good fortune which next befell me.

"For you must know that when, after laying in stores at a neighbouring village, I had driven my donkey forward for nearly a week over barren and uninhabited mountains, and when I had nearly exhausted my provision of dried cakes and wine (a beverage which our religion allows us to consume when no one is by), I was delighted to come upon a fertile valley entirely closed in by high, precipitous cliffs save at one issue, where a rough track led from this enchanted region to the outer world. In this valley I discovered, to my astonishment, manners to be so primitive or intelligence so low that the whole art of money-dealing was ignored by the inhabitants and by the very Governors themselves.

"The King (who, I am glad to say, was of the Faithful) had, indeed, promulgated laws against certain forms of fraud which he imagined to be denounced in the Koran; but these were of so infantile a character that a man of judgment could very easily avoid them in any plans he might frame for the people's betterment and his own. The population consisted entirely of soldiers and rustics, among all of whom not one could be discovered capable of calculating with justice a compound interest for ten years.

" Under these circumstances my only difficulty lay in choosing what form my first enterprise should take. After a little thought I decided that what we call in Bagdad an Amalgamation of Competing Interests would be no bad beginning.

" I began with due caution by investing a couple of thousand dinars in the merchandise of a potter who had recently died and whose widow needed ready cash to satisfy the sacred demands of the dead. She spent the money in the ornamentation of his tomb, with which unproductive expenditure the foolish woman was in no small degree concerned."

Here the eldest of the nephews interrupted Mahmoud to ask, most respectfully, why with a capital of twelve thousand dinars he had used but two, and why he had begun his experiment upon the petty business of a poor widow.

" My son," said his uncle affectionately, " you do well to ask these questions. They show a reasoned interest in the great art of Getting. Well then, as to the smallness of my beginning, it was, I hope, due to humility. For ostentation is hateful. But a good deed is never thrown away—and how useful I found this reserve of ten thousand dinars (which I had in my meekness kept aside) you shall soon learn.

" As to why I began operations in the kiln of this poor widow, it was because I have ever loved the little ones of this world and aided them to my best endeavour. This charitable action also turned out to be wise, as such actions often do ; for I could thus proceed at first unnoticed and begin my new adventures without exciting any embarrassing attention.

" I continued to live in the same small hut I had hired on my arrival, under the floor of which I kept my modest capital ; and I put it about, as modesty demanded, that I was almost destitute.

" As it was indifferent to me for the moment whether I obtained a return upon this paltry investment or no, I was able to sell my wares at very much the same sum as they had cost me, and as I had bought the whole stock cheap, that sum was less than the cost of manufacture. There was a considerable store of pipkins in the old sheds, and while I sold them off at charitable rates (very disconcerting to other merchants), I had time to consider my next step.

" Upon this next step I soon determined. When, with due delay, my original stock of pipkins had been sold, I purchased a small consignment of clay, I relit the fires in the kiln, I hired a couple of starving potters, and I began to manufacture.

" The fame of my very cheap pipkins had spread, as was but natural, and secured me an increasing number of customers for my newly made wares. But I thought it wrong to debauch the peasants by selling them their pots under cost price any longer. I was constrained by the plainest rule of duty to raise my prices to the cost of manufacture—though no more, keeping Justice as my guiding star. For, depend upon it, my dear nephews, in business as in every other walk of life an exact rectitude alone can lead us to the most dazzling rewards.

" This price of mine was still lower than that of all the other pipkin-makers, who had been accustomed from

immemorial time to the base idea of profit, and were
in a perpetual surmise what secret powers I had to permit me such quotations. But I made no mystery of
the affair. I allowed all my friends to visit my simple
factory and I explained to their satisfaction how organ-
ization and a close attention to costings were sufficient
to account for my prosperity.

" Still, as my sales continued to grow, new doubts
arose, and with them, I am glad to say, new respect for
my skill in affairs.

" The simple folk wondered by what art I had con-
trived so difficult a financial operation, but as it was
traditional among them that one who sold goods cheap
was a benefactor to the community, my action was
lauded, my fame spread, and the number of my customers continually increased.

" You will not be slow to perceive, my dear boys,
that my competitors in the bazaar, being compelled to
compete with my ruinous prices, were all embarrassed,
and that the less attentive or privileged soon began to
fall into financial difficulties, the first of course being
those who were the most renowned among these sim-
pletons for their cunning, their silence, their lying,
and their commercial skill in general. These, as they
were perpetually trying new combinations to discover
or to defeat my supposed schemes, were an easy prey.
Even the straightforward fellows who knew of no art
more subtle than the charging of ten per cent. above
cost price, and who did not play into my hands by any
wearisome financial strategy, began to be roped into
my net as the area of my operations spread. For when
I had acquired, at a calculated loss, a good half of the
pottery business in this sequestered paradise, I could,
by what is known as the Fluctuation of the Market

(but I will not confuse you with technical terms), put my remaining competitors into alternate fevers of panic and expectation very destructive to a Sound Business Judgment.

" Upon one day I would declare that a large consignment of pottery being about to reach me, I could sell pipkins at half the usual price. Pipkins fell heavily, and I bought through my agent every pipkin I could lay hold of. The supposed consignment, I would then put about, had been broken to atoms by an avalanche which had overwhelmed the caravan at the very boundaries of the State. Price leapt upward, and as I was the author of the rumour I was also the first to take advantage of the rise in price. But the very moment, my dear nephews, that my sluggish competitors attempted to follow suit the market would, oddly enough, fluctuate again in a *downward* direction.

" Upon a certain morning when one Abdullah (who was my boon companion and the next merchant in importance to myself) decided to mark his best pipkins at ten dinars the dozen I happened most prudently to have offered my own at eight and a half dinars to my favourite customers.

" And all this while I lived upon my hidden hoard.

" Poor Abdullah came to me in a sweat, very early the next morning, and after some meaningless compliments and many pauses, asked me to go into partnership. ' For ' (said he) ' though he admitted he had not my capacities, yet he had a long experience in the trade, a large connection and many influential friends in the allied lines of Pipkin brokerage, Pipkin insurance, Pipkin discount, Pipkin remainders, and—a most important branch—the buying and selling of Imaginary Pipkins.'

" He could—he anxiously assured me—be of great
service as an ally, but he was free to confess that if he
continued as he was he would be ruined ; for, to tell the
truth, he had already come to the end of his resources
and had not a dinar in the house.

" I heard him out with a grave and sympathetic
countenance, heaving deep sighs when he touched upon
his fears, nodding and smiling when he spoke of his
advantages, patting him affectionately when he professed his devotion to myself, and assuming a look of
anguish when he spoke of his approaching ruin.

"But when he had concluded—almost in tears—I told
him in tones somewhat slower and graver than my
ordinary, that I had one fixed principle in life, be-
queathed me by my dear father, now in Paradise, *never
to enter into partnership :* no, not with my nearest and
dearest, but ever to remain alone in my transactions.
I frankly admitted that this made me a poor man and
would keep me poor.   It would be greatly to my advantage, in the despicable goods of this world, to have at
my disposal Abdullah's marvellous experience, his great
array of family and business connections (to which my
wretched birth could make no claim), and above all
his genius for following the market.   But the goods of
this world were perishable—especially earthenware
—and the sacred pledge given to my sainted parent
counted more with me than all the baked mud in the
world

" As I thus spoke Abdullah's breast heaved with
tempestuous sobs, provoked by the affecting example
of my filial piety, but also, I fear, by the black prospect
of his own future.

" I could not bear to witness his distress.   I hastened
to relieve it.   Though my vow (I said) forbade me

solemnly to enter into partnership, yet I could be of service to him in another manner. I would lend him money at a low rate of interest to the value of half his stock upon the security of the whole. Times would change. The present ruinous price of pipkins (by which I myself suffered severely) could not long endure. He would lift his head again and could repay me at his leisure.

" He thanked me profusely, kissed my hand again and again, and gave me an appointment next day to view his merchandise and draw up the contract.

" I visited him at the hour agreed. The public notaries drew up an inventory of his whole stock, including his house and furniture, his prayer beads (which I was interested in, for they were of a costly Persian make), his dead wife's jewels, all his clothes, his bed, and his pet cat—an animal of no recorded pedigree but reputed to be of the pure Kashmir breed. I carefully noted all flaws, however slight, in each pipkin of his warehouse and set all such damaged goods aside as a makeweight. The sound pipkins I made no bones of but accepted frankly at their market value, and when the whole was added up the valuation came to no less than 20,000 dinars. Yet so hide-bound in routine were the inhabitants of the place that Abdullah—if you will believe me !—had actually set his business stock down in his old books at four-fold that amount !

" As I had had to carry on, I had not now left by me my full hoard of 10,000 dinars. I had but 8,000 left. Yet I was in no difficulty. Half 20,000 is 10,000 —but there would be deductions !

" The costs of all this inventory and mortage were, of course, set down against my valued friend Abdullah, but since he had not the ready cash wherewith to pay the notaries, their clerks, the demurrage fees, the stamps, the royal licence, the enregistration, the triplicates, the broker's commission, the . . "

" Pray, uncle," cried the youngest of the nephews, " what are all these ? "

" You must not interrupt me, my boy," answered the great merchant, a little testily, " they are the necessary accompaniments of such transactions. . . . Well, as I was saying, the broker's commission, the porter's wages, the gratuities to the notaries' servants, the cleaning up of the warehouse after all was over, and a hundred other petty items, I generously allowed them to be deducted from the loan ; for our Prophet has said, ' *Blessed is he that shall grant delay to his debtor.*' That very evening, with every phrase of goodwill and expressed hopes for his speedy recovery of fortune, I counted out to my dear friend Abdullah the full balance of 16,325 dinars and one half-dinar, and left him overjoyed at the possession of so much immediate wealth.

" But, alas ! no man can forecast the morrow, and all things were written at the beginning to be as they shall be. So far from pipkins rising, the price fell slowly and regularly for three months, during which time I was careful to restrict my own production somewhat, though my poor dear friend, in his necessity, produced more feverishly than ever, and thereby did but lower still further the now really infamous price of pipkins.

" At last he came to a dead stop, and could produce no more. I gladly allowed the first, the second and even the third arrears of interest to be added to the principal at a most moderate compound rate, but there was some fatality upon him, and I was inexpressibly shocked to hear one morning that Abdullah had drowned himself over night in a beautiful little lake which his long dead wife had designed for him in his once charming pleasure grounds."

" Oh ! Poor man ! " cried all the nephews in chorus.

" Poor man ! Poor man indeed ! " echoed their benevolent uncle, " I was a stranger in that country. He was the closest tie I had to it, and, indeed, in my loneliness, the nearest companion I had in the whole world." And here the good old man paused to breathe a prayer for the departed companion of his long-past youth. He then sighed deeply and continued :

" I used what had now become my considerable influence with the government to provide him a costly funeral at the public expense—for he had left no effects, nor even children to follow him. I walked behind the coffin as chief mourner, and though I attempted to control my grief, all the vast crowd assembled were moved by my manly sorrow, and several spoke to me upon it at the conclusion of the sad rites.

" I allowed the decent interval of three days to elapse and then did what I had no choice but to do. I took over Abdullah's factory on foreclosure and added it to my own.

" In this way the valuable kilns and stores of clay and wheels and vehicles, etc., all became my property. I had them valued, and was pleasurably surprised to discover that they were worth at least 25,000 dinars.

" A full two years had now passed since my first coming to this happy and secluded valley where Allah had poured out upon me His blessings in so marvellous a fashion. I was lonely, as you may imagine, but I manfully faced my duty. I continued to supervise and extend my manufactory of pipkins which now provided these articles for more than half the households of the

State. I therefore could and did put the price of these useful articles upon a basis which, if it was somewhat higher than that to which people had grown accustomed during my earlier manipulations, had the priceless advantage of security, so that the housewife could always know exactly what she had to disburse—and I what I should receive. As I manufactured upon so large a scale my overhead charges . . ."

" What are overhead . . ." began the eldest nephew,. when his uncle, visibly perturbed, shouted " Silence ! . . . You have made me forget what I was going to say ! "

There was an awkward pause, during which the old man restored his ruffled temper and proceeded :

" I was able to buy clay more cheaply and better than the private pipkin-makers (for so they were now called, with well merited contempt) who still vainly attempted to compete with me, and my business automatically grew as the poor remnant of theirs declined.

" Not only did I continually increase in wealth by these somewhat obvious methods, but also in the power of controlling property ; for when some fresh fool among my fellow pipkin-makers found himself in difficulties, it was my practice to seek him secretly, to condole with him upon what I had heard was his approaching misfortune, and to save him from ruin by taking over the whole of his stock. Nay ! I would do more. I would rescue him from the sad necessity of attempting some new unknown trade by taking him into my own employment at a generous salary (but upon a monthly agreement) ; with a pretty concession to sentiment I would even leave him to manage his own dear old booth in the bazaar to which so many years had now accustomed him. I look back with pleasure upon the tears of gratitude which stood in the eyes of those to whom I extended such favours.

" So things went on for one more year, and another, and another, till the fifth year of my sojourn among these simple people was completed.

" I was in complete control of the pipkin trade, making all the pipkins that the nation needed, and free from any rival.   The house which I had built for myself was the finest in the place, but covered, I humbly add, with many a sacred text.   Above its vast horse-shoe gate, ablaze with azure tiles, was inscribed in gold the sentence, ' Wealth is of God alone.'

" I was popularly known as ' Melek-al-Tawajin,' or the Pipkin King, but officially decorated with the local title of ' Warzan Dahur,' which was the highest they knew and signifies ' Leader in battle.'   I was entitled to wear a sword with a silver hilt in a jewelled scabbard, an ornament of which I was justly proud, but the blade of which I very sensibly kept blunt lest my servant should cut himself when he polished it, or even I should inadvertently do myself a mischief when I pulled it out with a flourish to display it to my guests, or saluted with it on parade.   I had become a most intimate companion of the Court and was the most trusted counsellor of the King, to whose wives also I often lent small sums of money ; nor did I ask to be repaid.

" In such a situation I mused upon my condition, and felt within me strange promptings for a new and larger life.   I was now well advanced in manhood, I was filled with desires for action and device which the narrow field of that happy but restricted place could not fulfil.   I longed for adventurous action in a larger world.

" The output and consumption of pipkins was at an

exact unchangeable level ; the revenue a fixed amount. The profit of the trade I held came to some 20,000 dinars in the year, the full purchase of which should be, say, 200,000 dinars.

" I prayed earnestly for guidance, and one night as I so prayed an idea was revealed to me by the Most High.

" I approached the King and told him how, all my life, I had nourished the secret belief that a trade necessary to the whole community should not, in justice, be controlled by a private individual, but should rather be the full property of the State, of which His Majesty was the sole guardian.

" The King listened to me with rapt attention as I unfolded with an inspired eloquence my faith that no one man should intercept profits which were due to the work of all. ' It is your majesty,' I cried, ' who alone should have control over what concerns the body corporate of your people.' He and he alone should superintend the purchase of pipkins, should regulate their sales, should receive all sums paid for them, and should use that revenue as he might think best for himself and the commonwealth. ' While I was struggling in the dust and confusion of commercial life,' I concluded, ' I had no leisure to work out my scheme in its entirety, nor even to appreciate its serene equity—but now . . . now, I see, I understand, I know ! '

"Carried away by the fire of my conviction, my Royal Master could no longer brook delay. He bade me put the idea in its main lines before him at once, and assured me it should at once be put into execution.

" I thereupon pulled out a paper showing that since I was fully agreeable to take no more than the cash value of the tradè *plus* goodwill and *plus* certain probable gains which I might reasonably expect in the future, I would be amply compensated if I were to hand all over to the Commonwealth for the merely nominal sum of half a million dinars—500,000. ' A sum which,' I continued, ' is of little moment to your Majesty ; especially as it will be met by the taxation of your willing and loyal subjects.'

" The matter was at once concluded. My great act of renunciation was everywhere acclaimed with transports of public joy. Every honour was heaped upon me. The King himself pronounced my panegyric at the farewell banquet given in my honour, and an inscription was ordered to be encrusted in the most gorgeous tiles on the chief gate of the city : ' On the tenth day of the month Shaaban in the three hundred and third year from the Flight of the Prophet, by the act of Mahmoud the Magnificent all citizens became in the matter of PIPKINS his common heirs.' "

The Merchant had been so moved by these old memories that he had difficulty in proceeding. He was silent for a few moments, and then ended in a more subdued tone.

" The sum of 500,000 dinars, well packed, will load without discomfort some dozen camels. These and their drivers were provided me by a grateful nation. I passed out of the town at sunrise, attended by a vast concourse of the populace who pressed round me in a delirium of grateful cries, and so took my way eastward across the mountains and left this happy vale for ever."

At that moment the detestable falsetto of the Muezzin was heard from the neighbouring minaret, and the boys, all dazed at the recital of such triumphs, left the presence of their uncle as though it had been that of a God.

القنطرة

AL-KANTARA

That is:

"THE BRIDGE"

CHAPTER IV

ENTITLED *AL-KANTARA*, OR THE BRIDGE

WHEN the hour of public executions had arrived and the boys were assembled once more at their uncle's feet to hear the story of his fortunes, (their minds full of his last success,) the old man, still occupied with that pleasing memory, began at once the continuation of his life.

" I left the valley, as I told you, my dear nephews, nourished by the memory of a whole people's gratitude and giving thanks to God who had made me the humble instrument of so great a good. They err who think that great wealth is marked with oppression, or that the rich man has despoiled the populace. Upon the contrary, the fortunes of the wealthy are but an index of what excellent work they have done for all ; and I, for my part, equally joined in my heart the memory of all the benefits I had conferred upon my kind in the matter of Pipkins, and my overflowing satisfaction at the heavy bags of coin which swayed upon the backs of my camels.

" Day after day we proceeded, my caravan and I, through the high hills, pitching our camp each evening by some wooded torrent side and nourishing ourselves with the provisions with which I had amply stored my company at my departure.

" Such scenes were solemn and inclined the mind to reverence. Never had my prayers been more sincere and deep than they were during the long watches I passed in the cloudless nights of those mountains, in the solemnity of their vast woods; and the holy thoughts of grateful affluence harmonized with the ceaseless voices of the forest.

"I had during this long journey through the barrier range but little opportunity to exercise those gifts in which I may humbly say I excel. For the villages were few and poor and the opportunities for talent were rare. It was indeed my duty to keep my hand in, as the saying goes, and not to let my wealth diminish as I passed. Thus I would, for mere practice, strike some little bargain from time to time. I would purchase obsolete arms from some village less backward than the rest and sell them at some further stage onward to rude mountaineers who had not even heard of such ancient weapons. I was not above offering to carry, as my caravan passed, sundry goods from one farm to another at an agreed price, and these (after selecting what from among them seemed to me best worth keeping) I would punctually deliver to their consignees.

"I amused myself at my leisure, also, when I was in no haste, with occasional experiments in engineering such as suit the more educated man among his fellows. Thus I would let the water out from a dam as I passed it and then, at a considerable price, repair the ravages the escaping water might have made in the valley below. And I was even agreeable to retrace my steps and repair the damage which the flood had inevitably occasioned to the barrier itself: charging a suitable sum for both operations.

"Sometimes—when the occasion offered—I did business on a somewhat larger scale. I remember

purchasing a whole train of wheat which was on its way
to one of the larger hamlets, and when I arrived there
keeping the people in some suspense (but not to the
point of actual famine) until their necessity very
naturally produced an excellent price for the grain.
I also negotiated ransoms from time to time upon
commission when I found myself in a district of brigands—simple folk—and I picked up some very curious
carvings and pieces of metal work at a price satisfying to
their rude owners yet promising an enormous profit
when I should reach the plains.

"But all these were mere jests and pastimes, the
occupation of enforced idleness as my long journey
through the hills continued. At last I came to a place
which had been described to me by a trusty servant,
where, from the height of a pass I saw some thousands
of feet below me the foothills descending rapidly on to
an even plain which stretched, brown and sun-burned,
to the horizon. Not far from the base of the mountains, at the edge of this plain, a noble river wandered
in many branches, separated by sand-banks; for I
had been seven weeks in the hills and it was now the
height of summer, the snows had long since melted
away on the heights, and the stream was low.

"I pitched my last camp a mile or two from the
hither bank of this great river, and sent forward
certain of my servants to discover how best it might
be crossed. They returned the next morning and told
me that in several of its branches it was too deep to
be forded, but at the place where the shores seemed
to approach each other (where there was no interrupting island, but one continuous sea of water four
furlongs wide), a ferry had been established from a
road-end and plied regularly for the passage of mer-

chants, pilgrims and other travellers who there went
over from the hills to the Kingdom of the Plain upon
the further bank.   I sent them back with an appointment for the ferry to be prepared to take my numerous
caravan from the first hour after sunrise on the morrow.
We packed all our gear, struck camp in the first dusk
of dawn and duly reached the ferry head where a large
flat boat manned with a dozen rowers captained by
the old ferryman of the place waited us on a sort of
wharf.

" The passage was tedious, and would take the whole
day ; for the stream was swift and no more than one
camel could cross at a time.

" I was in some little hesitation how to act.   If
I remained upon the hither bank until all had passed
over I could not be certain that my servants who had
gone ahead would not play me a trick.   If I crossed
first I could not overlook the doings of my servants
who had yet to cross ; and though I had no reason to
doubt their perfect honesty, neither had I any reason
to doubt their vile thievish character.   At last I made
the following plan : I discharged all the camels of
their packs, putting the packs on board in one heap,
being very careful to put on board all the food as well
as the coin.   With this and one camel which I attended
myself and hobbled, I crossed alone.   I then went back
again with the ferryman and his crew, still keeping
my provisions and my coin, and brought over another
camel and his driver, and so on until the whole of my
company was transferred.   Not till all the camels
and their drivers were assembled, clamouring with
hunger, upon the further bank, did I allow the coin
and food to be landed under my very eye.

" The time which all this took made my retinue

ravenously hungry, as I have said, and as the day wore on I was indeed touched by the earnest prayers they made for a little food, but I was too wise to yield, and it was not until the whole of my company was gathered together on the further bank, and I with it, that I permitted the cases to be landed and gave them all a hearty meal.

" It was by that time near sunset. We pitched our camp and waited till the morning to find a more regular habitation, for I had noticed a very little way off from the further bank, and somewhat up-stream, not a few scattered houses standing in gardens and shaded in a grove of trees.

" I had as yet no plan how I might use the sums of which I was possessed. I was rather waiting for a venture to come to me than going out myself to seek it, when a chance word from the old ferryman, as I paid him the fares (which I had already contracted for at a great reduction, seeing how numerous we were); started me upon a train of thought.

" And here, my nephews, I will beg you to observe that any hint of opportunity must be seized at once. It is thus that great things are done.

" What the ferryman said was, ' A curse on those who come so loaded ' (for he grumbled and contended that his old crazy craft might have sprung a leak under such a pressure of traffic).

" 'Yet,' said I in reply, ' you have no lack of custom. As it is this day's business has left many disappointed, and I see upon the further bank the fires of those who have been kept waiting the whole day. They will be a hundred or more to claim your services by morning.'

" ' That is true,' he answered, ' but luckily few come as loaded as you or with so many beasts. This is none the less a good place of traffic, for it is the only passage across the water for many miles up and down stream, and serves the main road through the kingdom.'

" I asked him why had he not thought to meet the pressure by purchasing larger boats, or more of them, and hiring more men ; since it was clear there was profit in the place, and a greater demand of travellers than he could accommodate.

" He answered again in the surly tone which people use when they boast of changeless custom, that the old boat had been good enough for his father and had served him all his own life, and was good enough for him. By this reply I saw that he was without the funds for replacing his old boat by more and better craft. This my discovery was the beginning of all that followed.

" Before striking my camp the next day I first put the old ferryman in a reasonable humour by giving him good food and drink and treating him honestly in my conversation. When I saw that he was in a mood to be approached I suggested that we should enter a kind of partnership.

" ' I am,' said I, ' quite at my leisure. I am under no need to go forward until I choose. I have thought of hiring some one of these habitations which I see in yonder grove, and of making a long sojourn here, for the perpetual spectacle of all this traffic crossing and re-crossing a great river under the mountains is a delight.'

" The old ferryman answered that he needed no partner, that he earned all that he needed by his trade and that he preferred to be alone. He also said that my foreign face was distasteful to him, and that grand people were often less trustworthy than they seemed.

" ' Your sentiments,' I answered, 'are a proof of your wisdom, and also do you honour. But has it not occurred to you that if in the place of this one old craft half a dozen good new boats, much larger and properly manned, were provided, more comers would be tempted to pass here, there would be less delay, both the volume of traffic and the pace would be increased ? I cannot but think it an excellent proposition.'

" I have found, my dear nephews, that obstinate old men are easier to shepherd into financial schemes than any other sort : nor was I here disappointed.

" The old mule made the admission which all such men make after the first conventional delays. He said : ' That is all very well, but who is to pay for them ? '

" I replied quietly that I would. ' I shall be delighted,' said I, ' to furnish half a dozen new boats and to pay for the men to row them until the new turnover begins. All I ask is that you shall still keep your present earnings, but share with me in equal amounts the new and extra earnings which my plan will almost certainly produce.'

" It took me some time to rub into his rusty head the terms of my very favourable proposal. He kept on mixing up the division of any future profits and the division of his present income. Never did I appreciate more than during my conversations with this stupid granfer the necessity for patience in spreading a commercial snare. I was at fearful pains to get the thing into his obtuse brain. He *could* be no poorer, for I asked nothing of his present earnings : he *might* be much richer, for he would have half any future additions. I would guarantee him the income he was already earning on condition that the much larger income to be earned by my methods should, over and above that guaranteed revenue of his, be equally divided between us.

" He still seemed to think that there was some flaw or catch somewhere. He wanted the thing, simple as it was, explained to him over and over again. At last he got it clear ; he got by heart and repeated the refrain : ' Cannot be poorer, may be richer.' Nor did it occur to him to wonder why I was so oddly generous.

" I had our contract drawn up in due form, witnessed and sealed. I then caused to be constructed by the local shipwrights four first-class flat boats, some ten *diram* long by five wide. I saw to it that they should be painted in gay colours and in general have that vulgar violence so attractive to the masses. On their completion I added them to the existing capital of the ferry line.

" At the same time I pointed out to him who was now my partner something which that same stupidity of his had made him miss, to wit, that as he had a monopoly his charges were far too low. ' Moreover,' said I, ' when you consider what fine new boats I have put into service and how, as a consequence, the stream of traffic is increasing, to neglect the opportunity of profit is a great sin for which you will be answerable on the Day of Resurrection. Why, it was but yesterday that you passed over twice as many people, you assured me, as ever you did in any other one day in your life ! '

" So wedded to custom was the old gentleman that he still hesitated, but remembering how right I had been in my innovation and unable to contest the evidence of his own eyes how from day to day the volume of traffic increased, he at last somewhat reluctantly consented. The fares were doubled, yet the applications of people desiring to cross the river grew no less. There arose a substantial profit, over and above the old ferryman's original income, to be divided between us, and judged by the cost of the new boats I was making some ten per cent. upon my money, a very reasonable profit under the circumstances. . . ."

Here Mahmoud the great merchant paused, shut his eyes for a few moments, and continued in a murmur. "A very reasonable profit. Ten per cent., a very reasonable profit." Then, suddenly opening his eyes fiercely, he fixed them upon his alarmed nephews and cried.

"Was it not strange for a man of my temperament to remain thus pottering with a few boats and leaving sacks full of coin unused ? You have only heard the beginning of the scheme upon which I was engaged !

"I had already purchased a very nice little property with a convenient house upon it, standing some yards back from the bank of the river and perhaps one hundred yards above the ferry.

"I next purchased a field upon the further bank, exactly opposite this house and its garden. I amused myself sometimes by rowing across the river from the steps at the foot of my ground to the field which I had purchased upon the other side. I sowed that field with beans of a particular kind with which (so I assured my neighbours), I was experimenting after an agricultural fashion. They were much interested, for agriculture is highly developed in that part, with the result that the highest arts, especially those of finance, are shamefully neglected.

"I allowed a few months to pass, during which the use of the ferry under my improved methods had more than trebled. It attracted to itself, now that the passage was so much easier, forms of traffic which it had hitherto not known. I even added to the fleet one huge pontoon for the special service of an elephant which we had warning was to pass, and when this was known, those great animals, which had previously used a ford several days up-stream, were attracted to the shorter mountain road by the ferry.

" When all this was so prosperously established, I informed a few of the friends I had made in the neighbourhood that I must indulge in the fancy of a rich man and amuse myself by throwing a bridge between my house and the field I had bought upon the other shore. ' It will save me,' said I, ' the perpetual trouble of rowing across in my little skiff and also occupy my leisure ; for I am something of an engineer.'

" In truth very little engineering was required. All I had to do was to drive strong piles at intervals into the stream, lay trestles upon them, stay them with large baulks upon either side, and so make a good working bridge. It was no more than fit for foot traffic, but for this it was very convenient.

" Having now this communication I bought more land upon the further bank and developed there a very nice little model farm. I will not deny that foot passengers would occasionally ask my leave to cross by the bridge in order to save them the tedious passage by water. These I always refused lest it should prejudice the interests of my friend the ferryman ; I made an exception only for one or two neighbours whom I desired to favour, and occasionally for really important people with whom the ferryman would not desire to quarrel. But I have a good heart, and at last I began to wink at the use of the bridge by more than these.

Children especially (for I am very fond of young people) I could not bear to condemn to the troublesome passage by ferry, and I gave orders to my people to allow their trespass.

" At last a regular path got established through my farm, and whether from slackness or generosity I know not, but I allowed the crossing of the river by my bridge to increase in volume and to become a daily practice. When it had reached a certain volume my detestation of disorder compelled me to make certain regulations. I put up a gate at either end and charged a purely nominal sum which went, as I pointed out, to the upkeep of the bridge ; though, of course, it did not nearly meet that expenditure.

" To avoid the length and inconvenience of the passage by water this toll was cheerfully paid, and as the season advanced my bridge was more and more used.

" My partner, the old ferryman,. saw all this with a confused eye. He had the sense to see that I would not hurt my own investment by competition, yet he could not but perceive that there was here an increasing rivalry to his own long-established route.

" At last he approached me and asked me if we could not come to some pact ; I said that I saw no occasion for that. There was plenty of room for both. I was a wealthy man, and an act of generosity was a kind of luxury for me ; I could hardly ask people who had now grown used to so easy a passage to go back to the monopoly of the boats with their primitive, slow and clumsy business of embarking and disembarking, and their necessary delays and crowding. I pointed out to my revered partner that the boats were still necessary for all heavy merchandise and for animals, and

I also pointed out very strongly to the ferryman what he could not deny, that I would hardly do anything to prejudice him since that would be also to prejudice myself, as I was his partner. I even ridiculed him for not perceiving the force of such an argument before coming to me, and for troubling me with what was obviously nonsense.

" He still grumbled, however, He said that he was no scholar, that it sounded all right, but that he did not feel comfortable. I answered that I could not help his feelings, but it was a plain matter of common sense, and so dismissed him.

" I then announced my intention of strengthening the bridge considerably and making it sufficient to support any kind of traffic. And so I did, at a very considerable expense. When I had completed the task it was a fine structure which would take every kind of beast of burden and vehicle, and a constant stream of foot-passengers. The only exception I made was for elephants, which animal (I said) I might allow later, but not until I had had the whole thing thoroughly tested. These beasts, therefore, still had to use the ferry : but as they were few in number and difficult to handle they only increased my partner's troubles.

" Meanwhile the fame of my bridge spread throughout all the neighbouring countries, it gathered upon itself the whole volume of commerce.

" The old ferryman came to me in a mixed mood of anger, panic and delirious complaint. He said that his revenue was falling with alarming rapidity, added (a little spitefully I thought) that my share of that revenue would be not a quarter of what it had been in the past year, and said very plainly that if I did not make some change in my regulations my own profit would disappear altogether : that nothing would be left but his original revenue and that even this was now in doubt. As I answered nothing to all this long plea but let him talk himself out he ended up by asking, with some irony, whether I was one of those rich fools who liked to throw away their money.

" Then it was that I answered him as he deserved to be answered, for I do not easily brook insult. I told him that I had mortgaged my share in the enterprise of the boats sometime before to a neighbour at a very good price before ever the bridge had appeared, that I was sufficiently pestered by this man who ascribed to me the continued decline in the revenue which I received and handed over to him, and that I would not have added to this perpetual annoyance the further complaints of my inept partner. I drove him from my presence and told him I desired never to see him again.

" I have no doubt that if I had been approached properly I would have made some sort of compensation to the neighbour to whom I had mortgaged at a fine figure my original share in the profits of the ferry. I had enjoyed a large sum which he could now never recover, and I might have let him have a fifth or a quarter of it back, merely as a piece of generosity. But when I discovered that he had himself resold his interest to an ignoramus who was at that moment trying to find a purchaser for his rapidly shrinking property I lost all patience with the combination of them and put every thought of the ferry out of my mind. The new purchaser foreclosed on his mortgage and got for the ferry one-third of what he had lent on it.

" It was shortly after this transaction that the old

ferryman went mad. It began by his coming to my
house daily and making scenes outside the doors.
Then he took to breaking the windows, and at last
to gathering crowds and haranguing them on his
imaginary persecution at my hands. I was compelled
to have him locked up in his own defence, and I am
glad to say that a merciful fever soon relieved him of
what had become incurable delusions. He did not
recover his sanity, however, as is so often the case,
even in the last few hours before death. He continued
to call me the most dreadful names, and to rave, in his
mania of persecution, shouting that he had been robbed
and ruined. It was a pitiful ending to what had long
been a useful if obscure life.

" As I could not bear to see the men whom he had
employed starve I took them into my own employ for
the making of a roadway to the bridge, for the further
strengthening of it, the painting of it and so on, and
sent all the ferry-boats down the river where they would
be of more use than at this part where by my enterprise and public spirit the bridge had come into
existence. I purchased them as old timber from the
owners and made an insignificant profit of some few
thousand dinars.

" It is a pretty example of the way in which names
cling to places that the point on the bank where the
ferry used to ply is still called ' The Madman's Grave.'
For, indeed, the old fellow was buried, I heard, by
his own request, close to where his boat used to ply.

" It was now high time to consider the whole
question of the bridge and its finances. Through my
goodness of heart and generous carelessness—defects
or amiable frailties against which I have always
to be upon my guard—the whole thing had got into

a very unbusiness-like condition. The tolls were not
more than customary payments, though I had raised
them from time to time. There was no careful
distinction between the different kinds of traffic.
There were no regulations for the hours at which the
bridge should be used, nor ready means of checking
the accounts.

" The new Bridge had caused the town to increase
largely. Its governors and those of the adjoining
districts were rightly concerned in its proper ordering.

" The authorities of the neighbourhood fully agreed
with me that it was necessary to put the thing upon a
more regular footing. I suggested to them that before
going further it would be but a kindly and reasonable act
to consult those who made regular use of the bridge upon
a large scale, and especially the merchants of the place
and of the more distant towns upon the farther bank
who crossed and recrossed at stated intervals and with
considerable trains of traffic. These, therefore, were
courteously convened. They were regarded as repre-
senting the mass of humbler foot-folk and between us
all we drew up an excellent arrangement.

" First we made ourselves into a Council. Next we
voted ourselves full powers to do what we liked in
managing the Bridge.

" The merchants who were regular users of the
bridge and who passed and repassed with their trains
upon an average once a month, were to be free of toll
on condition that they should pay an annual subscrip-
tion to the upkeep of the structure. It came to an
average, for each of their beasts of burden, to about
one-quarter of the public toll, and for each of their
servants to less than one-half.

" The common folk of the town and the villages,

the herdsmen and all the humbler multitude which
used the bridge in less lucrative fashion were to pay a
toll double the original, which, after all, was only fair
when one considered that they were compelled to
use the bridge as there was now no other passage
across the stream. I should add that the local authorities which sat with us upon this Council, after
drawing up the Ordinances, passed a local By-law
full of common sense and the spirit of order. In this
By-law they forbade the use of any boats whatsoever
for the crossing of the water, under the excellent
plea that men had in the past occasionally been drowned
from these and that, anyhow, there was now a good
bridge and no necessity for this old-fashioned and
backward kind of travel.

" People were also forbidden to swim the river between sunset and sunrise upon the grounds of security
and police control, and between sunrise and sunset upon
grounds of decency.

" After the new regulations had been passed the
gates were strengthened, regular officers were appointed
to take the toll and I was public-spirited enough to
permit my own servants to be withdrawn and these
officials to be named (and paid) by the new Council,
retaining to myself no more than the right of receiving
the tolls and taking on of course the burden of upkeep
as against the sums which I received from the regular
merchants. I also reserved to myself the right,
whenever the Council or the local authorities thought
it necessary to have the bridge strengthened or repaired
or painted, or ornamented, or decorated upon feast
days, or covered with an awning during the great
heats, to take up the contract for all these services
at a price to be agreed upon between myself and the

Council and the local authorities, at the head of whom was my dear old friend the Sheik.

" When all these arrangements had been made, the thing was on a proper basis and formed, I am glad to say, for many other similar arrangements a precedent, in which the advantages of the public and a proper return on capital were both considered. My ' Bridge Council ' as it was called was copied in many another enterprise in those parts, to not a few of which I was admitted as a director.

" But one must march with the times. It could not be denied that this conservative and established way of recouping expenses and interest by tolls, excellent in its time, no doubt, had its drawbacks. There was something rather absurd in these progressive days (such was the phrase used to me by my friend the Sheik of the place—which was now growing under the influence of my bridge to be a very large town), there was something rather absurd in the spectacle of gates put up to block that very passage which had only been erected for the convenience of the community! What would not posterity think of us if they heard that we built a bridge and then put up gates to interfere with its constant and easy use ? It was a burden also upon the community that officials should have to be employed at either end checking payments, keeping books and all the rest of it.

" What was worse, there seemed to be some leakage. Officials could not always be trusted to make an exact return (for they were of the baser sort at a small salary). It was suspected that their relatives and friends had been allowed to cross free of toll, for we could not keep a big watch at night and there was I fear a good deal of illicit use of the bridge.

" All of this, quite apart from the bad example it gave and the feeling of disorder it created, was also a source of anxiety to those who were concerned with the finance of the enterprise. The feeling grew rapidly —at least it grew very strongly in me and I made every effort to spread it in others—that Progress and sundry other virtues with which the Plain prided itself (as against the half-barbaric people of the mountains) demanded that all these anomalies should cease, and that the simple policy of ' THE FREE BRIDGE ' should triumph."

As the aged merchant described the last stage of his adventure his face took on an animated look ; he spoke with decision ; there was a freedom in his gesture which recalled his old oratorical triumphs when he had occasion as a younger man to combine the practice of commerce, investment and finance with the public speeches which had rendered him famous. He seemed, for the moment, not so much the Merchant as the Senator, the Free Bridgeite of the great old days, and his nephews could not but admire the lofty air, the direct glance, the eloquent vibration of voice which accompanied this mood.

" I for my part," continued the old gentleman, now transformed by the recollection of his part in public life, " did not fear to speak openly in the Council and (such was my love for my fellow-citizens) even in the market-place. I was untiring in explaining the simple economic principles underlying the policy of The Free Bridge. I was delighted to observe, as my efforts proceeded, two parties forming—the Free Bridgeites, who had the tide with them and were in the spirit their day, and another party which, for lack of a better name, I will call the Recalcitrants, who were but a hotchpotch of evil-minded malcontents, dolts, public enemies, and in general a body who had no argument save that things were very well as they were and it was a pity to change.

" I need scarcely tell you which of these competing interests won. Intelligence, business enterprise, public spirit, common sense, justice and eighteen or nineteen other things which for the moment escape me supported the glorious triumph of The Free Bridge. At last, when the moment was ripe for it to be voted upon, we swept our opponents out of existence at the polls, securing out of every 100 votes no less than fifty-three for our project.

" The Sheik who, in the growing importance of the community was now confirmed in his office by his Sovereign under the title of Excellent, delivered an unforgettable harangue, saying that the Day when the tolls should be taken off the Bridge and the gates thrown down would stand in the annals of his country next to its historic Charter and its acceptance of the True Faith. Amid the deafening shouts of a vast concourse, composed, as I was amused to discover, of both parties indifferently, but all out for the occasion, this great official proceeded in state to the entrance of the bridge, cut symbolically the silken thread with which the gates upon either end had been tied and in loud tones declared the bridge open in the name of Allah and his Prophet. Women wept profusely and even strong men had difficulty in hiding their emotion ; only the younger of the children and the animals accompanying the procession appeared indifferent. Of the four officials deputed for the watching of the tolls two were thrown into jail on the charge of malversation : the other two were, on my making an appeal for them, allowed to leave the country.

" The head of the opposing party who had done his best to defeat this great and necessary reform now, upon payment, openly admitted that he was converted ; whatever sentimental attachment he might still cherish for his old views, he now clearly saw that they were no longer practical politics.

" The gardens of the city were illuminated for three successive nights, cannon were fired and in view of the quite exceptional character of the occasion many criminals were pardoned, including the young brother of the head of the opposition who, under an assumed name, had languished in jail for several months.

" In all this enthusiasm it was easier to get through the practical details of the change, as the obstacle of petty detailed criticism proceeding from an ignorant public was removed.

" A new Constitution was happily agreed upon in place of the old revenue from tolls. This old revenue had fluctuated between the annual amounts of 15,000 and 25,000 dinars. To replace it and to allow for all contingencies a fixed sum of 30,000 dinars was put aside as an annual charge upon the public rates to be allocated to the Service of the Bridge. This sum would, of course, in the natural course of things have been paid annually to myself. But I had other plans.

" After this decision to allocate 30,000 dinars had been arrived at by a unanimous vote I created a very favourable impression when I rose in my place and said that I would never occupy the privileged and, in my view, corrupt position of a citizen drawing a regular pension from my fellows. However great my services had been in the past, I was glad that they should be at the disposal of my country—for so I called the place, having lived in it now two years and more. I could not bear to think that I was, as it were, sucking the very life-blood of the community and drawing into my private coffers pence which had been contributed, for the most part, by the humblest of my dear countrymen.

" Agreement had already been shown with this announcement—which came from the depth of my heart—when the Council was overjoyed to hear my conclusion. It was, if anything, even more sincere. ' I will accept,' said I, ' *if you really insist upon it,* a sum of money down which might represent the capitalized value of the revenue, but I absolutely refuse upon any terms whatsoever to remain a mere drone supported by this active commercial community, skimming the cream off the taxes and feeling myself a burden where I should be an aid.'

" Applause was almost unknown in the dignified debates of our assembly, but upon this occasion it could not be restrained ; for some minutes together the grave but voluminous cheers of my colleagues assured me that I had done right and amply compensated me for any loss that I might suffer, supposing (which was, after all, improbable) the revenue from the bridge in the future would largely rise.

" Such is the frailty of human nature that perhaps the recognition of my good deed would have been less frank, or less simple, had the Council themselves been compelled to find the money out of their own pockets. But there was no question of this. The burden must fall, as was only just, upon the whole body of citizens, since all used the bridge. My proposal met therefore with enthusiastic assent from every side, and one speaker in the ensuing debate (a friend who, in his humble way, was associated with other of my lesser enterprises) pointed out what I could not in decency have alluded to, that I also was a tax-payer, and a large one ; so that any public payment was borne partly by myself. The Sheik, in closing the discussion, after a few compliments which my natural modesty forbids me to repeat, said that clearly nothing was now left but to make a computation— a mere matter of book-keeping—and that this detail might safely be left to a small committee of three, which was nominated upon the spot ; their work was of course honorary, for they were men of high standing ; but I saw to it that all their expenses and other disburse-ments should be met and I gave them much hospitality. The committee met at intervals during the ensuing three weeks. I appeared frequently before this Committee in the capacity of witness, I produced all my books and had, I am glad to say, the restraint and good feeling to let things take their course and not to haggle as though this great public settlement had been a private commer-cial deal. It is enough to say that at the end of this proceeding the sum of 1,400,000 dinars was awarded to me by the arbitrators and that I, after protesting against what I called the excessive generosity of the State, then added to my popularity by erecting at my own charges a fine gate of entry at the city end of the bridge which absorbed half the odd 400,000 ; the other half I gave in a burst of generosity to the members of the committee : not of course in their public capacity but privately, as being my personal friends, and in reward for their untiring public spirit.

" I was left with a million.

" I was fully content.

" I desired no more.

" But, uncle," timidly interrupted the eldest of the nephews, " I am puzzled by one thing. Will you allow me to ask you a question upon it ? "

" Certainly, my dear lad," said the old man, stroking his beard and awaiting the query.

" Why, uncle," said the boy, still hesitating somewhat, " it is this. I do not quite see how it came that you should have a million dinars. You came to this place with *half* a million, how then did it become *one* million ? "

The folly of the question raised a titter from his brothers, who had always regarded their senior as the least brilliant of their clan. But their uncle was more lenient and checked their mirth (which was especially loud in the youngest), and said :

" My dear boy, do you see anything extraordinary in an accretion of fortune to a man who served the community so well ? "

" No, not exactly that," said the elder nephew, still hesitating, " far from it, dear uncle ; but what I do not quite clearly.see is where the other half-million came from."

" Foolish lad ! " answered his relative, now touched with annoyance. " It came from my untiring devotion to the public service, from my foresight in providing a magnificent bridge which for all those years no one had attempted ; from the freely expressed desire of my fellow-citizens through their honoured representatives. It was, indeed, but a small recompense for all the good I had done and all the immeasurable advantage to this town which my energy had created."

" Yes, dear uncle, but . . ." went on the blushing lad.

" Oh, don't listen to him," cried his brothers in chorus. " You will never make him understand ! Our father has always said that he could not even do his arithmetic," and the shrill laugh of the youngest was heard at the end of this protest.

" Well, well," said Mahmoud good-naturedly, " we will not quarrel about it."

At that moment the intolerable shriek of the Muezzin calling the Faithful to prayer was heard from the neighbouring minaret and the somewhat strained situation was relieved.

MILH

That is:

"SALT"

CHAPTER V

ENTITLED *MILH*, OR "SALT"

WHEN his nephews next filed into the presence of Mahmoud at the hour of public executions their first act was to stand in a line and salaam ; their next to push forward the eldest, who with much catching up of himself and in the humblest tones, desired to apologize to his uncle for the interruption of which he had been guilty during their last audience.

" It is not my fault, Revered Sir," said he, " that I was born a little thick-headed in the matter of figures. The whole thing has been explained to me most fully by my father, my mother, my brothers, and sundry guests that came in last night after the evening meal : to which (alas !) we could not afford to invite them. I now see very clearly where and how a million can become two without breeding, and I only hope that in the further story of your adventures we shall find miraculously increasing with every year the fortune which the Almighty bestowed upon you in reward for your ceaseless efforts to benefit mankind."

Having said this the lad bowed once more in deep obeisance, while, at a signal from one of their uncle's attendant slaves, all the brothers sank cross-legged to the floor and assumed expressions of the most enraptured attention.

" There was no need," said the old man kindly,

" to refer again to this unfortunate little affair; but since you have done so I am indeed glad to learn that your difficulties have been explained away. No doubt your excellent father, my brother, and his guests made it plain to you that, if anything, my reward had been far below that to which I was morally entitled. For a man who not only builds for a city a fine bridge but also, from a pure public spirit, leaves it open and free to all, is worthy of very high reward indeed at the hands of the Commonwealth. But, to tell the truth, though I am not indifferent to success in any task I take up, I was not so much concerned with the worldly advantage of my increased fortune as with the good I had done, and with the knowledge that it would add to my glory in paradise. For it is written: ' *Three works are remembered on high : The building of a bridge, the digging of a well, and the pulling down of poor men's houses.*'

" In the last part of what you said (my dear nephews), I fear you will be disappointed; for the story I have to tell to-day " (and here his voice fell to a graver tone) " is one of strange disaster.

" I desire you to bear my losses even more closely in mind than the previous accounts of my rising fortunes or than those other accounts which will follow and will show how I recovered my standing in the world. For it would indeed be a poor service I should do you young people if I were to leave you under the error that energy and adventure alone add gold to gold : no, nor even cunning. For there is also the Will of the Supreme.

" What is the Sleight of Hand or Eye, without Him ? " asked the old Merchant in a rapture (as his youngest nephew cleverly swallowed a yawn). " Do you hope for gain by the folly of your dupe or even by your own stupidity ? It is far otherwise !

" Our Sacred Books present us with many an example of good men whom the Infinite Mercy has seen fit to try. It is our conduct under these ordeals which are the true test of character and the only foundations of our future and eternal reward. By so much as I ascribe to the Mercy of Allah whatever goods have befallen me, by so much do I ascribe to His inscrutable wisdom and kindness even the sharp reverses of this life. For by these we learn that there is an element of speculation in all business ; that we are surrounded by the competition of rivals whom we should never despise ; that our friends ever lie in wait to outwit us. It is only by the humble acceptation of such lessons that we become even more acute in dealing with our fellow-beings than we were before we had suffered loss.

" However, I will not delay, but proceed at once to the harrowing tale. For you must now follow your poor uncle through dark and distressing days." As he said these words the features of his young relatives betrayed the utmost concern ; none more than those of the youngest, the great pathos of whose expression oddly assorted with innocence of his years.

" You must know, then," began the old man, " that my prime error at this moment in my career, was a desire for ease. I thought (I say it to my shame !) that I had made enough. To use the familiar language of the market I regarded my present fortune of a million dinars as my ' pile.' To use another phrase which you will come across very frequently in your maturer years, I was ready to retire.

" Oh, fatal error ! Oh, profound ingratitude !

Here was I, still in the vigour of early manhood—for I had but just attained my thirtieth year, on the full tide of an apparent success, blessed in all my doings —and yet already with a paltry million in hand so ungrateful to God as to entertain a shameful temptation to leisure ! The result shall be a warning to you, I hope, and to any who may come across this recital.

" The insidious poison of content had, all unknown to myself, wormed its way into my heart. I had (for the moment at least) wearied of getting the better of others—which should be the chief activity of a man ; I was already toying with such fripperies as the reading of books, the contemplation of fine manuscripts, the designing of a house for myself, the planning of gardens, futile conversation with the learned, and, worst of all, the taking of an interest in the past. Beyond this foolish bent for acquiring knowledge of dead things, I descended to the pen ! I actually began to write. To the writing of verse (I humbly thank God !) I never fell, but had not a sharp chastisement brought me to my senses I might have come to it.

·" You know, perhaps, my dear nephews, that there are some men so lost to all shame that on finding themselves possessed of a considerable sum they will not embark it in commerce nor even lend it out at interest to the widow and the orphan, to the teachers of our holy religion, or to districts struck by famine ; indeed, they make no lucrative employment of it, but, yielding to a base appetite for repose, they draw upon it as they need until it is wholly exhausted."

" Oh, how shocking ! " piped a shrill voice, interrupting the merchant in his eloquence. The cry proceeded from the youngest.

" You feel strongly, my little fellow," said his uncle,

"and you are quite right. I am delighted to find that one so young has already so sound a sense of our duty in the battle of life. There are, I repeat, men so despicable that they will put their substance aside, taking from it what they need from day to day, until one of these two events befalls them : at the worst they live too long and spend their last miserable years in destitution : at the best (and it is a poor best) they live too short, and have the infinite mortification, in the agony of death, to discover that they might have had some slightly larger income had they made a more exact calculation.

"I am speaking frankly to you, my nephews (in spite of the difference in our ages and of the respect you owe me as the head of the family), when I confess so great a depth of degradation as this. I did not put this million which I had acquired aside. I used it fruitfully. But my mind was occupied (even after so many years I blush to recall it !) in seeking some secure and permanent form of revenue, so that I should be free henceforth from the labour and risk of buying cheap and selling dear, and from the duty of hunting the dupe and the incompetent.

"While I was revolving in my mind how best I might obtain this leisure there came to me my temptation. For a traveller arriving in the City of the Bridge let it be known to the merchants of the place that the King of an Island called Izmar, one day's sail from the coast (a kingdom renowned throughout Asia for its fidelity to the Prophet, the antiquity of its customs, the solidity of its institutions), required a loan.

"'For what purpose ? ' I asked him.

"'I know not,' he answered, ' but I think it is in order to pay back another loan which he contracted

some years ago in the effort to pay another loan which
his father had contracted when a few years previously
he had been compelled to repay an earlier loan.'

" I admired the scrupulous anxiety of this monarch
and was the more confirmed in the project that was
forming in my mind.   That very night I bade farewell,
not without grief, to the City of the Bridge.   I sold
my slaves and my house at some loss (such was my
infatuation !) and before it was light started out upon
a good horse, carrying with me my million dinars
reduced to one hundred thousand pieces of gold
which, in this form, could easily be carried upon a
few pack animals that followed me with their drivers.

" My passage of the sea was easy.   I saw, at the
rising of the sun, fine mountains against the South
and very soon I discerned at their base on the shore,
the walls, the piers, the minarets of a great city, its
flanks upon the edges of the sea.   So did I land under
a good augury.

" Everything in the place, as I passed through it,
smiled at my project.   The wealth of the great houses,
the busy commerce of the streets, the port quite filled
with shipping from every place, the sounds of strange
tongues (men not only from all Islam, but Nazarenes
also, and Kafir, and merchants of China), the excellent
order everywhere about, all these promised me the
security which I desired.

" I put on my best raiment, finely fringed, and all
my jewels and presented myself to the Port-Master
as upon a matter of state business, handing him at
the same time, in a lofty manner, a roll which I begged
to have delivered to the Controllers of the Treasury
The Master of the Port treated me with the reverence
my wealth deserved.   I reposed for an hour in the

court of his house, resting to the pleasant trickle of
a fountain and waiting the pleasure of the authorities.
At the end of that time a dozen horsemen magnificently
mounted and bearing the insignia of the King formed
before the porch of my host.   Their commander set
foot to the ground and begged me with a very low
salaam to mount and ride.   It would be his privilege,
he said, to hold my bridle.

" It was my design to maintain my state, and thus,
in great pomp, was I led through the busy streets till
I came to a vast archway all emblazoned with holy
texts.   Passing through this, I came into a more magnificent court than I had thought men could have built.
in this world.   Indeed, the folk had made stories of
it that it was not of human handicraft, but that its
delicate piers and alabaster columns and lovely arches,
lighter and lighter as they rose to heaven, had sprung
up in a moment at the command of spirits in the days
of Soleiman, from whom the monarchs of this happy
island claimed descent.

" My advent was greeted with a flourish of trumpets
as though I were some sort of ambassador, such an
effect had my robes and jewels and letter produced,
and, without delay, I was conducted by servants of
the palace into the presence of the Council.

" The morning was already far advanced, the heat
increasing, but the apartment in which I found myself
(which was ablaze with the most costly tiles and hangings of the Indies) was very cool ; and again the
pleasant sound of water plashing from a scented
fountain refreshed the air.

" Before the throne stood, in respectful order, the
twelve councillors of the King ; and He himself, upon
a marble throne, exquisite in workmanship and vener-

able with age, sat : a young man of a dreamy, melancholy, but pleasing countenance, who bowed his head
very slightly at my approach, smiled gently as he did
so and welcomed me. Such was the King. I in my
turn cast myself down before him with a full obeisance
until he bade me rise.

" Our business was not long in concluding. The
Grand Vizier, who stepped up and stood on the right
hand of the throne, put me certain questions—Whether
I had my treasure with me ? Whether I could produce
it by such a date ? And so forth. I satisfied him by
signalling to my attendants with their burdens. The
packages were opened before the eyes of the Council
and at that sitting all was arranged. For the terms
which I proposed were discovered suitable enough.
I have told you, my dear nephews (and I do confess it
again to my shame), that desire for ease had now taken
place in my mind, whereas further gain should have
occupied it. I very modestly asked for no more
than five dinars yearly on the hundred, I told the
Council and his Majesty that for the million dinars
which could here be counted I should ask annually
but fifty thousand for revenue, and that paid on such
dates as they thought fit.

All nodded gravely ; the King gently complimented
me upon my public spirit, for now (as he was good
enough to say) he regarded me as a subject.

" He looked round among his councillors as though
seeking a suggestion, when one of them, Tarib by
name (whom I distinguished by his fine intelligent
face and felt drawn towards already), said in a firm
voice, ' The Salt Tax,' and all, including the King
himself, murmured approval.

" Then did I learn that for many generations past

the people of this wealthy and fortunate realm had paid to the State a fixed tax upon salt, which amounted yearly, upon the average, to the sum I had demanded. It was regularly received ; for all the salt of this land came over sea and the toll was levied at the ports of entry. A Charter was drawn up by the Council in simple terms. It was agreed by my own wish that my name should not be published to the people, lest, perhaps, the odium of receiving tribute should attach to one so recently come among them. But the King assured me, as he signed, that not odium, but gratitude, was my due : he for his part would never cease to believe that I had been moved to make so generous an offer by some particular affection for himself and his people.

" Rooms within the palace were set at my disposal until I should have time to choose some house in the city, and through the importance of my connexion with the State I was sworn of the Council with the rest.

" As I read my Charter through all alone in the privacy of my room I noted with pleasure the short and simple phrasing of this great commercial people :

" ' *To Mahmoud, his assignees and heirs for ever and ever, so long as the State shall last, and the Salt Tax be gathered* '

ran the what is called among the mighty ' The Operative Clause : the Words of Power.' I had them by heart in a moment. I could not forbear to write them down in my own hand more than once, for the pleasure it gave me.

" Here then was my every wish fulfilled ! Here was the best of company, the most dignified of positions, the most charming of climates, surroundings of wealth,

luxury and ease ; the culture of a thousand years ;
all that our religion permits in art and entertainment.
Books of every language and climate. Stores of good
from every sky under heaven, from every people and
of every age. Here, indeed, might I live my life
without further adventure or negotiation. What
pleased me most was to think that I would be able to
escape some little strains I might have to put upon my
honour—though not I am glad to say upon my con-
science—in the rude struggle of the outer world. No
one here knew my humble beginnings, or in too much
detail the particular abilities whereby I had so rapidly
enriched myself.

" I was now one of the great lords, and very soon
the foundation of my fortune would be lost in the
mists of time. Men would easily come to believe that
my fathers had acquired it, sword in hand, when first
the banner of the Prophet was seen upon those hills
three hundred years before.

" I will not detain you with the happy disposition
of my time, nor with more than the statement of my
supreme enjoyment. Scrolls from every land I
accumulated in my library, I had about me the most
costly stuffs and upon my person and upon those of
my attendants the rarest gems. My chief delight was
to gather at my table a small, but various, band of
intimates ; chief of whom was that earnest, intelligent
young man of the Council whom I noted on my first
arrival. Tarib, as I have told you, was his simple
name ; and I learned how his father had been no
more than a respected merchant in offal. Dying, he
had left his son a sufficient income, and that son had
so added to it by occasions of public service that he
had now risen to one of the highest offices of State

It was his special function in the Council to represent and to retail to the King whatever popular movement was abroad, for he was known to every class in the city. He was the intermediary between King and people, was regarded in some way as a Tribune : or, as his title went, ' The Doubler,' which term, already centuries old, some derived from his double function, others from the attitude which etiquette demanded him to assume to Monarch and subjects alike. Others again put it down to the emoluments of his post.

" Through him I learned to understand this kindly, industrious and most loyal people. In my walks with him, and by my regular attendance at his public addresses, I grew intimate with that character in the people of Izmar which had led to their great reputation throughout the world.

" It was their pride that they never shook the State by violent change, but with gradual and well-weighed reforms adapted themselves generation by generation to the movement of the world. They thought disdainfully of nationalities controlled by less powerful traditions ; for a man of great fortune like myself, it was therefore an ever-pleasing thought— the foundation I might say of my happiness—to consider the peace and solidity all about me. That portion of the populace (about one half) which lay upon the verge of starvation were manfully content with their lot, or, if ever they showed some beginning of complaint, were at once appeased when they had pointed out to them their superiority over the miserable foreigners of the Mainland ; while those who (like myself) were possessed of vast revenues and lived in great palaces were far too devoted to the Commonwealth to dream of grumbling at their lot.

They would, upon the contrary, frequently express their devotion to State and King, and prove it by doing for the common weal, unpaid, as much as three hours' work in a day ; or even four when there was a press of business.

" Thus, one would maintain the magnificent breed of horses by his devotion to the chase ; another would support the industry of the goldsmith by his frequent purchase of ornaments ; another would, as a local magistrate, condemn the poorest of his district to various terms of imprisonment ; another, though in no way bound to do so, would write a book—the description, perhaps, of his tastes in food, or a recollection of those men and women of the wealthier sort whom he had met in the course of his useful life. Yet another would contribute to the health of the State by the continual practice of commerce, to which these people were very much devoted. There was hardly one of this rich class in which I now mixed, but had his chosen work thoroughly accomplished. The content of the poor, the public spirit of the rich, welded the whole of that society into a sort of paradise ; but most noble of all and most worthy of this people was this young Tribune Tarib.

" He it was who talked most incessantly and before the largest gatherings, thus creating a taste for public discussion. He it was who discussed practical remedies whenever discontent appeared, and he who worked out every detail in the interesting reports upon the condition of the starving. To the thousands whom he addressed his manner never grew stale. His eloquence was sober, his speeches with praise of Izmar and quotations from the Sacred Books, as also with known jests —things which this practical people infinitely preferred

to empty theories of the Mainland.   So all went well ;
and I (blind to the future, alas !) went down that path
of statesmanship along which my friend led me, little
knowing whither it would lead me.

" I did not often speak myself at the public meetings
so frequently held (they were indeed the noble pastime
of this patriot folk), lest my foreign accent should hurt
my dignity,   For I had not yet a complete command
of the language, though it was now two years since I
had become a citizen and subject of the Monarch to
whom we were all so devoted.   But I would sit by
the side of my friend Tarib and others as they harangued
the populace in the open places of the city or, upon
occasions, in the mosques.   On such occasions I would
show by my smiles and applause my approval of all
that was said for the betterment of the poor or the
rich, as the case might be, and I always laughed at
the ritual jests, sometimes even before they were
delivered.   In this way I grew familiar with most of
those in the capital and with many of the provincial
towns, and hoped to conquer general favour.

" I was present when Ibn Rashn delivered his great
harangue to a vast assembly, denouncing the foreign
practice of marrying a fifth wife—which abomination
there was some danger of seeing introduced into his
beloved island.   I was present also when the same
great and eloquent man gave his second great harangue,
insisting upon the necessity of fifth wives and carrying
that reform by acclamation as a law.   Seated with
others on the raised platform which surrounded the
orator I applauded the Grand Vizier in his solemn
declaration against shaving, a thing (said he) abhorrent
to every true believer, and heard the sway of argument
for and against this custom ;   which (I am glad to

say) was afterwards put down with the utmost severity of the law. But my happiest memories are still of those numerous days when my intimate the Tribune Tarib—who could never be accused of any petty thing —poured forth his soul upon the poverty of the commons and extolled to them the national pride and glory of doing nothing to change it : in which principles he was applauded with frenzy. This spirit was peculiar to this happy land and no one expressed it in wiser or more memorable terms than he who was now my bosom friend.

" But there came a time—I had been in Izmar about three years—when it was clearly necessary to strike a new note.

" There was at the moment of which I speak some little commotion in the city on account of a dearth of rice, the diet of the poorer classes, or at least the diet of the poorer classes when they could obtain it ; for there was a custom deeply rooted in this conservative people that when the poorer classes could not obtain rice, they should do without it.

" At this juncture the difficulty had risen to the middle classes, and these joined with the populace. Ill ease grew general. A complaint of stringency was abroad, from the ranks of those who starved to death up to the merchants and the lords themselves. Even the moderately rich could no longer afford the services of more than a dozen dancing girls.

" The whole Island was in a ferment and the capital was so disturbed that one might have thought oneself at times among the degraded tribes of the Mainland.

" Processions had appeared in the streets, sometimes actually accompanied by musical instruments of a loud and distressing order. Banners had been carried, and upon one occasion the litter of no less a person than the Lord Executioner had been detained for half an hour in a block caused by the multitudes proceeding to hear a favourite orator. The Council had taken note of these things and my friend the Tribune Tarib, the Lord Doubler, was naturally deputed to deal with them in his own inimitable way.

"He went on foot to the vast meeting that had been convened in the Mosque of Nasr-ed-din the founder of the Dynasty. We also went with him thus humbly, the better to please the public eye. With some dozen others of my rank I sat upon a rug immediately at the foot of the orator and listened entranced to his impassioned words.

"Never had I heard him more inspired! It was a great volume of sound, the words in which followed each other in quick succession, often meaningless but never pedantic, and throughout the speech he was careful to interpolate short passages which the meanest intellect could clearly follow and which exactly corresponded to the desires of his hearers. 'Why should you starve?' cried he, 'while all around you is wealth? Which the wealthy will be the first to forego.' Murmurs of applause burst from the lips of the Treasurer and the Grand Vizier, while I myself—I am not ashamed to say—cried aloud in my enthusiasm for the sentiment. 'Why,' said he, 'do you lack your poor pittance of rice while the bloated rich'—and he looked round at the galleries as though to find them there—'have their fill of the tenderest lamb stuffed with pistachio nuts? And who shall blame them?' Again there rose a wave of applause in which I joined more heartily than ever, for the words reminded me of that delicious viand, which I had, but an hour before, very plentifully consumed. ' Why,'—he shouted in louder tones—' Why do you permit yourselves to be loaded with an intolerable burden of taxation ? Which our wealthier classes bear also in an immoderate degree ? '

" At this phrase the exultation of the Lord Chief Treasurer knew no bounds, and he led the stream of cheering which it so richly deserved. ' How long are we to wait for that reform which our fathers—especially among the gentry—demanded and so nearly obtained ? ' He looked round upon them for a moment in a dramatic pause, and then said in solemn tones, ' A tax upon the *worthless* rich, and more especially ' (yet louder) ' upon the *alien* rich and more especially still ' (his voice now booming like a hammering of drums) ' upon the alien rich who stand *idle* battening upon the revenues of the State, this I say . . .' But the delirium of acquiescence aroused by this noble sentiment cut off the rest of his phrase and drowned his voice for the space in which a man might recite the prayer for the Caliph.

" Used as I was to this style of public eloquence and the expression of opinions universal to this happy people (bound up, as I thought, with the very atmosphere of their race) I naturally expected that when the dying down of the applause should have allowed him to be heard we should have that second part of which his speeches had always consisted—an appeal to the conservative instincts of our race, to their noble patience and to their dogged tenacity in doing nothing which had made them the envy of their less-gifted neighbours.

" Bitterly was I undeceived !

" For what were his very next words ? I could

hardly believe my ears as those words fell upon me.
' Why,' said he in grave and tragic tones, slowly separating them syllable by syllable, ' why do you thus
remain ground down by such an iniquity as the tax
upon SALT ? '

" My heart stood still. I ventured discreetly to
touch his foot with that one of my own which was
nearest. He replied by treading heavily upon my toe,
which I interpreted as a signal of secret friendship.
But I was terribly concerned to note that the native
Lords around, squatted upon the same platform as
myself, wagged their beards in unison when this monstrous suggestion was made, and by their murmurs
of agreement interrupted the awful silence which
followed.

" That silence did not last for long. Once more,
but with stronger decision, with larger hope, there
arose from the vast assembly the same tumult of applause. Every man rose to his feet. Someone began
to sing, then all sang in unison their famous hymn,
which asks in stirring words and air whether one
Hussein shall die and asserts with the utmost vehe-
mence that if this most unfortunate event should come
to pass no less than twenty thousand inhabitants of
the peninsula province of Bar-el-sul would demand a
full explanation of the occurrence. The words might
not seem apposite to a stranger, but in the dignified
and strongly national atmosphere of Izmar their
purport is well understood. They can be suited to
almost any occasion of popular passion, and at this
moment most undoubtedly might be interpreted to
mean ' *To Eblis with the Salt Tax.*'

" I was by this time frozen to my marrow. I was
bewildered. I could hardly doubt the friendship

between Tarib and myself. I had shown him so many favours. Even now, as I looked at him, I found him very sympathetic—and so familiar! I could not doubt the force of familiar converse, I could not doubt my hosts and colleagues, the Councillors, who had for now three years sat with me round His Majesty in Divan and worked with me as one of the Chief Ministers there.

" The next words slightly, but only slightly, reassured me. They were more after the style I knew so well, when, in the past, the national glory in doing nothing had been expressed with peculiar skill. The Lord Doubler assumed a piteous expression and his mouth, the shape of which might now be compared to that of a horse-shoe, opened. ' Let me not stir you up, my friends,' said he, ' to a violent anger. We can leave froth and vindictive folly to the pitiful peoples of the mainland. We in Izmar, thanks be to Allah, will never lose our dignity in mere brawling. Let us confine ourselves to constitutional means, the only ones whereby anything practical can be accomplished.' Applause also met these sentiments, more subdued, indeed, than that which we had first heard, but sincere. ' My friends around me,' and he smiled on all the Councillors, including myself, ' will deliberate, as we always do, for the public good, and you will find that our recommendations thus laid before His Majesty, with the ensuing Proclamation, will be the beginning of better things. We cannot say that all this evil shall be redressed at once. We are a practical people, as I think I have remarked before. You have indeed cried to me for redress ; but we are, I say it again, a practical people. We do not attempt the impossible or tear up the ancient framework of our State. Step by step is our motto. One thing at a time. The advance of His Majesty's subjects in freedom and happiness has increased in breadth by imperceptible degrees from one decision in the past to another, as our great poet has so admirably put it ; and again, not once or twice in the far from smooth sequence of our insular activities has the mere fulfilment of our daily tasks proved an approach to distinction.' These verses (which in the original form noble lines of poetry) made a fitting conclusion to one of those great speeches which from time to time determined the fate of Izmar.

" We all rose ; the audience and the Councillors and the orator himself united in chanting that portion of the Koran which details Mahomet's visit to the moon (a religious exercise dear to this folk). We then sang an invocation to Allah that he might protect His Majesty the King and throw any hypothetical enemies of that monarch into the utmost confusion. Then we filed out of the Mosque in our thousands to the coolness of the declining day. That great, that historic, that fatal meeting had occupied four hours !

" The Council was immediately summoned, and their first action, after their obeisance to the King upon his throne, was to assure me, individual by individual, that no idea of any attack upon me had been for one moment intended.

" ' It is, my dear Mahmoud,' said the Grand Vizier, placing his hand familiarly upon mine as it lay listless upon my knee, ' it is the *principle* of the matter which we must consider. That is it.' He pressed my hand on the other side. ' For yourself, Mahmoud, as you know, we have a respect which exceeds all bounds, but we must move with the times. Things are not what they were. Evolution is better than revolution. If we do not reform ourselves, things will reform us. Mend it or end it. What did the Sultan Omar say in the thirty-seventh year of the Flight of the Prophet ? '

" These commonplaces fell mournfully upon my ears. I made no attempt to reply. His Majesty was pleased to say a few sympathetic words. The Tribune Tarib, who evidently felt embarrassed by my position and by his memories of our past friendship, most earnestly protested that his whole object had been to stem the growing dangerous demand—nay, he would go so far as to say perilous demand ; nay more, a minatory demand ; yea, a threatening demand. Had he not stemmed the demand as he had it would have had tremendous consequences in the way of demand. The great lord whose special function on the Council was solemnity and who was known by the title of His Impressiveness, opened his mouth in the midst of his prodigious beard to say that he thoroughly agreed with these sentiments.

" For my part I said nothing, but sat mournfully, seeing no issue and attending the pleasure of those who could do what they would with me and mine. I heard their debate : I was asked to sign their conclusions. I did so with a reluctant, unwilling hand ; and as I signed my name in its place and affixed my seal I glanced at the wording of the Proclamation and felt some relief to discover that the Salt Tax was not abolished, but only halved, while the loss so occasioned was to be made good by a tax upon revenue of one dinar in each hundred—a very moderate amount.

" After this dreadful session (the date will remain

engraved upon my soul to my dying day !—it was the
anniversary of the day upon which my grandfather,
your great grandfather, dear boys, had been hanged)
I paced up and down in my courtyard alone, no longer
soothed by the ceaseless whisper of my beloved fountains, in no mood for taking down any one of my famous
scrolls, nor even for toying with the numerous Cir-
cassians whom I had imported at vast expense during
the preceding months.   My bosom and my brow were
contracted and I was weary of life.

" But after some hours of these mournful reflections
some considerations of hope occurred to me.   ' After
all,' said I to myself, ' there must be ups and downs.
Many a man has lost a furtune and recovered it.   My
income is halved, but what remains is still ample.'   I
could yet call myself an extremely wealthy man—
among the wealthiest in the State.   The small tax
put upon my revenue I could not grudge, since it fell
also upon the revenues of others.

" But I was to learn what bitter truth there lay
behind the oft-repeated boast of these people that
they proceeded step by step, slowly, one thing at a
time, etc., etc., etc.   Not a month had passed but a
modification was issued to the first regulation and it
was ordained, in view of certain rumours which had
been heard in the market-place, that the tax on revenue
should be of a more complicated kind.   It was *to
begin*, indeed, at one dinar in the hundred, but since
it was harsh to apply even this small burden to the
poorer citizens, only those receiving at least one
thousand dinars should pay, and the proportion was
to rise rapidly with the larger fortunes until, for such
a man as myself, the proportion reached one quarter
of the total !   But worse was to come.

" Yielding to the vigorous popular clamour, the tax was doubled for those of alien birth. For those whose income was derived in any way from the revenues of State the tax was doubled again. Exception was made for the Councillors, for (so ran the Proclamation) their salaries are paid by his Majesty, and a diminution of them would but take money with one hand to give it back to the other. I hoped for one wild moment that I should come within so clear a category. But no! In a further clause it was specially indicated that this should apply only to salaries actually paid by the Treasury and not to annuities guaranteed by, or derived from, the public revenue directly—and my payment alone was of this kind in all the Council!

" Still more was to follow. An infamous new regulation appeared whereby a man should pay, not upon that which he actually received, but upon that which he had received in the course of three years— a space of time exactly corresponding to my presence in the island and attaching to my vast income of the past. It was clear that I was ruined. I made a brief calculation on the night after the last of these official Acts had been published. After taking this survey of my remaining wealth (I had already sold the most part of my movables, and had removed from my great palace to a humble lodging) I discovered that I had left in my hands, all told, less than one thousand dinars.

" I knew not how to look upon the world. My whole being seemed to have departed. I watched the day fading, and with it faded my spirit. I returned to my poor room and, very late, lost, or half-lost, my miseries in an imperfect slumber."

The old man concluded and bowed his head in a solemn silence. His young nephews appreciating how sacred a thing is death, especially the death of Money, glided on tiptoe out of the room and vanished.

الوكلاء

AL-WUKALÁ

That is :

"THE LAWYERS"

CHAPTER VI

ENTITLED *AL-WUKALÁ*, OR "THE LAWYERS"

WHEN the nephews next entered their uncle's presence at the Hour of Public Executions, it was in a subdued manner, as to a funeral, for their thoughts were full of that Great Loss, the story of which was in progress. They sat upon the floor before him in due order, and Mahmoud began :

" Upon the dawn that followed that hopeless night, my hopes were again raised, only for my further bitterness and disappointment. I had risen before day and gone out of doors. A chance acquaintance ran across me as I paced aimlessly in the narrow streets of the city, watching the shadows shortening under the rising sun, listening to the clear voices of the water-sellers and to the cries of the mariners at their calling.

" This acquaintance was one learned in the law. Not that he was himself a scrivener, or pleader, still less a judge—on the contrary, he was born wealthy, and those so circumstanced are (in Izmar) very much averse to the tedium of a profession. But in youth he had been compelled by his grandfather to read whole libraries of books upon the legal system of his beloved country, and had further been compelled to pay considerable sums to one of the most renowned pleaders of the day in whose office he had passed three miserable years. Seeing he was so educated, and knowing well my misfortunes, he kindly took me by the arm (I could not help suspecting a certain patronage) and said :

" ' Alas, my poor Mahmoud! How we do all feel for you ! And how we respect the way in which you have borne inevitable misfortune ! But though I praise you as much as any other for your conduct and resignation, do you not push it a little too far ? We, the free inhabitants of this our beloved Izmar, have a most glorious privilege, which is, that not the King himself (the glory of Allah be upon him) has any privilege as against the humblest of his subjects, when it comes to the issue of law. Our judges, as you know, stand above all mortal frailty and are, as we devoutly and firmly believe, filled with the spirit of God Himself. Though His Majesty and his Ministers be your opponents in a case, that case will be decided with serene indifference to the position or wealth or power of the parties. You believe this, do you not ? ' he insisted earnestly, for doubts upon so final a doctrine of religion are horrible to the imperial race of Izmar.

" ' Yes, I believe it,' said I with a sigh, though I confess that my short acquaintance with misfortune had shaken me in many points of loyalty to my new country.

" ' Why, then,' said he, ' do you not come into Court with your plaint ? Our lawyers have the skill to discover a claim in anything, and you may be sure that all that can be said in your favour would be allowed in the freest manner, and if there is a single loophole, the whole or part of your former fortunes may be restored at whatever cost. For it is a maxim peculiar to our island law that if a case is decided in favour of the plaintiff, then the plaintiff has the decision in his favour.'

" I confess that my acquaintance with the manners and habits of the foreign people among whom I had had the wretched luck to be born had made me think it futile indeed to approach the august judges in a matter where a king was concerned, or to ask relief from State officials for what the State had done to me. He stoutly denied the idea I had that the judges were State officials. Said he : ' Have you never read the famous oath which every judge makes on taking office ? Do you not know how we elect him ? '

" ' Yes,' said I, in tones which betrayed no enthusiasm, ' I know indeed how the judges are appointed and the oath they take. They are appointed—(how often have I not seen the Firman signed in Council ! How often have I not affixed my own poor name to it !)—they are appointed, as the rule goes, " *by his Sacred Majesty, that is, by the familiars, the wives, and the secretaries of the Richest Men, indifferently.*" Such are the very words of the Statute.'

" ' You answer rightly,' said my friend, with a noble carriage of his head. ' Surely so impartial a source of office must make you feel secure ! On the odious Mainland the king appoints his own judges : it is a tyranny to which we in Izmar have long refused to submit. *Our* Monarch is the ruler of free men ! He would disdain to influence an appointment. He leaves that to his gentry, and they, in turn, leave it to their women and other dependants. Thus we alone of all nations secure a Bench of judges wholly independent ! But there is more : Have you forgotten the oath they take, my friend— the oath they take on appointment ? '

" ' No,' said I, still wearily.   ' I remember it well enough. Indeed, I have it all by heart, for I have read it a hundred times :— *" I swear by the Almighty God and by the contents of this book that I will not depart from justice in anything, either for orders, or favours, or personal advantage, or any consideration whatsoever, save in the political interests of my class or family, of the Lawyers' Guild to which I belong, or for such other considerations as may occur to me."* '

" ' That is right ! ' said my friend in triumphant tones. ' Well, can you want a better guarantee ? '

" ' No,' said I, ' I suppose not.'

" ' Well, then,' he cried, rising, ' let me take you to a friend of mine among the most able Scriveners of the city, and be assured that whatever can be done for you will be done.'

" ' I have no great part of my fortune left,' said I timidly, rising as he did, but unwilling to follow him.

" ' Fear nothing,' he returned heartily. ' Justice in Izmar is not bought and sold. There are, of course, certain necessary fees. But the law compels you to hire no pleader. You can appear yourself in Court. That freedom is one of our great privileges ; and, believe me, you will be heard as patiently and directed as honestly as though you were one of the greatest pleaders in the city.'

" Half persuaded by such insistence, I followed my friend to a house where, seated in the midst of commentaries upon the law, of metal boxes containing the shameful secrets of great families and the record of their indebtedness, sat an elderly man, whose face reminded me, I know not why, of a vulture.

" ' I have brought you, Kazib,' said he, ' a client. You will recognize him, I think.'

" ' I do, indeed,' said the Scrivener, rising gravely and bowing to me. ' He is no less than My Lord the Councillor Mahmoud.'

" ' The title is superfluous now,' said I a little sadly.

" The Scrivener, however, continued to give it to me in his great courtesy, and when my friend had left us together, I poured out my story. As the more important details fell from my lips my host jotted them down upon a small tablet with a fine quill that he carried. When I had concluded he spoke as follows :

" ' Such a case as yours would appear first in the Court of Sweetmeats.'

" ' Of Sweetmeats ? ' said I.

" ' It is an old term,' said he. ' We love these historic traditions.'

" ' Exactly,' I answered humbly.

" ' Well, it would appear, I say, in the Court of Sweetmeats.'

" ' Yes,' said I.

" ' After it had gone to the Court of Sweetmeats, it would almost certainly be transferred to the Court of Wrecks, Lighthouses and Divorce, or to the Department of Wills.'

" ' Indeed ? ' said I.

" ' It is so,' said the Scrivener. ' Whichever of these dealt with it, an appeal would lie, of course, to a superior court, which is generally known as the Court of Mules.'

" ' Why is . . . ' I began.

" ' Oh, sir ! ' interrupted the Scrivener, with some impatience, ' these things are immaterial ! We must use such historic names. . . . From this Court again the appeal would lie, of course, to His Majesty in Council, which is the supreme authority in the land.'

" ' What,' said I, ' to His Majesty in Council—the very authors of the injustice ? '

" ' Of course,' said the Scrivener.

" ' But,' said I, ' if the verdict is in my favour, what reason should I have for appealing ? '

" ' None,' said he, simply. ' But your opponents would.'

" ' My opponents are the King and his Council,' said I.

" ' In quite another aspect,' said the Scrivener, looking on the ground and falling silent. ' Under these circumstances,' said he, after a pause, ' you will do very well to proceed.'

" ' But,' said I, ' in case these appeals . . .'

" He waved his hands. ' We will not talk of appeals yet,' he said quickly. ' After all, you lose nothing by first instance. Have you your Charter with you ? '

" ' I said I had, and brought it out for him. He read it slowly, consulted a book for a moment, and then said :

" ' An excellent case ! ' (you may judge, my dear nephews, how my heart leapt at these words !) ' An excellent case ! . . . You have your Charter and its terms are clear. By it there is bound to be paid to you and your heirs for ever the revenue from the Salt Tax, and the issue will lie, I think, upon whether the clause implies payment undiminished and perpetual, or whether the recent Proclamations make a gumbo-rumbo of the original.'

" ' A what ? ' said I.

" ' It is a legal term,' said he, a little wearily, ' and signifies a mixalum-malory or general contortation. . . . But let us not at this stage go into technicalities of that sort. We must first state our case.'

" ' Precisely,' said I.

" ' My own fee,' said he, ' is fixed by statute, and I must ask you for ten dinars—a nominal matter.' With this, before I could stop him, he seized a large metal disc, wet a corner of a parchment, put the disc upon it, struck it with a hammer, and then held out his hand for the fee. Luckily I had my pouch with me, and so, very reluctantly, paid over this first drop of my disastrous leakage.

" Good ! ' said the Scrivener. ' We must next ask the opinion of two eminent Pleaders.'

" ' Why ? ' said I.

" ' The law demands it,' said the Scrivener.

" ' But you have already given me yours, and told me it is worth my while to proceed.'

" ' My opinion,' said the Scrivener, shaking his head vigorously, ' may serve to guide you, indeed ; but it would be altogether irregular to go into court upon that alone. So, I will draw up a statement, as we call it, and have it put before two men of the first standing—it is always better in these cases to use the highest talent. In the long run it is worth while.'

" I asked timidly how much this further step would cost, and was somewhat relieved to learn that fifty dinars to each of these eminent men would be sufficient. He asked me to return on the third day when he would give me the responses ; and he particularly reminded me that I should upon that occasion not forget to bring with me at least 150 dinars.

" ' But why the other fifty ? ' said I.

" ' Stamps and fees,' said the Scrivener shortly, and then, with infinite courtesy, dismissed me from his presence.

" On the third day I returned, bearing with me the

150 dinars from my little hoard, which I put upon the
Scrivener's table to save all further difficulties in the
matter.   He poured the money meditatively into a
little metal case, beautifully engraved, and dating,
I should say, from the second century of the Flight
of the Prophet ; it was probably (to my practised eye)
of Syrian workmanship.

   " ' Here,' said he, ' are the responses.'

   " ' Have you them written ? ' said I.

   " ' No,' said he.   ' We must wait for that.   The first
Pleader, by name the Most Noble Ghǎddēr, is of the
opinion that you have a case founded upon the great
principle of our Common Law, of which you, perhaps,
as a foreigner, have not heard—it is the principle that
" The subjects of the King can suffer no wrong."   But
he warns you against relying upon the Statute passed
in the first year of His Majesty's father's reign, called
" A Statute for the Prevention of the Loss of Money
by the Rich."   For this has been the subject of so many
contradictory decisions that it is a very poor ground.
He says, further, that there are certain case precedents
which are interesting, and two of which, at least, in his
judgment, could be urged upon your side.   In one of
these it was decided that if a man had more than a
certain income no Order or Proclamation should be
regarded as capable of prejudicing him or reducing
his wealth.   The question would thus lie as to whether
or no at the time when the first change took place you
fell within these limits.   The second Pleader is of
an exactly opposite opinion.   He says . . .'

   " ' It is enough ! ' said I.   ' The first learned Pleader
shall be my guide.   I am content to hear from him that
I have a good case, which doubtless he will continue for
me in court.'

" ' What ? ' said the Scrivener, in astonishment, ' do you suppose that such men lend their valuable services in court for fifty dinars ? '

" ' Evidently,' said I, ' as they have been so kind as to give opinions with such nicety ! '

" The Scrivener laughed as heartily as such men can, and begged me to be disabused. ' These are but the formal stages. The hiring of pleaders is quite another matter. Let me proceed to the second response. The second Pleader, the Most Noble Makhar—who, it may interest you to know, is a negro by descent—we have many such at our Bar, they have marvellous abilities, that strange race—is of an opinion, I say, exactly contrary to the other. He thinks your chance under the Common Law very doubtful. But he thinks you are secure under the Statute passed for the Prevention of Cruelty to the Important —that is its general title—dated from the first year of the reign of His Majesty's late father. All the cases, he says, are against you ; but the general principle of the Statute stands.'

" When I had heard all this I said, ' Oh ! '

" The old Scrivener gazed down at the floor between his feet, where he sat upon his rug, and I gazed down at mine, not knowing what next to say.

" ' My fee for this second interview,' said he pleasantly, after what he thought was a sufficient interval, ' is the same as for the first, ten dinars.'

" ' I have not brought them with me,' I said, having only brought the 150 dinars previously asked for.

" ' It is nothing, My Lord,' he answered, waving his hand majestically (and again, I thought, as in the case of my friend, with a touch of patronage). ' We all know and respect your position of late Councillor, and I should be the last to press you.'

" I begged him to wait a moment until I should return. I hurried to my wretched lodgings and quickly came back with the sum which he required. He put it into the little metal box. I thought he was ready to dismiss me, and I was about to ask on what date the case might first be tried, when he said, to my surprise :

" ' But we must first have Pleader's Opinion.'

" ' But, Great Heavens ! ' said I, ' have we not got it ? '

" ' Why, no,' said he. ' We have not yet a Pleader's Opinion. We have, so far, only the Opinion of Pleaders.'

" ' And what in the name of Fatimeh and Katisha is the difference ? '

" ' Surely,' said he, ' you have heard of the distinction ? The Opinion of Pleaders is the verbal response made to the Scrivener, but the law requires that another response shall be added in writing, and this we call Pleader's Opinion.'

" Once more I could find no other commentary but a cry.

" ' And at what cost ? ' I moaned in a hollow voice.

" He turned to a written list of fees, then to a special memorandum of his own. He made a short calculation upon an abacus and answered, ' three hundred dinars.'

" I kept my mouth from blasphemy and asked him when the sum would be required.

" ' It is a mere formality,' said he, ' this written opinion, but we must have a record.'

" ' Yes, yes,' said I.

" ' And I will,' said he, take the opportunity of obtaining the same before you come again.'

"Once more I returned to my disgusting rooms, took money from my secret hoard and, returning, put into the Scrivener's hands a little parcel of 300 dinars. He dropped them thoughtfully through his fingers in little streams till they nearly filled his metal box.

"'It is a pretty box, is it not?' he said. 'I took it for a bad debt from one of my clients, who most unfortunately died by his own hand in a fit of melancholy after the most distressing disappointments in his suits at law.'

"'And as to the date?' I said.

"'The date?' Once more he consulted another document, then clapped his hands for the slave who sat in his outer apartment, and having asked him a question in some incomprehensible jargon, received an answer no less mysterious. Then he turned to me and said: 'It will come on at some date after the next New Moon but one.'

"'Cannot I have a precise date?' said I, for I was thinking anxiously of my diminishing capital and wondering how long I could maintain my poor life before my cash should be completely exhausted.

"'That is obviously impossible," he answered with a touch of indignation, which he evidently thought merited. 'No man can say how long the cases before yours will last, nor in what order it may please His Holiness the Judge to take them. It will probably come, by the way,' said he, peering at another list, 'before His Holiness Benshaitan.'

"With that I left him and waited my call to the Court.

"The time dragged wearily enough. I ate most sparingly and bought no raiment, nor even any game to pass my time, but my little stock dwindled day by day. My hours were spent gazing upon the busy life of the port, or sometimes standing on the edge of the pier and staring out to sea, as though I could read in the distant mainland beyond the horizon some hopes of a better fortune and a life restored. Daily, as the time approached for my case to be heard, as the second New Moon grew with every evening brighter in the last of its crescent, I consulted officials of the Court. I discovered it was customary to give each some small sum of five or six dinars before they would answer a question. It was upon the twelfth day, the moon being nearly full, that the case before mine (which turned upon whether a man without means should owe for a debt or should postpone payment, and had lasted five exciting days) was concluded. I heard that the precedent created was of the first importance, but would be subject to appeal.

" The sun sank. It was with the morrow that my case was to be called.

" I rose on that eventful day long before dawn. I put on my raiment with the utmost care, after having cleansed it with my own hands to make it as presentable as possible, lest the poverty of my appearance should in some way prejudice me. I had already given notice that I would appear myself ; for the fees asked by the Pleaders were quite beyond the poor remnant of my purse. I must confess that I had been strongly dissuaded from such action, but I had no choice. I found a great crowd assembled, for my name was familiar to all through the position I had enjoyed in the past ; and it is ever of an absorbing interest to watch the miseries of another.

" I took my seat at a place reserved for me immedi-

ately opposite the bench. I noted on my right the
Pleaders chosen by the Council, and beyond, among
the spectators, not a few of my former colleagues.

" The Pleaders were arranged in the vestments proper
to their great function, resembling the priests of a
religion, and bearing upon their heads, I noticed, what
they never showed outside, a strange headgear of
mule skin with twisted hair and long, furry ears. The
Judge, I saw, was clothed in the most magnificent
cloth of gold, inscribed with the sacred texts and loaded
with furs of such rare animals as the sacred Rat, the
white Jackal of Thibet, and the Skunk, and bore upon
his head a crown, which he lifted three times as a salute
to the Court, while all fell prostrate before him, murmuring in a buzz of low, prayerful whispers their praise
and incantation to him as the representative of God.

" These ceremonies concluded, there was a bustle
of men rising and taking their seats upon the rugs of
the court, the Judge himself upon a sort of throne overlooking the whole, and the proceedings began.

" A short man stood in front of the Judge's throne,
who rose and piped in a shrill voice, ' Mahmoud claims
against the King.' He then sat down, and from sundry
pushes and jerks which I received from my friends,
including the Scrivener, who was kind enough to
accompany me to the Court, I saw that I was expected
to rise from my carpet and put my case.

" I said : ' Your Holiness and Voice of God ' (for
such is the formula required, as a kind friend had
warned me : and if one word be omitted the culprit
is not only forbidden to plead but is thrust into a
dungeon of the most noisome kind). ' Your Holiness,' I
opened, ' and Voice of God. I had from the King and
his Councillors a Charter. It was given me as against

one million dinars paid to them in gold by me on such and such a date. I shall show the Charter to you, and you will see there the promise that I am to receive, as against the payment I made, the revenue from the Salt Tax for ever and ever, so long as the State shall endure and the tax be levied. This tax has been in great part remitted, and by special imposts the remaining part has been wiped out. I claim that this Charter gives me the right to the original revenue from the State in full.' And I then concluded with the magic formula with which my friends had very kindly provided me, ' *and that, Divine One, is my case.*' This formality completed, I sat down.

" I flattered myself I had done well, for all had been told with perfect ease, and, after all, there was nothing more to be said. But before I took my place, cross-legged upon my carpet, I handed up to those who served the Bench my original of the Charter, signed and sealed, the which I had consulted. The Judge rose from the throne where he was seated, put the Charter down carefully upon his throne, sat upon it, and ordered the case to proceed.

" In the chief of the Pleaders upon the other side, I was pleased to see an old guest of mine. He nodded to me familiarly, rose, and opened his statement, beginning, as I did, with the ritual phrase. ' Your Holiness and Voice of God,' said he, ' His Majesty and Council have instructed me. I admit that this is a case of peculiar subtlety and difficulty, nor do I doubt that it will employ many of my colleagues, not only in this Court but in superior courts, for many months to come. Indeed, to my certain knowledge, one of them has recently purchased a marvellous vehicle which travels rapidly of its own act without horses, a foreign

invention, in which he would not have invested had
he not foreseen the lengthy and lucrative nature of the
case.   But that is by the way.   I only mention it in
order to make Your Holiness understand that we have
here to settle an issue which indeed could hardly have
been brought before any Judge less divine than yourself.'

" There followed for about a quarter of an hour a
fine passage upon the majesty of the law and the
peculiar gifts and virtues of the Judges.   But through
the whole of it he insisted in every second sentence
upon the gravity of the case and its difficulty.   I
was flattered and surprised.   I had not thought that
my opponents would make so much of me ; but, on
the other hand, I remembered that their payment was
at the charge of the public and that every day added
to the sum they received.   He next touched upon the
folly of the Salt Tax, its iniquity, its old-fashionedness,
its absurdity, and after an hour of this paused a
moment to pull down and smooth the long furry ears
of his headgear.

" In the second hour he brought in the very words
of the Charter.   He first recited them, ' *for ever and for
ever, so long as the State shall endure and the salt tax be
paid.*'   He insisted, with repeated emphasis, upon the
word ' *and* '.   In the third and fourth hours he quoted
150 instances of cases in which this word had completely
changed the character of a document, as, for instance,
in the famous case known as Abraham's Will, where
the testator left all his property to his beloved wife,
Fatimah, *and* the remainder to her mother.   Next, he
quoted the case known as the ' Degree of Dignity,'
when it was ordered that all those apprehended for
speaking disrespectfully of the Grand Mufti should be
brought into his presence *and* decapitated.   Again

(what interested me very much, for it was connected with Money), the terms of the statute, now over one hundred years old, by which the Councillors of the King receive one dinar per day *and* whatever other sum they see fit to vote themselves out of the taxes.

" It was the word ' *and*,' said he, that made the difference in all these cases. He might call witnesses to show that the word was inserted in the Charter to render the phrase abortive, absurd, nonsensical and altogether of no effect. But, alternatively, supposing that the word ' *and* ' but confirmed my case in the decision of His Holiness, then he pleaded that the Charter, having been obtained by a stranger, not a subject of the King, was null and void. Supposing that it were upheld in spite of this, then, alternatively, that I, Mahmoud, was a subject of the King, a native born, and therefore subject to the King's decisions in Council. Finally, he concluded that in any case I must not win because, if I did, it would make His Majesty's Council and members thereof look a fool severally and collectively, than which no more deplorable thing could happen to the State. Further, even if His Holiness should decide that it mattered not a rusty nail whether the Council were made to look fools or no, there was, anyhow, no money to pay me. This established a default contumax and a discharge in alias of the second degree. I give his exact words, for I noted them at the time, and could guess vaguely that they must be of grave import. When he got so far I noticed a great commotion among his colleagues. Every man in court wore an expression of strained attention mixed with admiration, and the Judge himself could not withhold from his august features something of the same tribute to this Genius of Debate.

" ' Note also, Your Holiness,' continued the Pleader, wagging his arched forefinger (which was long and pointed) very significantly in the air, ' the contumax in advert to subvert . . . and the same regardant.' He added in a sort of sneering tone : ' I will not weary the Court with that ' (I could see that the Judge nodded), ' but even the plaintiff, learned as he is in the law, will admit,' and here he turned and addressed me with a very contemptuous expression, ' that plevin would not obtain in the case of recognisance, or at any rate in the defection thereof would be docketted as an endorsement pursuant. An endorsement pursuant would stand void,' he continued, with a renewed interest in his tone (he now excited a feverish attention in his audience), ' for that is in the very foundation, I take it, of our law of terce and perinomy and has been upheld by a long succession of your Holiness's predecessors from the origins of our Sacred Lawyers' Guild.'

" Here again I thought I noticed the trace of an uncertain nod from the august figure upon the bench. ' It comes, therefore,' concluded this eloquent man, ' in plain words, to this : we rely on the terms general, and the reference particular, each interconnected, and certainly maintain that guaranty lies overt.' Here he stopped dead, and then added in simple and lower tones : ' That is my case.' Then he sat down. I am told it was one of the most marvellous efforts in all the history of the Lawyers' Guild.

" Applause may be permitted even in the Mosque or the most sacred of Shrines, but not in the august presence of the law. Yet it was with difficulty that the enraptured pleaders present, the scriveners and their attendants, could forbear from open praise. A man whom I did not know and who sat next to me, cross-legged, upon his mat, one of the pleaders, I think (for he also wore the mule skin with long, furry ears upon his head), muttered to me that it was the finest opening he had heard since Achmet had opened for the Sheik-ul-Musrim in the Oyster Case, and that was saying a great deal.

" When this great Pleader had sat down there was a complete silence in court, which lasted for some time and seemed to me a little embarrassing. At last I perceived that I was in some way the object of too much attention, and my friend the Scrivener leant over with the suggestion that I should call my witnesses. ' But I have none,' whispered I over my shoulder in great trepidation. ' I have my Charter. That is enough, is it not ? '

" The Scrivener shrugged his shoulders as though in despair, and left me to my fate.

" Then was it that I heard the voice of the great Judge booming into my ears. ' What evidence is there for the plaintiff ? '

" I rose trembling. ' I have given you all I have, Your Holiness.'

" ' You have given me none,' thundered that tremendous personage. ' All you have done is to make an opening plea.'

" ' I thought,' stammered I, ' that I had stated all that I had to state.'

" The Judge glanced round at his fellow-lawyers with a look of despair, then leaning forward, with a sort of tenderness in his tone, he said : ' Be good enough to mount the Sacred Stool reserved for the witnesses.' With that a little block of wood was brought forward, and upon it I mounted, and so stood conscious and foolish before the Court.

" His Holiness the Judge leaned back on his throne
and surveyed me with the contempt I deserved, nor
did he repress the little titter that ran through the
assembly. An official squatted in front of the throne
put a scroll into my hand, bade me put it to my forehead and repeat after him certain words, the sense
of which I lost in my perturbation. But I did as I
was bidden. After that I remained dumb. ' Well,'
said His Holiness, sharply, after a long pause, ' how
much longer are we to wait ? '

" ' Pray, your Godship, what would you have ? '
said I.

" ' I would have your evidence,' said the Judge.

" ' I have no evidence to give,' I tremblingly replied,
' save what you have already heard.'

" ' I have heard none,' said he, and again the titter
went round the court.

" Moved to action, I repeated exactly what I had
said before, that the words were what they were in
the Charter, the clause was what it was. I repeated
it point by point.

" The Judge turned to the Pleader who had just sat
down and said : ' Now, brother Selim,' whereupon my
former friend and guest rose, looked me up and down
in a very offensive manner from head to foot three or
four times, and cried :

" ' You drunken scoundrel ! Do you still maintain
the abominable falsehood which you have had the
insolence to lay before the Court ? '

" I said there was no falsehood, but the truth.

" ' The truth ! ' he sneered. ' Remember, pray,
that you have taken an oath in the name of the Scroll,
and trivial as this may seem to a man of your depraved
character, others take the matter more seriously.'

" I stood silent under the rebuke and waited his further words.

" ' Well, well,' said he suddenly, ' where were you half an hour after sunrise on the fourth day of the Fast of Ramadan in the three hundred and seventh year from the Flight of the Prophet ? '

" As I stood aghast at the question, he touched one hand significantly with the finger of the other and said, ' I do not wish to press you.'

" ' I have not the least idea,' said I.

" The Pleader glanced significantly at the Judge and then continued :

" ' You haven't the least idea ? Can you tell me approximately where you were ? '

" ' No, I cannot,' said I. ' It is very long ago, and I was but a young and innocent child.

" Here the Judge interrupted me sharply : ' We are not concerned with your young and innocent child-hood. Answer the question, if you please, and make no speeches.'

" The Pleader consulted his notes, looked up to me again and said : ' You have told us the Charter was signed in your presence and delivered over to you. '

" ' Yes,' said I.

" ' Don't answer,' interrupted His Holiness, sharply, until you are asked a question.

" ' No,' said I.

" ' Take great care, witness,' said His Holiness in a menacing voice. ' Take very great care ! '

" ' Thank You, your Holiness,' said the Pleader. ' And now, sir,' said he, addressing me in a very firm tone indeed, as though he had caught red-handed some thief creeping into his household, ' will you please tell us where is that Charter now ? Can you produce it ? '

" ' His Holiness is sitting on it,' said I, simply.

" Here the Judge almost rose from his throne, so strongly was he moved.

" ' Were you not a layman and naturally ignorant of the forms of the Court, I should condemn you to some very severe penalty,' said he. ' I make allowance for your lack of custom ; but I warn you, you may go too far.'

" ' I will pass over the last remark, witness,' continued the Pleader in dignified tones. ' I think you were not quite yourself when you made it. Will you be good enough to answer my question ? Where is the Charter now ? '

" ' Well,' said I, all bewildered, " I handed it up for His Holiness to see what my case was, and to the best of my belief he——'

" ' Silence,' thundered the Judge. ' Brother Selim, I am afraid we shall get no further on this tack. The witness evidently does not or will not understand your drift. Allow me to ask him a question.' He then turned with a sort of false kindness upon his face and said to me in measured tones : ' What we want to know is, where is the Charter upon which you claim ? '

" ' I put it into Court . . . .' I began.

" At this the Judge gave a little gesture of despair and sighed. Then he spoke.

" ' It is a principle of the law of this country,' said His Holiness, leaning back in apparent weariness as though he were instructing a child, ' I should have thought a principle known even to the meanest of His Majesty's subjects, that a document must be proved. Have you proved the Charter of which you speak ? '

" ' I don't know what you mean, Your Holiness,' said I, in very genuine fear.

" The Judge leaned forward towards me and said in measured tones : ' Remember that I am treating you leniently. I am doing what I can for you, I understand the difficulty of your position. Take care ! Take very great care ! Brother Selim, have you any other questions to ask ? '

" ' I have one or two of some consequence, if I may be allowed, Your Holiness ? '

" ' Certainly, brother Selim. Pray continue. We are all ears.'

" The Pleader cleared his throat, again consulted his notes, looked up to me and said : ' What were your earnings in games of hazard during the year concluding with the opening of the last Feast of Ramadan ? '

" I answered that I had no exact calculation, but that I had small stomach for such pastimes, and might have won or lost anything between one hundred and two hundred dinars.

" ' Take care, take very great care ! ' said His Holiness, addressing me again.

" ' Between one or two hundred dinars,' said the Pleader, in a musing sort of voice, and I noticed that the Judge was taking a note of my reply. ' Now be good enough, you base fellow, to answer me this—and remember you are upon your oath—have you been in the habit of cheating at cards, loading dice, stacking packs, palming coins, and in other ways overreaching those who joined you in what they thought to be an innocent amusement ? '

" I was about to reply when he again thundered at me : ' Remember you are upon your oath,' and His Holiness was moved to add :

" ' Take care, witness, take very great care ! '

" ' No,' said I.

" At this moment I was astonished to see everybody, including the Pleader, sit down suddenly, cross-legged, upon the floor, while I stood there upon my little block of wood, most terribly conspicuous. It was due to a gesture from the Judge.

" ' So far,' said he, in a solemn and majestic manner, ' I have allowed things to take their course, because, as I have said, every latitude must be allowed to one who is foolish enough to plead his own case. But the dignity of His Majesty's Court forbids me to be silent upon hearing this last reply to a question of the most profound and searching kind, requiring an adequate reply. The witness has insolently answered " No ".' He then turned to me and said, with a severity that thrilled me to the marrow : ' This is a Civil Court ; but remember, sir,' and here he raised his voice in a very terrible manner, ' I can impound documents and present all that you have said to the Lord Prosecutor.'

" ' Yes, Your Holiness,' said I, now thoroughly at sea.

" ' Proceed,' said the Judge, simply, to the Pleader.

" ' I have only one more question to ask,' said the Pleader.

" ' Proceed, proceed, brother Selim,' said the Judge with geniality.

" ' Do you or do you not suffer from the itch ? '

" ' My lord,' said I, ' am I really to reply to——'

" His Holiness interrupted me with a violence which I little expected from one in so exalted a position. ' Answer the question ! ' he shouted, ' answer the question at once ! '

" ' Well,' said I, ' to tell the truth, I have some little affection of the sole of my left foot, but I conceive that with careful attention and proper medical advice——'

" ' That will do,' said the Pleader, putting up his hand. ' We have heard all we need to hear,' and he sat down again upon his mat.

" ' Any rebulgence ? ' said His Holiness, looking round with a pleasant smile upon all assembled.

" I had no idea what was meant, but my friend the Scrivener passed me up a little note, saying, ' Do you carefully re-examine yourself so as to undo the effect of this terrible cross-examination.'

" It was all Greek to me, but grasping at a straw I addressed His Holiness, and said ·

" ' Oh, Voice of God and Justice upon earth! I would like to ask myself certain questions.'

" ' By all means,' said he graciously. ' Let me inform you what is the custom of the Court. You have first to stand and ask yourself the question ; you shall then stand up again and reply to it.'

" Kneeling, I struck the pavement of the court three times with my forehead as is the custom, and rising again turned towards the empty space upon the little block of wood and said :

" ' Now, witness, remember you are upon your oath ; did you or did you not receive the Charter from the King and his Council in the terms you have mentioned? '

" I then leapt upon the little block of wood and turning to the place I had just occupied, I said :

" ' I did.'

" I then jumped down again (luckily I was still a young man and the exercise did not affect me or cause me loss of breath) and I asked :

" ' What did you do with that document ? '

" I leapt upon the little block of wood again and turned to the place I had just occupied and answered :

" ' I brought it into court.'

" Once more did I take up my place on the floor, standing beneath the little block of wood.

" ' Having brought it into court, what did you do with it ? '

" I returned to my little block of wood, faced the place I had just occupied and said :

" ' I handed it up to His Holiness.'

" The Judge then spoke, ' I have had enough of this and I refuse to waste the time of the Court longer. It is in my power to condemn you to the King's dungeons for ever, and I may say that never in my long experience of our august Courts have I come across anything to parallel your repeated insolence. I have already told you that you have not proved your document and therefore for the purposes of this Court it does not exist. Stand down.'

" The words ' stand down ' signify in the technical language of this great people ' sit down,' and can only be disobeyed under the most fearful penalties. I at once obeyed and resumed my place cross-legged upon the mat.

" The Judge was now free to give his decision, but first he turned to the Pleader who had opposed me and said in the most genial tones :

" ' Brother Selim, you have, I take it, proved your document, especially the word " and " ? '

" ' Oh, yes, my lord,' answered he, in a satisfied manner. ' I have further interpleaded for secondary and excised the four principal terminants, all of which are duly stamped, passed, filed, recorded, exuded, denoted, permuted, polluted and redeemed.' To each of these words the Judge nodded with greater and greater content, and then asked :

" ' Do you call any further witnesses, brother Selim ? '

" ' I call none,' replied the eminent man, ' for if I do the vile plaintiff would have an opportunity of cross-examining them and that would give away my whole case.'

" ' I think you have done wisely,' said His Holiness, by way of an obiter dictum. ' Things shall therefore turn upon the Charter alone.' With these words I perceived by the rustle all about me that the last phase of the trial had come and that my fate was sealed. I thought I had observed in the manner of its conduct I will not say a bias, but a sort of atmosphere unfavourable to my claims ; for though it was impossible to conceive that any personal or other feeling could affect His Holiness's mind, yet I dreaded his decision. None the less I awaited that decision with some interest, for, after all, nothing is certain until it is concluded.

" The judge put down his crown, assumed a headgear which resembled that of the Special Pleaders but gilded, and with the interior of the long furry ears carefully painted in silver by way of contrast ; for such the Custom of the Law demands when a decision is about to be delivered.

" He spoke :

" ' From the evidence that has been laid before me it is clear that there exists, or has existed, will exist, or may exist, or can exist or at some other time existed, demurrer notwithstanding, some Charter wherein the word AND is the point at issue. That form was admitted by the defence, I think ? ' All the Pleaders rose and bowed and then again were seated upon their carpets. ' But I gather ' (and here he looked sternly at me) ' that there was no acceptance by the Plaintiff. We have, I take it, an operative clause wherein the

operative word is AND.   " AND so long as the salt tax
endures." Many points brought forward in defence
of the Crown I am compelled to overlook.   It is the
glory of our courts of justice that they exercise an
absolutely even-handed dealing between man and
man, and that His Majesty himself is bound by their
decisions.' (Here there was a murmur of applause which
was instantly suppressed.)   ' I make therefore so bold
as to say that the Counsel engaged by his Majesty on
this occasion have said many things with which I do
not agree and others which I shall not take into account.
It is equally clear that the case presented by the
Plaintiff is, as he put it, no case at all, and that were I
to rely, as I shall not, upon the strict forms of law, he
is already out of Court.'   At this all looked severely
on me and I felt my stature singularly diminished,
and crouched lower upon my mat.   His Holiness continued :

" ' I shall treat this matter as though I had heard
no pleadings upon either side, for this I take to be the
true attitude of a judge concerned with justice alone.
We have, then, this operative " AND . . . " this
decisive word " AND." '   Here His Holiness leaned back
on his throne, cast his eyes upwards towards the rich
arabesques of the ceiling, sighed and continued :

" ' The word AND is among the most significant of
our ancient, glorious language.   It has been used upon
innumerable occasions.   Our industrial classes, our
nobility and even our middle classes, as well as the
poor in their humble station, are compelled to its
continual expression.   It is, if I may so express myself,
part of the heritage of our race.   He would indeed
be poor in spirit, and weak in his allegiance to the
imperial traditions of this island,' continued His

Holiness, warming to his subject, ' did he not appreciate the majesty, the significance, the grandeur upon occasions, the full effect and indeed the awful weight of this little word,' and here he dropped his voice, ' "AND." "AND so long as the salt tax . . .," etc. That is the point. AND . . . I trust I have made myself clear.'

" All heads nodded in unison, while a song in adoration of His Holiness was sung by an acolyte who entered at this stage of the proceedings (as is customary in courts of law), and a hidden chorus, distant, but just heard, added a short canticle of praise. His Holiness waited for the conclusion of these ceremonies, which are invariably interpolated during any important judgment, and then continued :

" ' AND so long,' What is the significance of that word " AND " ? I take it that it is affirmative, negative, copulative and restrictive ; but that is not all. I think it is also constructive, instructive, and destructive. It is only by using it in all these ways that we can fully appreciate its preponderant significance in the issue before us.' Once more all heads nodded and even I was constrained to follow the custom, although, in my ignorance, I could make neither head nor tail of the learned argument. The lawyers present bore a look of such intense absorption that one would have thought their lives depended on what was to come.

" ' The Plaintiff in reciting the clause,' said His Holiness quite suddenly, ' emphasized a very singular phrase " for ever and for ever," and also those other words, " so long as the state endures," but I noticed a curious hesitation upon his part when he came to this word AND.'

" Here some one in the back of the court yawned in so audible a manner that there was a sudden interruption signalling an ejection, and I learned later that the unfortunaté man had perished as he deserved.

" ' I appreciate fully,' continued the Judge, ' that my decision will, subject to appeal, determine in great part the future of this ancient State. Since we are destined soon to acquire and administer the whole world it may be said that my humble remarks upon this occasion will deflect the history of the human race itself. No one can be insensitive to such a responsibility. My duty is clear. The word " AND," standing as it does between the first and second parts of the phrase on which is based Plaintiff's claim under the Charter, clearly determines that claim. But to determine is to terminate. The Plaintiff has therefore no rights here, in the sense of the word " rights " as used by the august body of our Statute and Common Law. He is at the mercy of the Crown, and his claim is disallowed. He may think himself lucky that I have not taken advantage of my full powers and had him whipped at the cart's tail or thrown down a well. Let record be made and all adjudged as decided.' With this His Holiness majestically rose, granted a benediction to the kneeling multitude, and was about to leave the Court when the Pleader Selim interrupted with the words :

" ' What about costs, your Godship ? '

" ' With the Judgment,' said the judge wearily over his shoulder ; and I noticed to my dismay ten pens busily scribbling and wondered what was coming next.

" Indeed I was weary of the whole affair and desired nothing better than to hide my humble head in my poor lodging and on the morrow with what was left of my poor little hoard—at the most 400 dinars—to leave for the mainland, and there with this tiny capital attempt to reconstruct my fortunes.

"It was not to be as I imagined. Even as I approached the door of the Court · I was approached by the Pleader Selim, who repeated that phrase hitherto meaningless, ' What about costs ? ' and found I might not depart from the building till I had provided 350 dinars, leaving me with exactly fifty to face the world ! Luckily I had my pouch upon me. I hurriedly counted out this last poor remainder of my wealth ; then, fearing to return to my lodging (the rent of which I could no longer discharge) I paced hopelessly along the quays through the evening and on through the darkness, until, about midnight, I espied a master mariner about to board his vessel.

" ' For what sum,' I asked him, ' will you take me on deck to the mainland ? '

" ' It is a hundred dinars,' he said roughly.

" ' I have it not,' I answered. My stomach was already clamouring for food. ' I have but fifty dinars, and some part of that I must reserve for my nourishment lest I perish before reaching land.'

" ' Well,' said he a little less roughly but with no humanity in his tone, ' you may crawl up forward among the cordage if you like and give me forty-five of your coins ; the five you shall keep to feed yourself with when you land.'

" I thanked him humbly for his unexpected kindness. I tried to find some warmth in the chilly night, huddled amid coils of rope on the little deck forward. At dawn the last of the crew came aboard, two great sails were hoisted and we passed out upon the sea.

" Before the sun was high we had dropped over

the horizon, and left behind us the palaces of the land
where I had thought to find security and repose. There
I was, I who had so lately had the world at my disposal,
a beggar, hopeless for the coming days, and wondering
where on my landing I should find food to keep me
living for a week together."

As Mahmoud was concluding there rose a loud wail,
piercing and prolonged which startled him and all the
file of boys aligned cross-legged before him upon the
floor. It proceeded from the youngest of the nephews.

" What is it, my little fellow ? " said his uncle
in real alarm.

" Ah ! Ah ! " sobbed out the poor infant. " Lost !
lost ! All lost ! All that lovely money lost ! I
cannot bear it, uncle. I cannot bear it ! " and he
burst into floods of tears.

" For heaven's sake," said the old man, rolling upon
his seat in his concern for the child, " do not take
on so ! There is no cause for such a bother. You
make too much of it. It is but part of a tale. Do you
not see how I have been restored to great fortune ?
Are you not in this palace of mine with all my slaves
around you ? and splendid hangings upon the wall ?
Come, look about you and do not mix up these words
of the past with real things that you can touch and
see to-day."

The little boy tried to stifle his sobs, but they
returned with increased violence.

" Oh, uncle, to think that you, who had been so
rich, should become so poor ; to think that those who
gain great wealth cannot keep it for ever ! Consider
all your wealth ! Oh, it is terrible, the death and
destruction of it ! " Throwing himself down upon the
marble floor he buried his face in his crossed arms and

kicked either foot alternately in the air, in the violent paroxysm of his grief.

His uncle was so moved that he knelt beside the child to soothe him.

" Pray, pray, restrain yourself," he said. " You will do yourself some hurt. I admire you, my dear boy, I perceive your singular gifts. More than all your elder brothers do you seem to know that which the young should seek in life. You understand indeed what others do not always, all that money means. But it is terrible to see one of your age suffering such agonies from a mere recital of its loss. Indeed, I am moved to console you," here the old man was tempted to put his hand into his pouch and offer some small coin in consolation to the child, but he recollected himself and continued, " to console you with a pleasant draft of cold water, which I am afraid I forgot to tender to you and your brothers when I last had the pleasure of your attendance."

The little fellow sat up, still sobbing, but attempting to dry his eyes and moaning from time to time " All that money ! All that lovely money ! "

Pure, cold, crystal water was brought round and gratefully sipped by the boys, who when they had thus refreshed themselves at their uncle's expense, thanked him warmly and disappeared with reverence from his presence just at the moment when the voice of the Muezzin was heard from a neighbouring minaret boring the Faithful to tears with its repeated call to prayer.

GHANAMAT

That is:

"THE SHEEP"

CHAPTER VII

A S Mahmoud's nephews filed in just after the hour
of public executions to hear the continuation
of their uncle's absorbing tale, they wore an expression
different from that which he had observed on their
faces during so many days. The thought of this great
man subjected to misfortune like any other, and passing
through the trials of actual poverty, had shocked their
young and sensitive souls. They had been trained
indeed, even in their short experience, to the idea that
they and their poor father must suffer contempt ; but
that the head of the family should ever have passed
through such things shook their faith in the world.

The aged merchant, a little concerned with their
appearance, warned them that what he had to tell
them, not only upon that day but later too, would be
concerned with no happy relation. " These were, my
children," said he, " the days of my dereliction. They
served to humble me, and often when I have occasion
to turn a poor man out of his house or to prosecute
some starving widow for debt, or to see to the imprisonment of one who has failed to keep some contract I
may have imposed upon him, I sigh and chasten myself
with the thought that I myself might (but for the
infinite goodness of my God) have been in his or her
position. Though, frankly, I cannot say, considering
the ineptitude of such people, that I can ever imagine

143

them in mine." Having so prefaced what he had to tell, the merchant proceeded:

" I sat down, then, in the bows of the boat on that miserable night watching for land. I tried to make some plan, as is the habit of men of my temper, but none would form itself in my fatigued and unhappy brain. One asset I had and one only (over and above the few coins which could hardly last me for more than a day) and that was the dress I wore; for I still carried the fine clothes of my former rank. I had worn them on the occasion of the trial; indeed, I now had no others.

" This accoutrement and a certain proud manner of bearing which I had acquired during the past years of my affluence saved me from insult; though I am not sure that if I had been asked to carry some package for the wealthier of the passengers I should not have accepted the opportunity of reward. I spent about half my poor handful of cash on a meal; with the remainder I purchased provision for the evening.

" The town in which I found myself was—happily— too busy and populous a mart to pay attention to a chance wanderer. Lacking all direction, trusting as I had trusted long ago to fortune or rather to Providence, I betook myself after the worst heat of the day had passed, to a chance track which led first along the river side, above the harbour, and afterwards climbed through the gardens of the city to the hills beyond.

" The countryside was here of a nature more fertile than the countries through which I had hitherto passed. The dense trees of the woods made a grateful shade for me in that silent afternoon, and when I had passed beyond these on my upward journey I came to a great rolling land of sparse grass, feed for cattle.

" It was hired 'out, it would seem, to graziers ;
for I saw some little way off standing in the attitude
of a shepherd and holding his bent staff beside his
vigorous old frame, a very remarkable figure. I
approached him without any set idea of what my
adventure might lead to. I only knew that things
could not be worse. Perhaps I had somewhere in
my mind a guess, half-formed, that I could be of some
service at some small wage. At any rate I accosted
him. I have seldom seen an expression more haughty
and vigorous and marvelled that it should be that
of a hired man. He was perhaps sixty years of age
with a strong bearing, eyes luminous and almost
fierce, and a face in outline that of a hawk, or better,
that of an eagle. And as he stood there he watched,
grazing before him, a great flock of sheep, well fed,
and fat ; of a high breed, excellent to behold. There
were at least a thousand of these and it would seem
that the religion of this part (for they also were true
believers) did not forbid the use of bells. For I heard
a multitudinous tinkling come up from the flock as
it moved. Very far away the plateau made an edge
against the sky, and between that horizon and the
summit to which I had reached, folds, with water
pools concealed in them, diversified the great sweep.
But there were no trees. All was bare and majestic
under the sky as the light melted towards evening.

" The shepherd returned my salutation, accepted
my offer to share the very scanty food which I had
purchased and so sat down before me on the ground
to eat.

" As we ate we grew acquainted. I told him frankly
enough of my misfortune, though not in detail. ' I
was,' said I, ' only the day before yesterday a rich

man.   To-day I am what you see, and my last piece of
silver is gone.'   He looked at me gravely and said that
there was One Who gave and Who took away.   His
Name be exalted.   ' These sheep, for instance,' said
he, ' are the property of a man contemptible in every
way, foolish, irascible, a bad master and (one would
have thought) an unwise merchant.   Yet he pros-
pers while I, the shepherd, remain upon a hire too
small to permit me to save.   And so it has been for
years ! '

" ' I have not,' added he a little bitterly, ' the
faculties for that sort of life which my master pursues.
At any rate I am quite certain of this : that by any
common judgment of men he is the inferior and I
the lord.   Yet here I am ! . . . The world deals
harshly by poor men.'   He looked at me to see if the
words sank in.

" As he thus spoke (his sadness seemed to relieve
my own with a sense of our common dependence)
the sun now near the horizon warned us of prayer
and I was glad indeed to see that this new chance
companion was as much alive as I to the duties we
owe our Maker.   He fell upon his knees and bowed to
the evening prayer as I did beside him, and for some
moments, as we recited the sacred formula, all worldly
thoughts passed from my mind and I think from his
also.   We rose at the same moment from this exercise,
each filled, I felt, with brotherhood.   I was the first
to break the consecrated silence.

" I did so by asking him whether he had never
thought, in the course of his long years as a shepherd,
how money might be made by the stealing of his
master's sheep, or by some trick with them ?   Whether
he had never had the opportunity to blackmail his

master, or in some other way to increase his fortune ?
For it seemed intolerable to me that a man such as
he described his employer to be, should be wealthy
while he were poor. He shrugged his shoulders as
though in despair and answered simply :

" ' In the distant past I often attempted such things ;
but invariably have I failed. Indeed, the master
graziers of this part know me well for one who has
attempted at their expense every kind of bold chance,
and I would never have employment from them were
it not for my skill in lambing and in every other part
of the trade. As it is they watch me rigorously.
Their spies are everywhere. I could not, I fear, make
one dinar by any one of the methods you suggest.
I have in my time tried them all. I have forged
receipts ; I have sold sheep which afterwards I entered
as dead from accident ; I have falsified the returns of
the lambing ; I have sometimes raised a sum of
money upon the flock under pretence that it was my
own. My only reward has been fine and imprisonment and cruel torture. But the truth is that I have
not the faculties of the merchant. They are, I take
it, granted to some and withheld from others. For
my part I have despaired of their exercise and shall
never turn to them again.'

" His words filled me at once with pity and with
hope, and (since ingenuity is never long absent from
men of my temper) a scheme suddenly appeared.

" ' Why should not we,' I said, after I had gathered
wood and lit a fire to meet the approachng darkness,
' enter into partnership ? I think I may say without
boasting that I possess in a singular degree those
faculties which you say you lack. God made me in
every part for a merchant. I can conceal, distort,

forestall, outdo, bully, terrify and even boldly snatch, far better than any other man I have come across. Only once in my life have I fallen into the weakness of trusting others and as you see I have paid bitterly for that weakness.' So I spoke, not noticing that I was yet again committing the same error in suggesting partnership to a mere stranger. But in truth Allah had blinded me ; purposing to make me taste misfortune to the full that I might the better adore His later beneficence.

" ' All these talents I have in abundance and more also,' I continued, ' for God has been very good to me. You, on the other hand, have what I lack ; that is, a knowledge of the towns round about and of their markets ; of the value of sheep ; of the system which has been organized for the catching of ingenious men ; and of how that system may be avoided. Between us, then, we have all the things needed for our success. Come, let us determine with the very next breaking of the light to try our fortunes together.'

" After I had thus spoken the shepherd looked at me long and anxiously over the fire, the reflection of which shone in his piercing eyes. I wondered whether he were wavering and to what conclusion he would come. At last he spoke, slowly enough.

" ' I am not willing,' said he, ' I am not willing . . . but I will take the risk. The worst that can come to me I have already suffered. At the best ' —and he pointed towards the vast flock of sheep now a mass of glimmering white as they lay in the darkness —' at the best we should each acquire provision for many years.'

" ' Oh ! fool ! ' thought I, ' provision for many years ! Does he not know how money breeds ? '

But in open speech I said, ' Yes, we will divide the spoil and go our ways. I with my share and you with yours.'

" ' Precisely,' he answered, with a curious smile which, for the moment, intrigued me. ' You with your share and I with mine.'

" As the night passed I entertained him with the details of my plan. Since it was I who had to do the work while he would have to command (from his knowledge of the trade), I proposed that he should be the master and I the man. To all this he nodded assent. He was also prepared to meet me in my suggestion that he should put on my fine clothes and I his rags, the better to carry out our parts. ' This will,' said I, ' seem strange while you are driving the sheep, but as we approach the town and market to which you shall direct me, if there be one nearby, I will attempt to take over your task and under your direction I may at least complete it by bringing the flock to the place of sale. I will speak of you as the owner. My fine dress which you wear will carry out that deception and deceive all into thinking that it is an honest transaction. The sum upon which we shall agree with the purchaser shall be paid to *you*; and not until the whole transaction is over, and we well out of the gate, shall I ask for the division, which I take it should be in equal halves.'

" To all this also he agreed ; only asking whether I would not like (as, after all, I had only just met him) to have the money paid to both ?

" I urged him to keep to my plan. His receiving the money as master would seem natural and excite no surprise. We could divide in private at our leisure.

" To my surprise he made me a low bow at this ;

but I put it down to custom, and went on with my plan.

" For the sake of a rough calculation I asked him what sheep were fetching, and he said that in the neighbouring Ksar, which might be called a straggling market town or a large village, there was to be held, it so happened, the very next day a sheep market, where we must find ourselves shortly after sunrise. It was distant less than an hour across the uplands. The purchasers came from all parts, and as the bidding was likely to be brisk we might expect for the flock as a whole not less than 1,800 or even 2,000 pieces of gold. As he spoke I already felt that capital in my possession, or, at least, half of it, and I thought things would go hard with me if after our first successful transaction I could not carry on my partner to another and another, until at last I had manipulated him out of his share also.

" We discussed all further details through the night, rehearsed our parts, and had the whole perfect when the first glimmer of dawn showed in the East beyond the edges of the hills beneath a waning moon.

" We rose ; the flock was gathered ; our garments exchanged ; and I could not but admire my companion, now that he was dressed in what seemed a manner so much more suitable to his carriage and features. He looked a very Master, a prosperous lord of men, and I congratulated him upon the effect, which, I assured him, would allay all suspicion, since all would take him for a very great lord indeed.

" Again he smiled that intriguing smile and bowed too low. But I was a little nettled at his affecting to play the part thoroughly by addressing me in sharp tones and with the air of a superior. I, for my part, shivered in the dawn in the miserable rags which I had taken from him, and holding his staff awkwardly enough tramped on in my character of the servant.

" Soon, just as the sun rose, the dusty hedges and the cracked yellowish walls of the Ksar appeared in a hollow through which ran a muddy stream. From the enclosures within, rose the bleating of many sheep which had been driven to the same market, and we observed upon the folds of land beyond several flocks arriving in convergence upon the same place.

" My companion told me while we were still out of earshot that an early arrival would allow us to watch the movement of prices and, what was of more value to us, might enable us to get away before opportunity for pursuit should arise.

" He gave me my last instructions, recalling all that we had arranged in the night. ' I, for my part,' said he, as the first sheep of our great flock entered the narrow streets, ' shall fall behind you and take my way to the Pavement outside the Mosque reserved for the principal merchants, and there with all due dignity and honour await your report, while you go forward to the market place beyond the Mosque : when you have got a purchaser, come back and find me.   For such is here the custom.   It is the servant who nego- tiates, the master who confirms.   The servant leads the purchaser to his superior, and that superior takes the purchase money.   Do you, for your part, cast around until you hear the conversation of the bidders and see that you sell at a price not less than 2,000 pieces of gold.'   He then gave the number of our flock all told, which he made me repeat to a single point in ewes and in lambs.   When he had said this he fell behind me and went up a street which led to the Mosque ; while I, in some doubt of my capacity, but putting what bold face I could upon the matter, went straight before me along the broad way toward the market beyond. There I drove all the flock into a great pen, of which certain were reserved for the vendors in that mart.

" The market soon filled with buyers. They came in little groups, prodding the sheep, feeling the wool and sometimes looking into their mouths; and the flock which I had the honour of commanding was the most admired of all. I was asked by several if I would not sell singly; but estimating the eagerness of the buyers I shook my head and said that I could not sell for less than a reserve sum of two thousand pieces of gold, nor could I break the flock. I added that it was a pity to do so as it was a pedigree flock, every single animal being descended from the famous ram which had spoken in a human voice to the Holy Hassan three hundred years ago by order of the Most High. I admitted that this origin made little difference to the mutton, but I pointed out its extraordinary effect upon the wool.

" With that the bidding began and I noticed with great pleasure one tall, dark, very thin man among the rest, slow of gesture, fixed of eye, who never took his looks from my face and who, just after each last bid, would raise it by fifty pieces of gold. He was not to be beaten. One competitor after another dropped out. At last when the magnificent sum of 2,832 pieces of gold had been bid by the mysterious stranger I clapped my hands together as the signal and used the formula ' Heaven has decided.' The stranger approached me, drawing from his girdle a reed and a small horn of ink. I thought we were about to sign the transfer—it seemed to me an odd formality, seeing that he had but to drive the beasts away and leave me the bag of gold. I was undeceived. He presented me no charter of transfer, no deed, but a strange piece of writing such as I had not seen before and asked me for its counterpart. I was startled and a little confused. ' What counterpart ? ' said I.

" ' Do you mean,' said he in clear tones, so that the curious bystanders should overhear, ' that you have no permit ? '

" At this the audience tittered, and others, scenting amusement, crowded round to gaze and follow.

" ' Have you no permit ? ' he repeated severely.

" I felt myself growing hot and confused under the laughter which followed ; and even alarmed when I heard one buyer say contemptuously to his neighbour, ' They've caught another of 'em ! '

" I confessed that I had never even heard of such an instrument.

" ' Follow me,' said the stranger grimly, and whether from curiosity or from a conviction growing in me that he had authority, I followed humbly enough, leaving my large flock bleating in its pen.

" The stranger (for he now showed that he had upon him the keys of the market) locked the gate of the pen, appointed (another proof of his authority) a slave to stand by and see that no one interfered with the property I had transferred to him, and motioned to others to fall in behind us. He then led me away, and I was more concerned than ever to notice the strange smiles of those who saw the little procession which we made, he going first with his great staff, I treading behind.

" He led me to where the Sheiks of the neighbour-hood, the principal sheep owners and magistrates, sat in solemnity before the Mosque; an awe-inspiring company. Grand and splendid among them, in their very centre and clearly the most revered of them all, I perceived my late companion the shepherd, all dressed up in my own fine clothes, but having now added ornaments reserved for him, and looking for all the world like the king of the place.

"At our approach he turned an indignant glance upon me, rose to his feet, and addressing the stranger who had captured me, cried in a terrible voice:

"'Officer! Do you bring me yet another of these evil-doers? Whose sheep had he driven off? And is it a case of a forged permit or what?'

"I already saw how the land lay, and I quailed to think what was before me. The owners—I rightly guessed—had suffered from sheep stealing; had established permits, signed by them, in order to check fraudulent sales; had plotted to catch the chief culprits, and this perfidious man had disguised himself as a servant in order to catch such, and had caught *me*. The officer who had arrested me spoke:

"'My lord,' he said, 'we have caught this ruffian'—pointing to me—'selling *your* sheep without any permit at all! He must have driven them through the night. By the law which your Council proclaimed last year, just after the Fast, his punishment lies in your hands. The owner has the determination of it.'

"To my astonishment and horror my former companion looked on me with a dreadful face of scorn and said: 'Tell me all, that I may apportion the punishment due to him. I have had him in my employ for but a short time. I mistrusted him from the first. Tell me all!'

"'I have so found him selling your lordship's

sheep. They fetched nearly 3,000 pieces of gold,'
answered the officer grimly. ' He shall make an excellent example for, my lord, he is the first whom we have
caught in this market trying to sell without a permit.
There can be no doubt (I have witnesses to it) that he
proposed to take the purchase money and (perhaps
with some accomplice whom I have not traced)
to fly.'

" On hearing this my former companion, clenching
his hands and showing as intense a passion as his
dignity would allow—a magnificent figure in those
clothes of his (my clothes)—cried, ' What ? Is it
possible that one whom I have nourished, tended and
befriended should be guilty of so abominable a crime ?
How wise we were to make the regulation ! How
excellent and zealous are you in your office thus to
have found the first culprit who attempted theft in
this place ! How admirable that he should be brought
to justice before he could consummate his crime !
How marked is the work of Providence '—here he lifted
his eyes to heaven—' which has given him up to us
for an example ! Come, let us cut off his head with a
blunt saw.'

" The officer who had thus traitorously caught me
bowed low and said, ' Hearing and obedience ! But
if my lord will take council I would speak.'

" ' What is it you would say ? ' said my companion,
who resumed his seat but slowly and seemed displeased
at the interruption.

" ' My lord,' said the official, ' I suggest that if you
cut off his miserable head with a blunt saw, though
doubtless it would have a good effect for the moment
and strike terror into the hearts of those here who see
it, so that never more shall sheep be stolen from this

market, nor ever more shall we suffer as we have suffered in the past, yet it would be of slighter effect than what I shall propose. For to hear of a man's execution is one thing, but to hear his own relation of his sufferings is another. I propose therefore that he shall be beaten at great length but not to the point of death ; on the approaching of that consummation let him be released to crawl away and tell his story throughout our countries to whoever will listen. Such an example would be of far more service to the owners, my lord, than his death would be, and I promise that he shall be beaten in the most expert manner to the advantage of all posterity.'

" Even as he advised so was it done. I was given the bastinado without mercy until I thought I should have expired, and then under every circumstance of ignominy I was turned loose with a week's provision of coarse meal into that deserted country, to spread terror among the servants of the wealthy owners and by my example to deter them from ever attempting to play tricks with their masters' goods.

" I, who from my youth have abhorred the ill use of servants, I who had founded once so great a fortune and proved so kind a master to hosts of dependants, I in my ingenuousness and simple heart could not have believed that such trickery existed in the world ! I had been wholly duped !

" As I limped from village to village, begging my bread, I heard the whole story and it exactly confirmed the conclusion I had reached when I first stood trembling before the Sheiks at the Mosque.

" The shepherd in his poor clothes was the richest sheep owner in the country. He and his fellow-lords had for some years past suffered from surreptitious sales, they had appointed officers to watch the markets and even so had not always been able to recover the purchase money from their agents. They had therefore—as I guessed—instituted a system of Permits so that no man could sell in the market without their signed licences and so that each man so selling could be detected as a thief by the officers of the markets. But how should I, a poor stranger from over-sea, know anything of this? The blackness of the treason wounded me even more than the sufferings of my bastinado. I almost lost my faith in man; by the Everlasting Mercy I did not lose my faith in Heaven! . . . Nothing, my boys," said the old man, his voice trembling, as he remembered this terrible passage of the past, " nothing but Religion supported me during the fearful days that followed. I think I can say with humility that one less founded in a firm reliance upon his Maker would have grown embittered. I might have turned into one of those useless people who, as the result of misfortune, become railers, nourishing a perpetual quarrel against mankind. But our Holy Religion stood me in good stead, and as my wounds healed and as my wanderings led me further from the scene of my torture I recovered so much of my spirits as once more to attempt what might have seemed impossible; I faced the world again. It would seem that those for whom Heaven has high designs, those for whom, like myself, it intends the highest positions among men, must in the divine scheme pass first through the fire and the ordeal. Happy the men who (like myself) profit by such visitations and retain unclouded their childlike trust in God."

" Amen," murmured the eldest of the nephews.

" What was that you said ? " cried Mahmoud sharply?

" I said ' Amen,' Uncle," answered the lad in humble tones. His uncle scanned him narrowly.

" Well," he muttered, " I suppose you are too much a fool to have meant it ill. . . ."

At this the strident nasals of the Muezzin suddenly shrieked from the neighbouring minaret and the young lads with unaccustomed rapidity vacated the great merchant's apartment.

الْبُسْتان

AL-BUSTÁN

That is:
"THE ORCHARD"

CHAPTER VIII

ENTITLED *AL-BUSTĀN*, OR THE ORCHARD

WHEN Mahmoud's nephews reappeared before him at the hour of public executions it was in a certain weariness of spirit; for though they knew that the fortunes of their uncle must subsequently be recovered in the narrative (since there he was before them, rolling, or, as the phrase went in Bagdad, " dripping " with it) yet the blows of fate had fallen upon him with such violence in the recent tale that something of his then despair had entered their own souls. They sat down therefore with hanging heads to listen, as they feared, to little better than the further advance of intolerable things.

The old man began in a subdued voice of lamentable recollection :

" I wandered on through the bare uplands, miserable, weak, penniless and in rags. So far had my soul fallen that on the seventh day I came near to omitting my prayer at even . . . but I thank Heaven that this temptation was conquered ! I knelt down painfully upon the little carpet which was my last possession and submitted myself to the will of Allah.

" As though in answer to my prayer, and while I still knelt there, I saw afar off the figure of one who moved, as I could see from that distance, with a carriage of leisure, and I hoped—I dared to hope— that in answer to my prayer, I will not say a victim, but, at any rate, some provender was to be afforded me.

"I hastened my steps to catch up the stranger, and as I approached him remarked with pleasure his fine clothes and stately manner. 'I have here,' said I to myself, 'some Important Man, some one doubtless unused to the base necessities of commerce; simple, noble in mind, straightforward, generous, amply provided: the very companion whom I should desire.' I turned over in my mind (as I slackened my steps for a moment, so that he should not yet observe my arrival) various schemes whereby I might excuse my intrusion upon his solitary walk. At last I hit on that which seemed to me the most agreeable to his supposed circumstances and to my appearance. I strode up to him and bowing low asked him whether his Greatness could direct a poor wretch to a certain village the name of which I had heard and which lay more or less in the direction I had taken.

"The stranger turned to salute me and with that I felt an added delight. For he was the very thing I had prayed. Young, simple in manner, courteous, probably, by his dress, independent and wealthy; probably, as our language has it, 'his own father.'

"He wore rare ornaments; his cloak was of the finest wool and the cord that bound his headdress was interspersed with silver.

"By way of reply to my request, he told me in a pleasant, deep voice, speaking after the fashion of the rich, that he was himself strolling towards it so far as his own house and farm, which lay between, and that there he would put me upon my way. I expressed my gratitude, and my fear lest so bedraggled a companion might be distasteful to him. He smiled and assured me that he loved nothing better than converse. He had visited a neighbour that morning to ask advice on a certain set of pear trees of his which had not been doing well. He had left his servant to follow him with his mount, preferring this hour's stroll back homewards in the cool of the sunset hour which had now descended.

" As we went we talked of many things and I frankly told him the story of my life ; for I have discovered that nothing is more pleasing to men of his station than the account of how another has been reduced from wealth to poverty.

" ' I was not always,' said I, as I strolled by his side, ' the deplorable figure you now see me. Indeed, but a very few months ago I was the over-manager of a great fruit plantation some hundred miles to the north of this place. I had come with good recommendations from my former employers, planters of the Gulf. I had left these my original masters with the best of characters and the kindest of recommendations, and only because the eldest son of one of the partners had to be put into the business and there was no room for both of us. I had accumulated in some years of useful service a sufficient little capital which my kind masters were so exceedingly generous as to double, and I was able to put the total sum into the new business to which I had been recommended. For it is always better,' I added, ' to have some stake in the firm.'

" ' You are right,' said my new friend in hearty approval. ' There is no greater error than to offer a firm such intangible things as talent, honesty and the rest. Valuable as they are, if they are unaccompanied by metal they are without substance and void.'

" With an expression of great humility I applauded

his reply and told him how flattered I was to find that
my judgment had jumped with his. ' But, alas, Sir ! '
I continued deferentially, ' There is no controlling the
current of our destinies ! For there is One above——'

" ' I know, I know ! ' agreed my companion hurriedly,
in the tones of one to whom the sentiment was familiar
and at the same time doubtful, and I continued :

" ' By that Divine Will,' I went on, ' was I visited.
Heaven saw fit to try its servant. In the course of
my management I was sent to negotiate the purchase
of a cargo of lime-dressing at the nearest port, for
use upon the plantation. On my way I had the misfortune to be robbed at an inn of the pouch of gold
that had been confided to me. I ought, of course, to
have returned at once and told my partners and
employers what had happened, and to have offered,
perhaps, to repair out of my own property what might
look like the result of my own negligence ; but I was
afraid lest I should not be believed, and again lest, if
I were believed, the loss should prejudice me in their
eyes as an incompetent. What I did was to go forward to the port that very day, penniless, and trust to
the credit of my firm to complete the transaction I
had in hand.

" ' But once again I was unfortunate ! I carried
through the negotiations with success and purchased
the cargo upon very reasonable terms. I delayed to
the last moment the payment of earnest money and
then, when delay would no longer serve, I said carelessly, that full payment would follow by messenger
within two days. The merchant's face darkened. He
told me that he had been led on by false pretences,
roughly bade me begone and would hear no more of
the transaction. He refused to sign, and indeed left

me abruptly, saying that he was off to seek another
purchaser and telling me at the same time that he
was seriously considering whether or no to summon
me before the magistrate for having thus lost him a
whole day upon a false pretence.

" ' He was as good as his word, and I received a
summons from the magistrate that very evening to
attend his court the next day.

" ' It was unfortunate that during the night another
theft took place in the inn where I lay.   The bundles
of those staying at the place were searched.   My own
alone contained no valuables of any kind.   One would
have thought that such a circumstance would have
spoken in my favour.   It was exactly the other way.
It was argued that a man who will stay in an inn
without the means of paying must be a thief of some
sort and that since the sum stolen was not to be found
elsewhere it was probably I, thus manifestly suspect
of trickery, who was the culprit.   In my fright I
attempted to escape.   I was caught and roughly
handled, with the final result that I appeared in the
magistrate's court covered with blood, my garments
torn and in such a posture subjected to a double accusation upon the part of the innkeeper and also upon
the part of the foreign merchant who appeared upon
the original charge.

" ' In such distress I had no avenue of escape save a
reference to my honoured firm, the name of which,
though distant, was familiar to the Court.   The
magistrate expressed his doubt that I had any connection with such important people, and asked me if I
would risk the sending of a messenger to my so-called
partners.   I said I would do so gladly, but during the
two days' interval of the messenger's absence I was

closely confined in the public prison, where I regret to say the foreign merchant had the heartlessness to come and make faces at me through the bars, and where, having no money to give my gaolers, I was treated with the utmost harshness.

" ' My misfortunes were not at an end. As luck would have it the firm to which I belonged and of whose books I had the sole management, undertook a surprise audit on the very day of my departure, and discovered a most serious deficit in one item which the partners, in their ignorance, could not account for. Had I been present I could easily have explained what had happened. It was but an advance which I had made to a customer whose transactions with us were of the highest value. As much in my own interests as in those of my partners I was well justified in risking the money. I had acted foolishly perhaps in refusing to take a receipt or to enter the matter in the books, but the thing was only for a week and after so many years of prosperity I could not dream of so small a thing turning out untowardly. However, there it was. My partners hurriedly sent after me and learned to their dismay that I had left the first inn upon the road without payment, and giving no account of my future movements. They had sent a man post-haste on a swift horse. He had covered the distance to the port in twelve hours, but (as I was now in prison), could discover nothing of me in the town nor find any cargo I had bought or, indeed, any trace of me. He returned to my partners, as they had instructed him, upon another beast as swift (having sold his spent mount) and it was just as they received this grave news of my apparent absconding, just while my partners grew more and more convinced of my supposed guilt, that the messenger from the magistrate arrived and completed the accusation. They answered, not by coming in person, but by sending a letter of the most violent kind, calling me a notorious thief, expressing their pleasure that I had been laid by the heels and begging that, so far as they were concerned, the magistrate would not spare me in any punishment he might see fit to inflict for my other escapades. Meanwhile (they said) they would not trouble him to enter judgment for the sum I had taken, since they had replaced it out of my capital in the firm, which nearly, or exactly, made good the deficit.

" ' You may imagine, my Lord, the result of all this ! The magistrate read the Court a sermon on the justice of the law which spared no man for his rank or commerce, and concluded, " You have before you the sad spectacle of a man of substance fallen through temptation into poverty and disgrace." The foreign merchant contemptuously waived his action, the innkeeper with equal contempt expressed himself satisfied with the punishment I had already undergone, claiming only my clothes by way of payment, giving me these few rags in exchange. With yet another admonition the magistrate dismissed me. I went out from the court a broken man, wandered aimlessly southward, doing a little work here and there upon the farms, and I am now seeking the next village with the object of offering my services.

" ' Such, Sir,' I concluded, ' is my tale. . . . Here am I, with every commercial aptitude, and full training in the various transactions of business (but especially in the management of plantations) for no fault of my own unable to exercise these talents, rehabilitate my character, and recover my position in society.'

" The rich young man was deeply touched by my story, every word of which, I am glad to say, he seemed to believe ; for I·was not deceived in my reading of character and I had rightly guessed that a man under thirty, honest-faced and clearly enjoying leisure and wealth would be singularly open to the reception of any romantic tale that might be offered to him.

" ' It is indeed fortunate,' he answered, ' that you understand plantations. It is a matter in which I am for the moment interested. I have an orchard which is not doing well.' He had evidently forgotten his first sentence on our meeting which had given me my clue. But rich and generous natures are like that in early youth : hence, also, are they bad players in games of skill.

" ' Come with me,' he continued, ' and pass the night in my house yonder (it already lay before us in the hollow) ; ' the conversation on your past life, which is doubtless full of adventures, will entertain me at my meal. To-morrow I will see that you have occupation upon my farm, and after a short experiment I think we shall get along very well indeed together, particularly as I have recently planted by way of experiment a number of pear trees which—as I think I just told you—are not doing well. I thought myself able from my general knowledge to conduct this orchard, but I regret to say that some of the trees have died, and that the rest are in a poor way. I evidently lack the special experience required. Since plantations are your special line you may be of the greatest service to me in this little matter.'

" Here, my dear nephews, I was in something of a quandary. This, I am told, is a difficulty we men of affairs come across often enough in the conduct of

our negotiations. It is our duty, as I need hardly tell
you, to add details of a corroborative kind to the
statements we have to make in affairs. To omit
any detail is to court suspicion. On the other hand,
one never knows where the most necessary fictions may
lead one. Here I was confronted by the task of bringing to fruition an orchard . . . an orchard of pears
. . . and I knew nothing whatever of orchards and
of pears far less.

" I replied, therefore, with the greatest enthusiasm
that the opportunity was exactly what I should have
desired. Orchards were the *one* kind of plantation I
had most carefully studied, and of all fruits *pears* were
those upon which I had specialised most. Once I
had seen the kind of tree my kind host had planted I
should certainly be able to tell him what was the
matter.

" It was almost dark when we came to his enclosure,
but so eager was he on his new idea that he led me at
once to the back of the house where the trees were
planted. Very sickly indeed did their gaunt twigs
look in the gloaming. A good third of them were
shrivelled and dead, the rest drooped in various degrees,
one only gave a promise of fruit out of some three
hundred stems. The rich man surveyed the ruin
and gazed at me anxiously while I held my chin in
my hand as though meditating upon the best course
for him to pursue, but in reality considering my own.

" Then it was, my dear infants, that I received from
on High one of those illuminations which have always
been, with me, the forerunners of great things. I
deliberately kept the rich young man waiting for the
space of a long prayer and then said suddenly and with
determination, ' Scrap the lot ! . . . Excuse me,' I

added, ' I have used a phrase current in the barbaric cities of the north, which is somewhat corrupt in speech. My intention was to express to your Highness my conviction, formed upon this rapid survey in gathering darkness, that the orchard can no longer be saved, for I am sure my judgment will be confirmed when I make a more thorough examination to-morrow morning in broad day. I see also, even in this light, that the type of tree you have planted is wholly unsuited to the climate. May I be so bold as to ask where you purchased the stock ? '

" ' I was assured,' answered my new friend a little shamefacedly, ' that it was stock grown within this very region and peculiarly adapted for our dry climate : for the drought of our position which, as you know, stands too high for waterways.'

" I shook my head. ' You were deceived,' said I. ' Who sold you this unsuitable stock ? '

" He told me that it was a sound friend of his who had gone off for a while upon a journey, that he was quite sure he had not intended to deceive. ' Perhaps there was some error in the consignment shipped to you,' I answered cheerfully as we turned towards the house. ' This kind does admirably in the River Lowlands, and I take it your friend's servants by some mistake sent your consignment to some lowland client and *his* to *you* in these uplands. Anyhow, the orchard is manifestly doomed, as you can see, and for my part I make no doubt that the trouble has come from the use of a wrong species. Now what you want here,' I continued rapidly, turning over my chances well in my mind, and plumping for technical terms, ' is a pear neither palinate nor sublongate, nor, for that matter perforate, but daxullic, or, as we sometimes

call it in the trade " retarded "—at any rate in the
second and third stirp.'

" ' I see ; I understand ; I apprehend,' said the
rich young man. For thus, have I discovered, do
rich young men carry on a conversation which leaves
them entirely at sea.

" ' I do not,' I hastened to add, ' insist, of course,
upon the Persian stock, though that is the best. It
might be difficult to procure and it is *very* expensive.
What I mean is something of the same family. I
should advise, as a stock more easily purchased in
local markets, the pear called by the merchants " The
Glory of Heaven."

" ' It was introduced some few years ago by my
friend Nasredin and is now a favourite stock on the
Plateau of Reshed where the climate is very similar to
yours. It bears a large, luscious fruit, highly market-
able, and maturing early ; and it can be purchased
at a moderate expense. I will, if you like, go for you
to the nearest provider of such things and see what
I can do.'

" My host thanked me profusely. He remarked
how small the world was and at the same time how
manifest were the workings of Providence. He blessed
the day when he had met me. For though (he said)
the matter of expense did not weigh upon him, he had
made a particular point of success in the matter of
pear trees, and but for my advice he really did not
know what he should have done.

" He was so keen upon the affair that he pressed me
to start for the nearest nurseryman the very next
morning. There was an excellent nursery plantation,
he said, not more than half a day's ride away to the
West. It stood, with the owner's house in the midst,

M

just outside the gates of the town to which he would
direct me, either going himself or sending his bailiff
with me. He would also send a wagon for the convey-
ance of the young shoots. Indeed, as the meal progressed (for we were now dining), he grew more and
more enthusiastic on the matter and could hardly
bear the delay of the night. I saw which way the land
lay and saw fit to increase his keenness. I therefore
told him it was quite impossible to act with such
speed. ' The young shoots,' said I, ' must not be left
to lie untended and unplanted. We must first of all
prepare the ground. The old trees must be dug up,
the pits enlarged. It is the narrowness of the earthing
that has been half your trouble, for the smaller root
tendrils which we call " trips " are easily estopped in
hard groundings.' ' I see ! ' said he, sapiently. ' The
ground must be well soaked,' I continued, ' and man-
ured with a full dressing of lime, and only when all
this has been completed could I think of advising you
to plant.'

" I paused to concoct something new, and the amiable
youth filled the gap for me by murmuring : ' Precisely !
Exactly ! Now I understand.'

" I resumed : ' Further we must underpin the
runners and work up the earth herring-wise. And
then there is the daubing. . . . It will be a matter
of full three days' work. On the fourth day I can set
out before sunrise. You may take it that I will be
back by evening, and we will, if you please, plant the
very next morning—that is on the fifth day—lest the
stock should suffer ; for I have always found it,' I
added profoundly, ' of invariable service to plant
immediately. I have indeed lost in the past one or
two most valuable sets of trees—*pear* trees—by delaying

at this season of the year so much as twenty-four
hours before putting them in the ground.'

" As I thus spoke he nodded frequently, admiring.
my talent and knowledge of these affairs, and I took
occasion, as evening wore on, to ground him yet more
deeply in this fascinating subject, which I had already
begun to feel was mine.

" The next day with the first of the light we both
of us set out to the orchard.   He summoned his workmen and our labours engrossed us for many hours
during which I fed his enthusiasm with renewed tales
of marvels in the way of fruit-growing—and especially
of pear trees.   That particular pear called ' The Glory
of Heaven' increased wonderfully as I proceeded
until at last it had grown to such a size that each
individual fruit was as large as a child's head, and half
a dozen of them would fetch a piece of gold ' if ' (I
was careful to add) ' if they are properly packed !
For I regret to say that, simple as the detail is, the
neglect of good packing has been the ruin of most
speculators in this line.'

" During the second day of our labours I dilated
upon other details of the trade which occurred to me
as I went along.   I especially insisted upon what I
called the *maximum point*, and for this he was all ears.

" ' There is a limit,' I said, ' to your plantation,
after which the expenses of management begin to eat
into the profits earned.   A first small speculation of
300 trees, such as you have here, is, of course, a mere
bagatelle.   It would provide you with amusement,
but no appreciable income.   The most profitable 'size
of orchard is far larger. . . . In such a situation as
yours,' said I, looking round with the air of a connoisseur, ' and with such soil as this,' and with that I took

up a clod and carefully crumbled it in my fingers,
' possessing acidulated properties of this type, but
corrected by some slow exhaust of porphyritic matter,
it would need but a top dressing of bardulm and an
occasional picketing of charcoal to make some 3,000
trees produce a regular annual profit of not less than
200 pieces of gold—and that upon an original expenditure less than double the amount. I would estimate
your return with care and good fortune at quite fifty
per cent., but at any rate you could calculate upon
thirty per cent. But *more* than 3,000 trees,' said I,
musing, ' would, I fear, be an error : the earnings
after that get eaten into by expenses.'

" He interrupted me with the eager words : ' I should
be happy——' I lifted my hand to check him and
said, ' No ! I assure you, that even such a number as
3,500 would be just beyond the line, and as you approach
5,000 you would find the expense absorbing nearly all
your profit. It is as great an error to over-do these
things as to starve them. Let us fix the number at
3,000 and the capital expenditure at 400 pieces of gold.
Then I think you will not be disappointed.'

" The third day I spent overlooking the levelling
of the ground and its last preparation, as also in
making mysterious marks with little pegs and
jotting down notes in a book : all of which excited
the owner to the last degree, and left him (as the
phrase goes) with his tongue hanging out for the new
trees.

" That evening my kind host after some little
embarrassment made me an offer. Would I, he asked,
share in the profits of the enterprise ? I at once
refused. My decision surprised him : but, as he
pressed the project upon me I told him that gratitude

was only a part of my decision. I owed him everything; he had found me—it seemed a month ago
indeed, though it was but three days—in rags; he
had clothed me, fed me and, what was more, trusted
me. His trust, I assured him, would not be deceived.
'I shall be content,' I concluded, 'with the salary
proper to my position' (he at once mentioned a sum,
which I halved), 'but I will go so far as this; if,
upon the opening of the fourth year, your profits
shall be found to have *exceeded* what I have suggested,
if you make in the three years more than 600 pieces
of gold, at 200 pieces a year, which I suggest as the
probable result, I will accept, though reluctantly, one
half of the excess. For I am confident,' and here I
put an especially serious tone into my voice, 'that
we shall do better than I have said. I have ever held
it my duty to give a conservative estimate and to avoid
the disappointment of those who employ me. To
this, among other things, do I ascribe the great success
which attended me during my earlier years, and which
only failed me through the deplorable accidents I
related to you on our first meeting.'

" My host appeared a little confused at my probity,
or rather, at my scruples; but he told me that he had
always found such errors to be upon the right side, and
assured me that I should not lose by the austerity of
my temper. Nor did I. . . .

" We spent the rest of the evening looking at the
illuminations in his fine library. I expressed myself
enthralled by them all. I lingered with especial care
over every representation of an orchard in these
pictures, and spoke in the most learned manner of the
various fruits therein displayed. As luck would have it
we came to one particularly fine painting in which were

delineated the most enormous pears of a brilliant golden hue interspersed with soft leaves. ' This,' I cried delightedly, ' is the very fruit of which I have been speaking ! How interesting ! How exciting ! '

" ' Is that so ? , said my host, transported at the coincidence, ' Once more I must say it : how small is the world ! '

" ' Yes,' said I, ' it is that pear " Glory of Heaven," of which I have been speaking and which you may see, by comparison with the insects here portrayed and of the trellis work, to be most enormous fruit. Of its succulence I must leave you to judge when you shall gather your first harvest. Of its highly saleable quality in the markets of the north you will, I trust, soon have satisfactory experience.'

" ' I shall indeed ! ' said my host, now quite beside himself with the combined emotions of the collector and the man of property. He blessed again and again the day he had the good fortune to meet such a man as myself. Summoning his bailiff he gave orders for the wagon to be prepared over night and the horses to be ready by sunrise. ' No, no,' said I, ' an hour before sunrise, if you please ! I am determined, at whatever inconvenience to myself, to have the plants back here, at your house, on the night of the same day. I will risk no failure in this great affair ! ' Again he blessed and thanked me, and when his dependants were dismissed took me aside and prepared to count out the money which would be required for my expenditure.

" ' You said 400 pieces of gold,' said he, as he disposed the coins in little heaps of ten upon the table. ' You had better make it 500, for there may have been fluctuations in the market since you last purchased, and it is good that you should have a margin.'

" I told him I thought the provision a wise one, but that I would account for every penny when he should next see me. And this, curiously enough, was my true intention, though I could not have given him any very exact date for our next meeting. I wrote him out a formal receipt in spite of his protests, remarking that business was business ; and so that every formality should be accomplished I signed the document in the name of an old friend of mine, one Daoud-ben-Yacoub. I said I would further have affixed my seal had I possessed one, but placed as I was, no such instrument was available.

" ' The ball of your thumb will do,' said the young man carelessly. His words brought me up rather sharp, and it was not without trepidation that I acceded to this chance request. But once more the inspiration of Heaven served me. I dexterously substituted my middle finger for my thumb as I pressed the wax thereunder. This arrangement," said the old merchant, as he crossed the two fingers in the presence of his nephews, by way of illustration, " I recommend you upon every occasion of life. It is especially useful in those tyrannical countries where the police take the thumb-marks of innocent wayfarers. I have used it a dozen times. . . . But to return to my tale.

" I pattered on to my kind host as I pressed my finger down, and thus distracted his attention from too close a watch on my hand. ' This thumb mark,' said I, releasing my middle finger from the wax, ' this thumb mark is as good as any signature, I think ; for Allah has made it the sign manual of all honest men ; no two are alike. Remember, pray,' I added laughingly, ' that it was the thumb of my *right* hand.'

" ' I will,' said he, laughing in turn. ' As you say, these are mere formalities. I do not think the less of you for your insistence upon their performance.'

" With these words we parted in the greatest mutual satisfaction. He to dream of this fine new plantation and his coming wealth, but I to pour out my soul in prayer to my Maker and humbly to ask for further guidance.

" Next morning while it was yet dark I rose and mounted, the bailiff at my side, and the slaves taking the wagons behind. Early as was the hour my kind host was astir ; he gave me his blessing for the tenth time on my departure and poured out petitions for my safe return. I hung the pouch of gold to my saddle bow, where I securely fastened it ; I took the weapon with which he had kindly provided me in case of any misadventure by the road, and left him under the benediction of God. I thought a little sadly, as we rode out in silence through the gate and out on to the bare uplands again, how transitory were all human affections. How short had been this episode of friend-ship and hospitality ! How brief even in the short course of one human life are these passages of complete confidence and brotherly kindness ! When should we meet again ?

" Of my journey there is little to be related. We plodded on, our pace necessarily determined by that of the slow wagon following us and my mind still turned upon what my future action should be ; for, to tell you the truth, my dear nephews, Allah had vouchsafed me no revelation, in spite of my earnest prayers during the night, and I was still considering what turn I should give to the affair when once more that Infinite Mercy which has never failed me (or, at

any rate, only for some short few days and even so
but to chastise my pride) came to my rescue.

" There are, in this country, deep gullies called
nullahs, the course of streams which run but rarely
on these heights, but which, when they run, dig their
channels deeply into the friable soil. The crossing
of these gullies by any rolling vehicle is something of
a business. As we reached one, therefore (they came
at intervals of two or three miles) the bailiff and I
were careful to dismount and help the slaves with the
wheels.

" It was while thus engaged during our careful drop
into the second *nullah* that the inspiration from on high
flashed into my brain. I perceived that the wheels
of the waggon were fastened to the hub with wooden
pins, one of which, at the off-hind wheel which I was
holding back, looked a little loose. The slaves had
their backs turned to me, holding back the front wheels,
and checking the horses ; at the other hind wheel,
with the body of the front wagon between us and
concealing his view from mine, strained and heaved
the bailiff, a fat, elderly rogue, unaccustomed to such
work. I pulled out the pin, threw it into the depths
of the neighbouring scrub, and as I did so continued
to cry, ' Steady there ! Steady ! So ! Hold hard !
That's better ! Woa-oh ! Stand by ! ' and other words
of the sort, which showed my interest in the operation.
I could see the wheel wobbling as we crossed the flat
bed of the *nullah*. At the foot of the far rise it was
nearly off. The time had come. ' Now ! ' I cried
suddenly, ' *All together !* Whip up the horses and
shove ! ' The whips cracked, the slaves hauled at
the traces, the horses strained, up went the wagon,
off came the wheel and the whole collapsed upon one

side with a great din and with a sharp cracking, as though something had given way.

"And so it proved to be ; for the main axle, though not snapped, had split ; so there we were with the wagon out of service for the moment, the axle unsure, a hind wheel off, and the whole contraption on its side.

"The bailiff was seriously disturbed. It seemed that my kind host was a firm master, that he had his moments of sharp temper ; and the bailiff bewailed his fate and considered what awaited him on his return. I laughed good-naturedly and reassured him.

"'Come, come,' said I, 'it is no great matter ! I understand these things. Do you ride on towards the town. I will help the slaves put back the wheel. We will make some sort of jury pin to put into the hub, we will tie a rope round the cracked axle, and all will be well. We are men enough between us to repair the wagon, but you, as I say, ride forward. I shall soon catch you up.

"The bailiff was relieved at this proof of my efficiency and good will, and delighted to be released from work to which he was quite unused. He rode on at a moderate pace while the slaves and I heaved the wagon back upright. I fashioned a jury pin out of a piece of the scrub and I was careful to make it too weak for its work. We bound a piece of rope round the axle and when all this was done I bade them go forward carefully lest a further accident should befall. I then rode on smartly to catch up the bailiff, who had by this time got about a mile ahead. As I neared him I looked back from an intervening rise of land. It was as I had anticipated. The jury pin had given way, and the wagon was on its side again : but the lift of

land soon hid it from me and down on the further slope
I caught up the bailiff, ambling along. ' The wagon
is all right,' said I, ' but it will have to go rather
slow.' He gave a great sigh of content. ' Thanks
be ! ' said he. ' Truly you are a genius ! '

" ' Not at all ! ' said I modestly. ' It is quite a
small accident and of a sort to which I am accustomed ;
but do you ride back now that everything is well, for
the slaves are uneducated men ' (this sort of flattery
is honey to bailiffs), ' and will need some one of your
standing to moderate their pace and to check their
horses and to see that the wagon comes on in good
condition. Go very carefully, for the axle is weak.
When you shall reach the town we will get a proper
pin and have everything put right in an hour or
two, meanwhile I will go forward and we will make
an appointment at the market gardener's, which you
will reach, I think, some three-quarters of an hour after
myself. For we are now, I take it, some couple of
hours from the town.'

" ' You are right,' said the bailiff, ' you have but
to follow the track and we will come after you.' With
that he turned back. Once I had seen him disappear
behind the rise of the hill I dug my spurs sharply
into my poor horse and went at top speed across the
bled.

" I am a poor rider and had not my saddle been
ample and my stirrups weighty I should have fallen.
but Providence was with me once again. I came
through a gap of rocks and saw, immediately before
and below me, the white domes and flat roofs of a large
city, and just outside the gate a fine plantation of
young fruit trees, which I recognized as the nursery
gardener's.

" I had ridden past his house and grounds, and admired the young pear trees especially (a fine collection) when a useful thought occurred to me, and I acted on it at once, eager though I was to save time. I turned back and said to the slave at the gate of the plantation, ' I have a message for your master. Tell him that if any one asks for Daoud-ben-Jacoub, he has bidden me say that he went back by a short cut to help his companions with a broken wagon.' I then turned again and rode off towards the city walls.

" I approached the town and rode through the gate with dignity in the new fine clothes the young lord had given me. I nodded in a superior manner to the guard and made straight for the opposite entrance to the city. A horse fair was proceeding. I put up mine at an inn, took off the bag of gold (which was heavy, but not too heavy to be carried) walked towards the market and asked where I could best purchase a horse. The name of a horse-seller was given me. I approached him, failed to believe all that he told me with regard to the beast he offered, but said it would be enough for my purpose. I had not an idea whither to fly, yet fly I must, for sooner or later the bailiff or my late master himself must follow. I knew nothing of the country nor of the names of its towns nor of the roads. I took refuge in a piece of diplomacy. As I paid for the horse, I said to the seller, that I had to reach my mother's house in the next city before sundown, and that I hoped my purchase was able to carry me that far in the remaining half-day.

" ' Half a day's riding ? ' answered the merchant in astonishment. ' I know not how you ride ! If you mean the town of Taftah it is not more than three hours' going for any reasonable mount.'

" ' Is that so ? ' said I in surprise.   ' I am a stranger
and I can only believe what I was told.   But you
know how vague these country people are.   I was
assured that this was the road to Taftah,' and here
I pointed through the eastern gate.

" ' Yes ! That is the road,' he said.   ' You can
easily reach your mother's house before evening upon
this beast,' he said, clapping its crupper.   ' Without
doubt you will be there long before the prayer : and
God be with you, Hassan ! '   For, incidentally, it was
as Hassan that I had done business with him.

" I paid him ten pieces of gold for the beast.   (It
was more than it was worth.)   I humbly repeated his
prayer which I felt did apply with peculiar force to
me now, for I was conscious that I was once more
under the beneficent guidance of Heaven—who could
not be with that heavy pouch now hanging again on
his saddle ?   I rode out therefore confidently, quite
careless whether I killed the beast or no in my rapid
progress and brought it into Taftah well within three
hours in such a state that I was delighted to find a
purchaser (to whom I gave my name as Abdurram, and
my profession as that of a leather dresser), who offered
but five pieces of gold : I was glad to be rid of the
horse and him at that.

" Time still pressed.   I might be traced.   I knew
not what accidents had occurred upon the road behind
me, whether indeed those poor fools had managed to
mend the wagon again, if not, whether the bailiff would
have the courage to tell his master or ride on to find
me in the first town.   If he had so ridden on he might
find evidences of my departure, and even (more doubtfully) of my second horse and its purchase.

" But though time pressed it would have been fatal

to show any too great speed. I therefore sauntered very gradually in my fine clothes, afoot, bearing my pouch in my hand concealed under the fold of my garment, until I reached a gathering of merchants outside a sort of Exchange which this town of Taftah boasted, like others of the neighbourhood, in the vicinity of the governor's palace.

" It was there that, during a conversation which, for all my anxiety, I took care to make slow and dignified, I learned how *dates* were in great demand in a large city called Laknēs, about two weeks' journey beyond the hills. It was, to a business man like myself, a most fascinating story that I heard ! The people of that far country were passionately fond of dates and gave that fruit the briskest market imaginable. Their appetite had grown all the more formidable since the next people immediately beyond them had passed a law prohibiting the culture and sale of all dates on account of the toothache sometimes arising from that fruit. With this reduction of supply Laknēs became more of a bidder for dates than ever. Great rewards were offered to any taking the fruit to such a market. The last advices, not a month old, quoted thirty dinars the kantar and were rising. The merchants designed to despatch a caravan the day after the morrow.

" With equal leisure and dignity I left them after this little talk and made it my immediate business in the next half-hour to procure with the capital at my disposal a number of camels and a couple of bales of dates for each, together with a few slaves that should conduct the caravan to its destination ; I also hired a free man for a leader, as he was acquainted with the road.

" By this time it was nearly dark. I had given
orders (in order to conceal my movements) that I
should not start till late in the week, but I had also
given a child a small coin to come up to me, upon a
signal, with a piece of paper folded, upon which indeed
nothing was written. Just as the camels were being
driven off to their litter, I signalled to the child, who
ran up and gave me the note. I opened it before the
head man, put on an air of great perturbation, and
said, ' This message changes all my plans ! I fear I
disturb you, but will you start out to-night ? '

" ' Willingly,' said he. ' We have provisions, and
I know a good place on the road where we can purchase
more to-morrow. The weather is warm and if your
business demands haste, it may be better to march
during the cool.' The slaves (who were not consulted)
were no doubt agreeable enough. We set out and all
that night went our way.

" It was a monotonous journey through an arid
land, with few towns or villages, sufficient watering,
but no more. Though I pressed the pace we lost no
beasts, and on the twelfth day, with the cool of the
evening, we reached Laknēs.

" My camels were parked, I took my place in the
chief inn of the city (under the name of Ishmaïl-of-
Taftah, merchant), and my first act before ordering a
meal was, again, from the very bottom of my heart,
to thank Allah for the return of his mercies. My
capital was, indeed, nearly exhausted. I had but a
few pieces of gold left in my garment, and the pouch
was empty ; but there was my solid row of camels and
my fine cargo of dates. I made no doubt I should sell
at a good profit next day and that my career was
once more launched. I took care to speak to all

openly of my arrival, to hint at my wealth, to make all familiar with the name of Ishmaïl-of-Taftah, a merchant in dates which it was proposed to offer next day in the market. For there are occasions, my dear nephews, in commerce when it is perfectly advisable to tell the truth and even to spread it abroad."

With these unexpected words the merchant Mahmoud suddenly ceased his tale, for the shriek of the muezzin was heard rending the air. The nephews rose and bowed. "We trust," said the eldest, "that when we next appear we shall find you, my dear uncle,'climbing from greatness to greatness in the story you still have to unfold."

"Alas, my children," answered the venerable sage, "I fear you must hear of other disappointments before the goal is reached!"

At this the youngest boy put forth his lower lip, which trembled, and began screwing up his eyes.

"Stop!" said the merchant testily. "Stop! My little fellow! I have had enough of this!"

"Oh, Uncle," sobbed the boy, "I cannot bear to think that perhaps all that new wealth will be stolen from you."

"Stop, I say!" shouted Mahmoud angrily, and half-rising, "I tell you I have had enough of it! I appreciate your motive. I admire your judgment. It is marvellous in so young a child. But I cannot be disturbed with useless tears at things so long past. You show too great a sympathy. You are too sensitive, my dear."

The child saluted, assumed a more equable appearance, and followed his brothers out of the room, while Mahmoud, his equipoise a little disturbed by the incident, set himself right by the simple process of drawing from one sleeve a handful of coins and counting them out slowly into the other : a pastime which never failed to restore him to the best of tempers.

الجمل والنّخل

AL-JAMAL WA'L-NAKHL

That is:

"CAMELS AND DATES"

CHAPTER IX

WHEN the hour of public execution had arrived
the boys came timorously into their rich
uncle's presence, and seating themselves upon the
expensive carpet at the feet of his divan, prepared
to hear the continuation of his adventures.

That excellent old man began as follows :

" I warn you, my children, that the path to wealth,
which (by the Mercy of Allah) I have been allowed to
tread, is varied and difficult. Profit by my misad-
ventures ! Remain determined to enrich yourselves,
even after the worst mishaps ! Yea ! After wealth
and poverty (like mine) renewed wealth and (alas !)
renewed poverty never despair. Still hold to gold
and still determine your fate. Still thirst for money.
But all the while most reverently worship Him the
Supreme, the All-compelling, the Giver of Great
bags of coin. No talent in the deception of individuals
or the gulling of the crowd can of itself bring the great
reward. The acquirement of those immense sums
which are the chief glory of man, is, like all else, in
the Hand of God.

" My brother, your worthy though impecunious
father, has sufficiently grounded you in the essentials
of our holy religion. You will not repine if you turn
out to be one of the ninety-nine who end their lives

in the gutter, rather than the blessed hundredth who attains, as I have attained, to the possession of a palace and of innumerable slaves. . . ."

Having so spoken the aged merchant bent for a moment in silent prayer and then proceeded :

" You will remember that at the conclusion of my last adventure I had reached a position, not of affluence, but at least of tolerable fortune. I was possessed of a train of camels, each heavily laden with two large panniers of dates, and drivers to conduct the whole.

" You will further remember how, on my arrival in Laknēs, as I was anxious to make the best of my time I spoke freely to all of my merchandise, extolled its character, described how I intended to put it up for sale next day in the public markets, and spread abroad the name of Ismaïl-of-Taftah which happened for the moment to be mine.

" The rumour spread (as I had intended it should). I strolled through the narrow streets of the town after sunset, and was glad to hear my arrival discussed, and my wares. I had promise for the morrow. I returned to my men.

" I had already spread out my bed upon the corner of the yard, when there came up a slave magnificently dressed, who bowed to the ground, and approaching my presence asked whether he had the honour and felicity to address the renowned merchant Ismaïl. He bore an invitation from the greatest merchant in the city, whose name I had already heard half a dozen times in Taftah, and whom all the merchants there revered from afar for his enormous riches : a certain Yusouff ben Ahmed, also called ' El-Zafari,' or the Triumphant.

" Late as was the hour I purchased finery ; with my

last gold I hired a donkey of strange magnificence,
and arrived at the palace of Yusouff, dressed in a
fashion which I could ill afford, but which I regarded
as an investment.

" I had expected to find within this palace that
admirable simplicity of manner which is inseparable
from really great wealth : Nor was I disappointed.
The inner room to which I was led, encrusted everywhere with black marble, boasted no ornament
save three white alabaster jars as tall as a man and
of immense antiquity. They had formerly been the
property of a young noble whom Yusouff had ruined,
and *he* had them of the Sultan. In the midst shone
the single pure flame of a massive silver lamp,
rifled from the tomb of a saint. It now hung dependent
from a chain of the same metal, the height of which
was lost in the gloom of the lofty cupola.

" A fountain of scented water—I could not name
its odour precisely, but I guessed it to be Fior
de Goyim—plashed gently into a basin of porphyry
at the end of the apartment.

" Yusouff and two other guests (who alone had been
asked to meet me), rose from the exceedingly costly
rugs of Persia whereon they had reclined, and gravely
saluted me. The master of the house, after the
first salutations and an invocation upon my head of
the Mercy of Allah, told me that the feast was ready
prepared, but that before summoning it he would
ask me to honour the house and survey what poor
ornaments he might be able to show me.

" I was expressly delighted at his tone. It was
that which I had always heard to be native to princes of
commerce. He had already acquired, in the few years
that had elapsed since he had cleaned the streets for

a living, a well-bred restraint of gesture, and when he spoke it was in the tone of one who thought negligible the whole world, including his guest. I prayed fervently, as I accompanied the leisurely steps of my great entertainer, that when I should have achieved a similar fortune I should myself as quickly acquire this distinctive manner of the great. I watched him narrowly in order to imitate (when I should have left his presence) those peculiar little details which mark affluence and are of such service in negotiation. He would often interpose words of his own into the midst of another's sentence. It pleased him not to answer some repeated question. He would change the conversation at his pleasure without too much regard for what I might have been saying immediately before. He also turned to another guest while I was addressing him and in every way showed his superiority.

" When we had sat down to meat I was further edified by the varied information, the extensive culture of my host. He would lead the talk on to some subject which he had recently acquired from his numerous secretaries, and dally upon it at a length which would have been tedious in one of lesser station. But all this was done with such an air of *money* that it was impossible to feel the slightest tedium, though his minute description of things which we all knew by heart extended more than once to a full quarter of an hour.

" During the progress of this divine repast I noted with pleasure that the distinguished master of the house never once introduced the subject of my affairs.

" I would have you remember, my dear nephews," said Mahmoud at this point, " that nothing is less pleasing in a merchant, especially in one of approved success, than the introduction of profit and loss at a meal; for profit and loss are of such profound importance that their mere mention must distract from the legitimate pleasures of the table.

" It was not until a late hour, when the two other guests (whose insignificant names I have not attempted to retain) had arisen to depart, that affairs began.

" With the subtle tact of commercial genius my host retained me, gripping my arm. I ventured in the absence of any witness to say a few words upon what was nearest my heart : I asked him ' *How were dates ?* '

" To my delight he proved affable. He unbent in a degree unworthy of so small an occasion and listened with the greatest attention to my simple tale. I told him frankly that I had with me at the moment but few camels (I was under no necessity to confess that I had not another asset in the world). I suggested by my negligent tone that such a number could hardly be called a caravan and was little more than a distraction with which I amused myself on my travels. I then dropped the fact that I had loaded them— more as a pastime than anything else—with a few *dates*.

" At this second mention of the word ' *dates* ' the face of Yusouff-the-Blessed suddenly changed. He at first cast his eyes down in an expression of real concern. Then, looking up at me anxiously and steadily, he said :

" ' This is no affair of mine. . . . You may resent my interference.'

" I assured him that I desired nothing more than a hint from one so favoured of Heaven. How I had better dispose of my trifling merchandise ? I was more anxious to hear his reply than it is possible to say !

" He sighed heavily, shook his head, and answered with a certain familiarity that I could not resent :

" ' My poor friend . . . ! '

" He then sighed again and added :

" ' I really do not see how I can advise you. . . . The truth is that dates will from henceforth be almost unsaleable here. There has lately taken place—indeed it was but last week—an extraordinary thing. The mother of our Emir—the dowager—has left by will the whole of her immense date groves in trust to the nation with orders that regular weekly distribution shall be made *free* to all the citizens. We are bidden praise her generosity and the masses are of course delighted. But it is ruin for the poor merchants whose stocks of dates are now so much dross. They cannot sell to our neighbours in the country over the border, for these hold dates to be evil from their effect in giving the toothache. Their new law, called the Date Prohibition Act, is of the most rigorous kind. I have myself (from a sense of public duty) bought up the greater portion at a ruinous loss to prevent the failure of smaller men and to avoid a panic. I have sacrificed myself to the public good.' He sighed heavily once more and was silent.

" You may imagine, my dear nephews, the effect of this news upon your unfortunate uncle ! The panniers of dates (two for each camel) were, save the animals themselves, all that I had in the world. I had traversed the waste at the cost of much labour, infinite privation, and mortal perils, precisely because this district had the reputation of being by far the best market for dates, and here was I, with an enemy left behind me, alone in the world, and my sole venture ruined. . . . I remembered my dreadful poverty, only so recently past, and I shuddered as I considered those unsaleable dates and my black future! Before me was a country where dates were rigorously forbidden by law; behind me a hue and cry. Despair was in my heart!

"Though I trust I have a sufficient degree of the arts essential to our profession, Yusouff must have guessed my thoughts. Ignoring my former statement that the goods I had with me were but a toy, and that I was indifferent to their fate, he expressed the deepest sympathy with my plight and begged me to bear with him while he reflected within himself how he might be of service.

"Having said this he covered his face with his right hand, bowed his head, leant his elbow upon his knee, and for some moments was plunged in what merchants use as thought. When he raised his face I was shocked to see how haggard it had become, and I marvelled that one so circumstanced should care so much for the chance misfortunes of a stranger. But I had read that these Princes of Commerce were often of tenderest heart and that one should never be surprised at any freak of generosity on their part.

"Judge therefore of my delight on hearing Yusouff say in a determined voice that he had concluded upon the only issue and that he would purchase my dates himself!

"'I cannot' (he frankly added) 'give you as good a price even as I could have given a day or two ago; the old Queen's idea of free dates has swamped everything. But I will pay a good quarter of the customary price—which is far more than you now could obtain elsewhere. I am very wealthy. You are a stranger and, as it were, our guest in this town. A good deed is never thrown away. Perhaps some day I shall be glad of your aid also. I have seen you a few hours only, but I think we know each other's hearts already. Moreover, I do not conceal it from you, I *may* save much of the loss. I have special correspondents in distant towns, and opportunities of sale which others do not possess. . . . Come! I'll do it! I will offer you this price of one-third. It is but a poor price,' said he, sighing yet again most heavily, ' but it is far, far better than no price at all.'

" My relief was beyond words. I had seen myself leaving my merchandise unsold or sacrificing it at a ruinous nothing. That which Yusouff offered me was the difference between despair and a shred of hope, and though the loss was severe it left me at least with some capital for a further venture.

" Great men have a sort of simplicity in their dealings. Hardly had Yusouff discovered my gratitude and my immediate acceptance of his gift (for I could call it by no other name), than the princely fellow clapped his hands, sent for his treasurer, and had counted to me upon the spot a hundred pieces of gold. I gave him my writing of delivery, which he handed to another slave with a few words in a low voice. Then he continued to talk to me, for he was determined to detain me far into the night. Indeed it was near dawn before he whom I will now call my friend, and to whom I felt bound for life by the greatest ties of grateful affection, allowed me to pass his gates and to return to my hostelry.

" There I found that my panniers had already been removed and their contents conveyed to the purchaser's

warehouse. I admired the promptitude in business
which so often accompanies a generous heart.

*   *   *   *   *

" With the early hours of the next day, before the
sun had yet acquired too great power, I strolled through
the bazaar, not so much cast down at the thought of
my loss as cheered by the recollection that I possessed,
after all, one hundred good pieces of solid gold.

" With a malicious pleasure I approached the stall
of a fruit-seller. Putting down a small copper coin
I begged him for a handful of dates.

" ' I need not full measure,' said I, ' only a handful
to munch as I go along.' For I knew that in the state
of the market my penny might have purchased a
gallon. I desired to show a neglect for small sums.

To my surprise the fruit-seller stared at me and
said :

" ' Dates ? From what country do you come that
you ask for *dates* in our town ? '

" ' Why ! ' said I, ' is there not a glut of these ? I
am told the place is overflowing with them.'

" ' There is One-who-judges,' said the fruit-seller
resignedly. ' But as for dates—you will not find
one in the whole town ; our last month's arrival was
pillaged by robbers in the hills. If you will but procure me a single gallon I will readily give in return two
pieces of gold, so great is the demand. Of supply there
is none whatever, nor, alas ! any prospect of such.'

" I was so bewildered that I hardly know what next
I said, but at any rate, in reply to it, my new acquaintance told me that there were, indeed, *suspected* to be
certain dates in the possession of Yusouff-the-Triumphant, ' who ' (he remarked aside) ' has all the luck.'
He next said it was also rumoured that Yusouff's slaves

had been seen in the last hours of the night going in
procession with a great number of panniers laden on
mules towards Yusouff's warehouse, and those who
brought the news swore that they could smell the
smell of dates.

" ' But beyond that smell,' he ended, " we have
had nothing of dates in the place for three weeks.   And
if you understood our habit in the matter of food you
would feel for us ! '

" I have already described to you, my dear nephews,
my admiration for Yusouff-the-Triumphant.   Long before I had seen him his distant reputation had inflamed
me. My brief acquaintance with him had exalted that
feeling to what I had thought the highest pitch.   But
now it passed all bounds.   A man so subtle in negotiation !   So ready in affairs !   So rapid and conclusive
in a bargain !   With so marvellous a command of
feature and of tone !   A man (in a word) so infinitely
my superior in that profession of commerce to which
Allah calls all great souls and in which I also was
engaged !   Such a man I had never thought to meet !
Nay—I had never thought such a one to exist upon
this poor earth.   I could have kissed the ground upon
which he walked or have borne upon me for ever,
as a relic, some thread of his purse.

" ' Here,' I exclaimed, ' is the true merchant !
Here is the model of all that a man of affairs should
be !   Oh ! Mahmoud, you thought yourself something
in your trade, but you have met your master, and more
than your master !   You have met one who is to you
as the most holy of saintly men is to the basest of the
Kafir.   There is *none* on earth like him.   Allah has
raised him beyond all others.

" But it is not enough, my dear nephews," continued

the old man, whose eyes were now filled with a sort of sacred light, " it is not enough to admire those who set us great examples. We should also imitate them. I determined after so rare an experience to follow as best I might in the footsteps of one who had shown himself raised high above the level of mortality.

" ' Him,' said I to myself, ' him will I copy! *He* shall be my guide! *His* manner and his tone, on that unforgettable evening, shall be my exact model! Then perhaps in time I shall do as he has done and accumulate so great a store of money as shall put me among the greatest of mankind.'

" I hastened to summon my slaves. I paid my score for the stabling, and as I looked at my small capital and surveyed my beasts I hesitated what I should do. Yusouff-the-Triumphant had, by God's special grace overshadowing him, got hold of my substance. Nothing was left me but the camels. In such a strait I abandoned the thought of men and turned at once to heaven. I lifted up my heart to my Maker and prayed for guidance. He that has never for very long abandoned His servant answered my prayer with singular alacrity, for even as I prayed I heard two men who passed me muttering one to the other.

" The first, as they hurried along, was saying in fearful undertones :

" ' They have not yet a camel among them! Yet camels they must have or the terrible sentence will be pronounced!'

" ' Yes!' returned his companion in a horrified whisper, ' I fear greatly for my relatives in that town, and I am proceeding there to make certain that they shall have at least *one* camel in so terrible a time!

For if a sufficiency of camels is not there by to-morrow noon I hear they are all to be impaled ! '

" So speaking in subdued accents of terror, little knowing they were overheard, they walked on while I followed and noted every word.

" My mind was immediately made up. I continued, with stealthy feet, to follow these two anxious beings who were so engrossed in the coming misfortunes of their native place. At last, when we had come to an empty space where three streets met, I caught them up and faced them. Accosting them I said :

" ' Sirs, are you bound for such and such a place ? ' (naming a town of which they could never have heard —for indeed it did not exist).

" They stopped and looked at me in surprise.

" ' No, sir,' they answered me together, ' we are bound in all haste for our native place which is threatened with a great calamity. Its name is Mawur, but, alas, it is far distant from us—a matter of some twenty leagues—the desert lies between, and we shall hardly reach it within the day that remains. For we are poor men, and only with fast *camels* ' (at this word they glanced at each other and shuddered) ' could the journey be accomplished in the time.'

' I thanked them politely, regretted that I had disturbed them for so little, proceeded with the utmost haste to my caravan, inquired the road for Mawur (the track for which lay plain through the scrub and across the sand), and hastened with the utmost dispatch all that burning day and all the succeeding night without repose, until at dawn I passed with my exhausted train through the gates of the city. I had covered in twenty hours twice as many leagues.

" Five of my beasts I left upon the road ; and some

few of my slaves—how many I had not yet counted
—had fallen out and would presumably die in the
desert. But there was a good remainder.

" Unfortunately I was not alone in my venture,
for I discovered that early as was the hour another
man had arrived already with two camels and was
standing with them under the dawn in the market-
place. Poor beasts they were, and bearing every mark
of fatigue. But I was determined upon a monopoly.
I had hoped from the conversation I had overheard
that not a single camel would be present in the place.
I would secure myself against even the slightest competition. I approached the leader of the two sorry
camels and asked him there and then what he would
take for his cattle. He stared at me for a moment,
but to my astonishment when I offered him for a
beginning the derisory price of ten pieces of gold, he
accepted at once, put the coins into his pouch, smiled
evilly, and moved off at a great pace.

" To my chagrin there approached within a very
few moments yet another peasant, leading this time
but one camel, a rather finer beast than the others.
I hoped, I believed, he would be the last. I made
haste to follow the same tactics with him as with the
first. Like the first he took the five gold pieces without
so much as bargaining, but he looked me up and down
strangely before shrugging his shoulders and taking
himself off hastily down a side lane.

" And then (the people beginning to drift into the
street as the day rose) appeared a man leading not
less than ten camels in a file. I was seriously alarmed,
but I bethought me of my reading : how all great
fortunes had been acquired by speculation, how caution
and other petty virtues were the bane of true trade.

I boldly approached him and offered him my remaining gold for the whole bunch. Instead of meeting my offer with a higher claim, he asked to look narrowly at the pieces, and then looked as narrowly into my face. He took one of the gold pieces and bit it. He stooped and rang it upon the cobble-stones. He determined apparently that it was good, and without another word took my gold, appealed to those around us as witnesses to the transaction, handed me the leading cord, and with a burst of laughter ran off at top speed.

" Here, then, was I with my thirteen new camels and what was left of my original caravan. I will not deny that I was somewhat disturbed in mind ; but I could only trust in Allah. I did so with the utmost fervour, and implored Him to consider His servant, and to see to it that not another camel should reach the town before I began to sell.

" But what is man ? What is he that he should order the movements of the Most High ?

" I lifted up my eyes and saw approaching down the narrowness of the street a file of certainly not less than one hundred camels led by a great company of ragged men and walking with that insolent and foolish air which this beast affects and which at such a moment provoked me to rage.

" Then a slave, trembling lest he should give me offence, bade me come apart with him where steps led up the city wall. These I climbed, and from the summit I saw a sight that broke my heart.

" For there, across the plain that surrounded the city, came such a mass of camels as I hardly thought the universe contained. They came in batches of twenty, fifty, two hundred, herds and flocks of camels,

driven, led, ridden, conducted in every shape from one
direction and another, through the desert and cultivated land, from track and path, a very foison and
cataract of camels. It was as though all the camels
of Arabia, India, Bactria, and Syria had been summoned to this one place.

"And, alas, so they had! or at least as many as
the King of that region could command. . . .

"For this was the explanation. . . ."
Here the old man's eyes grew dim with tears,
his voice faltered, and in spite of his present riches
he broke down at the recollection of his past ill-fortune.

"Oh, my dear nephews," he said in broken accents,
"hardly will you believe the magnitude of my misfortune! For it turned out, as I eagerly questioned
the people of the place, that a war having broken out
against their King on account of the Date Prohibition
of which I have told you, that ruthless monarch had
ordered them to collect as best they might so many
thousands of camels to be present within the walls by
noon of that day, or suffer massacre. If the full tale
were not present every man, woman, and child would
be killed. For he had been suddenly alarmed by this
declaration of war and caught with an insufficient
provision of sumpter beasts. His Emirs had advised
him that his salvation lay in seizing without payment
every beast for leagues around.

"In proportion as my soul sank so did the hearts
of the townsmen rise, to see the number gradually
fulfilled. By noon all was well for them—but very
ill for me! The officers of the king arrived, the beasts
were counted and set apart, with not an ounce of
copper to pay for any one of them! All seized!
And my poor herd, alone and in that vast multitude,

suffered the fate of all the rest, and, what was worse, every one of my slaves—all were taken off to serve as drivers.

" There in a far land, alone, I stood, with not a gold piece left in my pouch and not a head of cattle to my name; once more quite destitute.

" I spent the remainder of that day debating whether to hang myself on a beam or throw myself from a minaret. The arguments in favour of either course were so evenly balanced that the sun set before I could decide between them, and even at sunset there appeared, through the Mercy of Allah, a new relief."

" There did ? " said the second of the nephews eagerly, but before his uncle could reply the intolerable noise of the Muezzin was heard and the boys, rising at the signal, bowed low to their uncle and were gone.

الحصان

AL-HISĀN

That is:
"THE HORSE"

CHAPTER X

ENTITLED *AL-HISĀN*, OR THE HORSE

WHEN the nephews of Mahmoud once again attended their uncle at the hour of public executions he gazed at them in his benevolent fashion, again stroking his long beard, the better to expose the jewels upon his fingers, and continued the tale of his fortunes.

" You left me, my dear children, at the end of my last recital in a very deplorable condition. You will remember that through the superior business ability of a merchant renowned for his organizing power, grasp of detail, sense of affairs, etc., etc., etc., I had been reduced in property to a few camels and their attendants, and that even this poor remainder of my fortune I had lost through a miscalculation of the camel market on the eve of war.

" Your filial affection will also recall the bitter mood in which I hesitated whether to precipitate myself from a minaret or to hang myself from a beam.

" Advantages and disadvantages appeared equally balanced between these two courses ; and though my long training in commerce had led me to make rapid decisions (as being the most certain way of forestalling competitors), yet I confess that in this debate I stood uncertain for nearly half an hour.

" It was well I did so ; for in that half-hour was

manifested in a triumphant manner the Mercy of Allah to them that fear Him.

" As I stood there, among strangers, without one single coin left in the world and utterly devoid of credit, with no knowledge even of how I should get food upon the following day, I heard cries and a confusion of horses' hoofs, and saw galloping down the street towards me a very finely-bred grey horse, with flowing mane and a loose bridle. It bore a noble saddle of Indian workmanship, but no rider ; while, some hundred yards behind, impotently ran and gesticulated a corpulent man who, from his dress, seemed of some wealth and consequence. My first instinct was to catch the runaway like any beggar and restore him to his master in hope of some small reward ; a few pence that might buy me food that evening and lodging for one night.

" But the beneficent Creator soon put other thoughts into the mind of his servant. I had caught the horse indeed. Its panting owner had slackened his pace and was coming towards me in a more dignified manner—when it struck me that the animal (which was restive) could be better controlled were I in the saddle.

" I am, my dear nephews, as I have told you three times, no horseman. My more habitual steed is the donkey and though I have, since my attainment to high rank, taken part in ceremonial processions, and even in the hunting to which His Majesty so kindly invites me, yet I must confess to you that whenever I have to ride *now* I take care to be provided with an animal not only trained in the most exact manner, but also previously soothed with drugs.

" I had, however, taken to the saddle when necessity

drove me, as you have seen. And on this occasion, although the beast was infinitely more mettlesome than any I had yet dared to face, I took the risk. Courage was granted to me from on High. I scrambled into the saddle, but found that my control of the creature was no better than it had been when I stood at his head.

" I cannot swear that, in the bewilderment of the moment, I kept a sufficiently tight rein. I will not even swear that the value of the opportunity was lost on me. I certainly remember delivering several violent kicks with either heel into the ribs of the unquiet brute. There followed a few minutes in which (under my direction, I must admit) he seemed to be galloping farther and farther away from his original master, and at full speed down the main street of the town. I heard cries arising behind me on every side, and upon attempting to look round (a difficult feat for one so unused to the saddle) I was aware of a now considerable mob, in the midst of which I saw the distant figure of the horse's wealthy owner frantically exclaiming and gesticulating.

" Nothing, my dear nephews, is more foolish than to treat generously, or even rationally, an excited crowd of human beings. All historians and philosophers will tell you that man in this state is but a wild beast, to be fled or mastered according to our abilities.

" As I had not ability to master them, then it was clearly my duty to flee them. Moreover, even as I urged the horse to further efforts, I confusedly appreciated what difficulty I should have in explaining my position, were I to attempt to return. We thundered through the open gate into the country outside, and by that time I had no course but frankly to take the track across the plain and shake off my pursuers for ever.

" Admire, my dear nephews, the steps by which Providence, when It desires to succour one of Its favourites, will lead him through one consequence after another until at last he stands secure in the possession of some considerable sum of money! Here was I, not ten minutes before, contemplating death as the only issue from my poverty, and now mounted on a fine steed, seated in a saddle of price, and free to try any new adventure.

" I kept my handsome mount at the gallop until the gates were far behind me and all echo of the confused cries of my pursuers was lost. I checked him to a sharp trot until we had passed the first low rise of rolling land which hid my movements from the city. I then judged it reasonable to proceed at a pace less trying to the poor animal who had so befriended me. I noted from his freshness that he could but recently have left the stable. I did not hesitate, though with intervals of repose, to continue all day long to put a greater and greater distance between myself and that unfortunate misunderstanding which I had left behind me.

" By evening my many hours' acquaintanceship with my horse had increased my pride in his possession, and I turned my mind away from all morbid considerations of his former owner. My only anxiety was for the night. Judge therefore of my satisfaction when, a full hour before the setting of the sun, I found myself, on emerging from a considerable wood, facing the walls of a new city, the gates of which stood about a league away from the spot whence I had first caught sight of it.

" I lingered in this pleasant pasture at the edge of the wood, loosening my horse's girths, unbridling his bit, and letting him graze at large on the delicious herbage.

" I reclined myself, for repose, upon that same grass, and mused upon the distant prospect of domes and minarets under the mellow light, my thoughts naturally turning to conjecture what sums I might acquire in cash from the citizens within those walls during my enjoyment of their hospitality.

" The sun was barely set when I rode into the town ; noting on the walls the usual proclamation against the eating of dates and receiving, as was due to one riding so well-accoutred and so fine a horse, the respectful looks of the passers-by, and the humble but prolonged gaze of the guard at the gate. As I noted their attitude I could not but thank heaven for one more mercy which was now revealed to me. Had I happened to find this horse after some days of misfortune my own outward appearance would have ill consorted with his. How manifest was the dispensation of Providence whereby I came upon him within an hour after losing my other property, and, therefore while I was still in my decent merchant's dress, cleanly, well-shaven, and groomed !

" There was in the central square of this town a runnel specially disposed for watering beasts of burden, and my horse (we had forded but one stream in all that day's journey) eagerly approached it. I fondly patted his neck and thought with pleasure of how noble a friend I had acquired ; for as you must have read, there is a sort of affinity between man and the horse which readily makes them intimate after even a short acquaintance : especially if the man be of a business turn of mind and the horse of considerable value.

" From this mood into which I had fallen while my handsome mount was taking his simple refreshment, you may guess the perturbation caused me when I heard at my side an eager voice deliberately pitched in a low key so that it might be heard by none but myself. That voice was full of passionate necessity, and was asking me whether it would be possible *now—here—at once*, for me to dispose of my mount to a man whose life depended on it.

" I turned and made out in the dusk under the shadow of his cowl (part of which he had pulled over his features to make a sort of veil) a young man whose agitation made me yearn instinctively to take some advantage of him.

" ' Sir,' he whispered hurriedly, ' my request is not only impertinent but extraordinary. I know that you will not understand it. I can only implore Heaven for a miracle. My time is very short. I know not how far my pursuers may be. My life is dear to me and·still dearer is my honour. The night is falling. Here is my opportunity, which, if I do not take, all is over with me.'

" He thereupon passed up to me a leather bag upon opening which I could see in the fading light a quantity of gold pieces, and he accompanied the gesture with so imploring a look as explained the vastness of his offer.

" Had I passed through any series of adventures less astonishing than those of the last day and night, I would not have listened for a moment to a first proposal. I would have attempted, as was indeed my duty, to raise his price, to obtain immediately some of his apparel as well as his purse ; and if possible a written promise of further payment as well. For he was distraught with fear and men in that condition are easily squeezed. But the rate at which I had been living, the perpetual succession, first of unfortunate and then of fortunate accidents, showed the manifest finger of God in all that had so far favoured me since the morning, and strangely convinced me. Without another word I took the bag of gold and dismounted.

" The young man, with a new expression such as I had never yet seen upon anyone's face, said not a word, no, not even of gratitude to his benefactor; turned the horse's head down the main street of the town, wisely refraining from too rapid an exit lest his passage should be remembered, and went at no more than a sharp trot through the gate into the falling darkness without. The last I saw of him he appeared, a dark figure rapidly dwindling against the darkening sky, framed in the tiled horseshoe of the Bab-El-Soued. . . . But even as I gazed a troop of mounted horsemen thundered past me and passed through that same gate into the night.

" For my part I thought no more of him, but turned back to the centre of the town. There I was, with three times the price of my horse in my pocket, and thus with solid ground on which to stand for the future.

" My first care was to make an excellent meal, my next to discover a good lodging for the night. In both I was fortunate. But before reciting my last evening prayers I took the precaution of informing a passing patrol that I had had a horse stolen from me ; for, in business, no opportunity should be neglected. I then recommended myself to the Divine protection and fell into a sweet repose.

" Next morning, after I had humbly and devoutly recited my early prayers, I thought I would, before proceeding to any lucrative task, divert myself a little so that I might later approach serious business with a more open mind.

" It is my custom, when I am in need of recreation from the cares of commerce, to frequent the criminal courts and to attend the sentences passed upon those brought before them, as well as to be a spectator of the ensuing executions. No pastime affords greater relief from the dull, everyday round of buying and selling ; while the contrast between one's own pleasant position and that of the pauper who is to be beheaded, adds a zest which I recommend to all men of affairs.

" I strolled, therefore, to the court in which I had heard that certain criminals were to be that morning briefly examined and presumably dispatched.

" Great was my surprise upon entering to find that I had come just in time to hear the last evidence given and sentence pronounced upon the same young man who had so imprudently bought my horse the night before ! Did I say ' imprudently' ?—Well ! The designs of Providence are hidden from us, and it is not for me to judge another ! . . . While I pitied him, therefore, I had nothing to reproach myself with, for I had fulfilled in the most honourable fashion the only contract with which I was concerned in the matter. The pursuers had arrested him before he had left the city more than a mile. He stood accused of eating dates : a practice (you will remember) forbidden throughout all those dominions. He had been seen in the act by the Sultan's officers a week before and his name and description had been sent round to every city. Indeed a troop was hot upon his trail at the moment he had come up the night before imploring for my mount. Sentence was pronounced, and the unfortunate young man was led out to execution.

" My natural love of such sights would have led me to follow him, when one more act of Heaven (I dare not ascribe the inspiration to my poor unaided soul) suddenly put an exceedingly valuable thought into my mind. I addressed the judge in a loud voice, complaining in the matter of my horse. At first he was disturbed and inclined to silence me, not understanding what plea I could have in this particular case ; but I made bold to arrest his attention and told him that the evidence I had chanced to hear proved clearly that the horse on which the unfortunate young man had tried to escape was one stolen from me but a few hours before. This I was prepared to prove. The officers of the court were examined and admitted my description to be exact as to the horse, and, what was a clinching piece of evidence, as to the details of the saddle, the workmanship of which they had noted.

" I informed the judge further that I had ridden into the town the evening before. I was prepared to bring witnesses from the guard at the gate who had seen me pass. And when these were summoned they agreed that I had entered riding a horse of the description I had just given. I could see that the judge inclined to the justice of my plea ; the officers of the court naturally fell in with his mood ; I made him, I think, the more gracious by my assurance that I would not dream of making too exact a claim. If the animal were but restored to me I should be satisfied, nor would I ask anything for dilapidation or loss of time. I was only too glad (I said) to have been of the most insignificant service to the court.

" The judge now smiled upon me with evident approval, and was further confirmed in his decision by remembering that even if I claimed any compensation it would not come out of his pocket but the public's ; and I have no doubt that this argument, though not explicitly put forward, was present in the mind of all the officers of the court as well.   The judge therefore ordered that the animal should be restored to me, and was pleased to use the following words. They are not my own.   I am not responsible for them. But I am glad that he used them.

" ' This honest merchant,' said he, ' who has given a very clear account of his movements, we are in some fashion beholden to, on account of the temporary loss which he has suffered in the filching of his mount by the criminal with whom we have just dealt.   He was indirectly the cause of that criminal's arrest. The least we can do, therefore, is to give him his property back with the least possible delay.   I order that the animal with all his accoutrements, having first been properly fed and groomed, shall be restored to him.'

" I very humbly bowed and thanked the court for its just decision.   But a new complication arose.

" The chief officer of the court, the captain of those who had arrested the young man (he had by this time lost his head, so that there was no trouble to be feared from *that* side), conferred with his colleagues and then prostrated himself upon the earth before the judge, begging to be allowed an explanation.   The judge assumed a disturbed expression and bade him be brief.   He arose and admitted with evident grief that the horse, in the excitement of the arrest, and in the darkness of the moment (for all this had passed in the night), had got loose and was lost.

" Seeing the rising anger of the judge I hastily intervened. I said that I yielded to no one in my admiration for the Mounted Police of the Anti-Date force, the renown of whose efficiency had reached me even in my own distant land. I said that I would be the last to cause the least injustice or even pain. I begged that his Importance (for such was the simple title of a judge in that country) would overlook the unfortunate accident whereby my horse had been lost. I concluded by saying that I would be perfectly content with what we merchants called ' a minimum valuation,' that is, a payment of the price the horse would have fetched from what we merchants also call ' a .willing seller.' In a phrase of which I confess I was secretly proud, I hinted that the doing of justice in this matter would not only be of no charge to the court, but even of some profit to them, seeing that there were certain to be fees of transfer, registration, and what not. As a layman I was ignorant of their amount, but I knew them to be attached to such affairs—all out of the taxes.

" The judge, the officers of the court, and every lawyer present, the very sweepers were moved to action. Sundry papers were signed (to which I put the name of Ali—it was the first that occurred to me). I was paid the sum of thirty pieces of gold, and after profound obeisances to all present, and especially to my benefactor the judge, I left the court, yet richer than I had entered it.

*   *   *   *   *

" My children, what next ?

" It is a universal rule in commerce to follow your profits and cut your losses, and men of my profession have a sort of instinct which tells them how long the tide will be flowing with them and when it will turn. I decided that there was yet one more step for me to take.

" The arrest had taken place not far from the edge of the wood whence I had first perceived the city. There my horse, the evening before, had found good pasture. There had I loosened his saddle. There had he known an excellent place of repose. Thither did I wisely suppose my lost friend to have repaired. I sauntered therefore out of the city as though engaged upon no more than a stroll, and sure enough, a league away, under the trees which afforded a grateful shade, the noble beast was reclining, hampered only by his saddle.

" I loosened the girths. He was grateful, and our friendship was renewed. But though my affection was increased by such a recovery, I steeled my heart for what I purposed next to do.

" It is a maxim of all sound business that a thing should be sold as often as possible, and it was clear that I now had an opportunity of selling this charming creature for the third time. It was equally clear that, if I delayed, the opportunity would pass ; for the story of my appearance in court would spread through the city, the officers would talk with their friends about the saddle and the description of the animal ; I might even get into a difficult tangle with the authorities.

" But the whole of this propitious day was in the hand of Heaven. For, while yet the sun was high, there came upon me through the pasture a shepherd

driving his sheep, and to him I told a tale that I had
been sent by my master to sell the horse I was leading,
and his saddle, to a certain dealer, who had already
seen them and bargained for them. I had been given
a writing with the name of the dealer in the neighbouring city, but I had lost the writing and could not
remember the name or direction.

" The shepherd told me that he only went to that
city from time to time, but he was well acquainted
with it ; the purchaser could be none other than
Abd-ul-Eblis.

" The moment he pronounced this name I clapped my
hands together and said : ' Abd-ul-Eblis ! That was
the name ! ' I thanked the shepherd for thus refresh-
ing my memory, and I carefully walked by the beast's
side as should a mere servant by his master's precious
possession. I avoided the main gate (which I had
now passed twice and where I might be too well
known) and entered the city by a little postern.
I found from inquiry of a blind man—which
was the more prudent—the way to Abd-ul-Eblis's
stables.

" I made no plan of what I should do, for on those
days when I am specially favoured by the Most High
I leave His Power to guide me . . . and to guide also
those with whom I do business. I went no farther
than to tell the groom that I had come to find a purchaser for the horse—not indeed in this city, where
I had been told the market was poor, but in a place
two days' journey away, where the news of the famous
beast's coming had already been spread. I then
wandered out into the streets to take the cool air of
the evening. It was as I had expected. When I
returned to see that my horse had been well fed,

Adb-ul-Eblis was present in the stable and eager to deal.

" He pointed out to me the advantages he enjoyed for disposing of horses, the dangers of the distant journey of which I had spoken to the groom, the possibility of what is called in the language of that country 'a proposition.' He showed me what, in my innocence, I might have forgotten, that it was not as though the horse was my own. That *I* could only be a gainer. That my master would be none the wiser. That I might pretend any accident to have taken place (for indeed such an accident was likely if I went on farther). He also was at the pains of repeating what I might have forgotten, that I was free to retain for myself some portion of the price, assuring me that he would keep silent upon the matter. In the end I promised to hand him over the horse for sixty pieces of gold.

" There are some men, my dear nephews, who even in these circumstances would have begun bargaining for a higher price. These are men who love the making of small sums and who do not understand the enormous weight of caprice and chance in human affairs. So far from attempting to get a higher price, I expressed my gratitude and said that for my part I was quite willing to take less, but that I somewhat feared my master's anger and could not return to him without at least fifty pieces of gold, adding that I considered ten pieces a sufficient reward for myself. At the same time I advised Abdul not to sell the saddle *with* the horse, nor did I omit to remind him that horses of a light colour are more easily dyed than those of a darker hue.

" At these suggestions of mine he looked upon me

mournfully for a few moments and then slowly counted
out sixty pieces of gold. I took a long farewell of the
kindly, patient, and beautiful animal, which had borne
me to this fortune in the short space of one day, and
then walked forth through the city into the evening,
preferring the chance of a lodging in the forest to
tempting further the singular Fate that had so far
befriended me.

" The weather was warm, the neighbouring wood, as
I knew by experience, hospitable. There would I
spend the few hours of darkness, building myself a
small fire to keep off the beasts and to cherish me.
Thence, I did not doubt, I could the next morning, with
now so satisfactory a capital, proceed to the re-edifica-
tion of my fortune.

" I reached the wooded hill which overlooked the
city. I recited my third night prayers. Before
building my fire and disposing myself to sleep, I
looked at the outline of the walls and domes and graceful minarets against the last of the evening, and I
revolved in my mind that thought which shall ever be
mine on my departure from any town. Let it also be
yours, my dear children, in all your travels.

" For just as when you come to a new city of a
morning, before you enter it, and after having prayed
God, you should muse within yourself what sums of
money you may hope to lift from its inhabitants ;
so when you leave any city at evening, never omit
(after due thanks to your Creator !) to calculate what
sums you have indeed subtracted from those to whom
you bid farewell."

As the old merchant ceased it was like the ending
of a strain of solemn music, the echoes of which linger
and continue in the memory. The strangely moving

words he had uttered stirred a profound chord in the depths of their young souls, and they sat with bowed heads until the horrid outrage of the Muezzin's call murdered that sacred silence.

At the signal the lads rose and filed out on tiptoe leaving their uncle with his eyes closed and his lips murmuring in prayer.

الولّى

AL-WALI

That is:

"THE HOLY ONE"

CHAPTER XI

ENTITLED *AL-WALI*, OR THE HOLY ONE

WHEN the hour of public executions had arrived (they were more numerous than usual) his young nephews respectfully assembled at the feet of the aged millionaire and received the further account of his fortunes.

"You might imagine, my children," he began, "that having this small capital so happily furnished me by Providence in the short space of a single day, I would again venture upon a commercial undertaking. That would have been indeed my natural course ; but you must remember that I could not, without great danger, enter the city I had just left, lest my able transactions should lead me into contact with those at whose expense they had been conducted. Further, I was in a strange country with no knowledge of my way and with nothing to guide me save the happy circumstance that I was still within the boundaries of our holy religion. Most of those I should meet would thus be True Believers, whose frailties I could better understand than those of the Kafir, and of whom therefore I could (under the all-powerful guidance of Heaven) more easily take advantage.

"Devoutly remembering the signal mercies shown to me by Allah in this last short day, I determined to follow the same course as I had when my good fortune came to me—to lie passive under the Mighty Hand directing me and to trust to luck.

" I took some sleep in the night beside my fire, but hardly had I awakened at dawn when I was aware of a group approaching me through the forest track. They were a party of a dozen or so, half of them on foot, half of them mounted ; of no great consequence if one might judge by their clothing, which, my dear nephews, is in most occasions in life the signal by which we may know whether to revere men or to despise them. Both beasts and humans in this group were travel-stained as having come from some great distance.

" As I saw them before they saw me, I naturally took the precaution of creeping up behind them through the trees in order to overhear the object of their journey. It appeared that they were bound on pilgrimage to the shrine of a Most Holy Man, to obtain his oracle in a matter which concerned their miserable village.

" My mind was at once made up. I ran back by a circuitous course through the trees, came to a place ahead of their progress, and there, spreading my little mat upon the sward, I prostrated myself in prayer. Indeed, I was thus able to kill two birds with one stone, for I had not yet said those morning prayers of the True Believer which I had never omitted in all my life, save when I happened to be flying from justice and therefore deprived of leisure.

" As I heard them coming up behind me I raised my head and voice at once, and fell into a perfect ecstasy of worship, which did not fail to impress the simple mountaineers. They halted respectfully until I saw fit to terminate my conversation with the Most

High. I pretended to be so absorbed in my contemplation of divine things as not to notice them : for to
keep them waiting secured religious as well as worldly
respect. They approached me with deference and
even awe. I told them I was bound for the shrine of
a Most Holy Man whose name I gave them. They
were overjoyed to discover that they had a companion
filled with the same sentiments as themselves.

" ' We also,' said their leader, ' are engaged upon
the same sacred mission. For we have been informed
by a messenger (whom we dispatched a month ago
from our village) that the Saint will graciously receive
us and give us a reply upon a doubtful matter of wild
hedge-pigs which has greatly excited our tribe, whether
they be pork or no.'

" I let them convey by chance phrases the direction
we had to travel and the distance of our goal. I was
delighted to discover that our way did not lie through
the city, and that we might hope to reach the Holy
One before night.

" The journey was tedious, passing over burnt land
with but a few wretched villages upon the track ; but
by the late afternoon we could see far off, coloured by
the declining rays of the sun, a small, white-domed
building, the tomb of a great saint long dead, by the
side of which a large group of tents and a considerable
assembly lying out in the open round them cooking
their evening meal, beasts of burden, and all the
movement of a camp, showed us that we were reaching
the term of our day's journey.

" When we reached the camp I joined the thickest
part of the throng, separating from the group with
which I had been marching. I made my evening prayers
in as conspicuous a place as possible, prolonged them

prodigiously, the better to impress my new neighbours, and then lay down, uncertain what the course of the next day should be.

" It was revealed to me in a dream.

" In that dream there appeared a bright and beneficent Being who with one hand was relieving of his superfluous wealth an unconscious pilgrim to his left, and with the other was conferring precisely the same favour on another to his right.   Each of the two pilgrims had his face turned away from the Blessed Genius thus engaged and seemed unconscious of the process to which he was subjected.   The Glorious Visitant, without interrupting its occupation or ceasing with mechanical regularity to dip its hands into the pouches of its unwitting neighbours, looked upon me with the most benign expression, winked, and disappeared.

" I awoke.   It was yet dark.   I pondered until dawn what the revelation might mean.   With the rising of the sun inner as well as outer light was bestowed upon me.   I interpreted in the following fashion the vision that had thus been vouchsafed to me and the event proved me to have divined the right reading by interpretation :

" In every place largely frequented by pilgrims you will, my dear nephews (if your commercial pursuits lead you to such spots in after life), discover two kinds of men.   There are those who have already spent their all under the influence of the Spirit and are about to depart.   These, being in a necessity to raise a viaticum for their return, will eagerly convert into cash at a vile price such wretched objects as remain to them. On the other hand, those arriving are flush of money and eager to acquire holy relics and memorials of the blessed days before them.

" With two such markets before one's eyes and clamouring for exploitation, all that is required is a little judgment upon which is which, who is who, and what is what. Such a judgment is essential to any commercial success, but especially to success with people in a state of religious exaltation. For whereas this mood often conduces to folly, it sometimes so supernaturally brightens the intellectual faculties of devotees as to procure most cruel rebuffs for him who attempts to take advantage of it.

" I mixed with my fellow-worshippers. I picked out those whom I judged from their anxious expression, coupled with their preparations for a journey, to be eager sellers. From these I acquired at prices quite surprisingly small, all manner of objects—sticks, chaplets, sandals, water-bottles, rags, and cords—while I dexterously sheered off the few who seemed too much inclined to bargain, and whom not even a prolonged residence at the shrine had wholly purged of avarice. The remainder were quite sufficient for my needs.

" With a stock thus acquired at the expenditure of not a tenth of my capital, I next proceeded to mix with the more prosperous new-comers, pressing on them now one object and now another (sandals, lace, rags, bits of bone and leather), as some things of peculiar sanctity, either as dedicated to the shrine of the Dead Holy Man or as having touched the person of the Living One. I discovered a very brisk market indeed, at prices varying from a hundred to a thousand times the original cost of the rubbish. To each bit of rag, bone, or what not I was careful to affix a pedigree written in various hands and proving it authentic.

" In these negotiations I was careful, at the least note of suspicion, to pretend a complete indifference ;

and to one or two more than usually guileful I even made the sacrifice of giving a yard of used cord or a hopelessly worn sandal, remarking as I did so that Sacred Things should not be made a matter of traffic.

" In this fashion I passed four days so absorbed in the interest of the occupation that I quite forgot (it was an error on my part) to present myself within the clamouring line of those who daily demanded the opportunity to fall down before the object of our pilgrimage and to offer him obeisance. It was a mistake which nearly cost me dear, for the Holy Man had his hired watchers among the crowd.

" On the evening of the fourth day, as I was privately counting my gains under a secluded bush where I hoped to be unobserved, I was disturbed by a smart tap upon the shoulder and a summons from an aged but tall and still strong man, armed with a formidable bludgeon. This person bade me follow him without comment, and told me I had been granted the singular favour of personal access to The Master.

" It was with mixed feelings that I accompanied my guide. We elbowed our way through the foremost ranks of worshippers to that inmost place wherein the Holy One communed with his Creator. They envied me and gazed with awe upon one so privileged, but for my part my heart sank lower and lower, and I waited in something approaching panic the interview that had been so graciously afforded.

" I was introduced through a curtain into a low hut, wholly devoid of ornament, built of dried mud and lit only by two small smoky lamps that stood upon the floor. I dimly perceived before me in this half-darkness the figure of a very aged man, incredibly emaciated with prolonged fast and vigil. He was upon his knees with a chaplet in his hands. His eyes were cast upon the ground, which his long but sparse white beard almost touched. He seemed oblivious to all the external world, and was plunged in profound communion with his Maker.

" The attendant in low but angry whispers bade me prostrate myself, which I was not slow in doing ; and in that posture I waited for a space of time so tedious that it seemed to me the greater part of one hour. But during all that time I dared not move ; for though I had never visited this particular shrine, I had heard tales of what had happened to those who underrate the Unseen Powers. I was relieved at last by a distinct and hollow voice bidding me in measured tones to rise. I arose, and found that we were alone. The attendants had been dismissed by a gesture while my face was yet buried on the ground, and though I have no doubt that they were within earshot, I suffered the added awe of loneliness.

" The Holy One still maintained for a moment his impassive attitude of prayer, then slowly pivoted round on his knees, turned his luminous eyes upon me, and sternly asked me what profit I had made by my infamous trade during the last few days. I felt that all was known to him. I did not (I thank Heaven for its mercies !) attempt to deceive him and thus jeopardize my life and reason. I told him the full tale and awaited his sentence.

" There was a long pause, during which what little was left of my courage ebbed away. I felt prepared to hear some short sentence of doom and resigned myself to my fate. But I had happily miscalculated the serene wisdom which accompanies holiness.

" The Saint spoke next in a more benevolent and

softer voice, bade me be seated cross-legged before him, and adopting the same attitude pronounced the following remarkable words :

" ' The Just, the Merciful (Whose name be exalted !), has given to different men different aptitudes. The fool attempts that of which he is incapable. The wise man recognizes his limitations.'

" In the silence that followed I turned these weighty phrases over in my mind and recognized excerpts from the Proverbs of Mar-Hakim, whose wisdom has been collected by the Persians, and has been famous since the times of the second Omar.

" After a short interval the voice continued :

" ' In mutual appreciation and in mutual benefits each acquires profit. The short-sighted forfeit advantage by too much grasping.'

" These words, which were chanted rather than said, I recognized to be from a totally different collection of popular sayings, formerly current in Arabia, and reduced to writing in the first century of Hegira by the learned of Rasht. It was clear that I was in the presence of a man unusually well informed, and my conviction was confirmed when after yet another solemn pause the voice continued as though in conclusion :

" ' In acquiring money there is profit, but in letting it slip there is none at all.'

" This last jewel of wisdom I immediately recalled as part of yet another collection, to wit, the Sacred Books of the Jews ; and from this further example of immense erudition my estimation of the Being possessed of it arose to the clouds.

" After such a preface I might have expected further general statements of a moral nature from my host,

when suddenly I perceived a total change in the tones
of his voice and a similar change in his attitude. He
put off the preoccupation of religion. He took on the
tone of familiar intercourse proper to temporal affairs.
He smiled genially and entered upon a conversation
such as one might enjoy in the bazaar of any city or
in the private hospitality of any merchant.

" ' There are some,' he said, ' who would have blamed
your conduct ; and in a sense I do so ; for I cannot
excuse your passage of four whole days without a
thought of heaven. But then, we are all agreed that
the driving of a trade, especially if it be remarkably
rapid and lucrative, is a very worthy occupation, and
it is one of my regrets that my professional devotion
to the Other World has curtailed my own activities
in the same line.

" ' I am visited by thousands of respectful worshippers. The small amounts of alms which they graciously
leave with my treasurer might easily be increased by
various commercial activities.

" ' Indeed, I have from time to time attempted to
establish such in this camp, but I regret to say with
no success. I opened a canteen here but two years ago
where refreshments were sold to the new arrivals at
from three to five times their value. But the evil
servant to whom I entrusted the management of this
concern decamped with the whole of the profits. I
obtained the satisfaction of having him put to death
by a distant friend, but I was never able to recover
his ill-gotten gains.

" ' At another time I entered into a contract with
certain brigands who hold the passes of the mountains.
It was clearly understood between us that they should
hold up the worshippers returning from my shrine and

that one-half of the ransoms they collected should be paid into my chests. But from that day to this I have not received a penny.

" ' On yet another occasion it occurred to me that I might fix a regular tribute to replace the voluntary alms which, though considerable, leave room for improvement. But the alarming falling off in receipts and the dwindling of my income made me withdraw the order within six months of its issue.

" ' All these experiences combined, my dear Mahmoud,' said he familiarly (thus showing that he knew my true name and disturbing me not a little), ' have convinced me that I have not what you men of affairs call " a business sense." I may have a latent talent, I may even have a genius, for religion. When I tell you that I sometimes pass three days without changing my position of prayer and without taking food or drink, the whole performance watched by a great crowd of astonished faithful, you will agree that I am not without capabilities of my own. But I am reluctantly convinced that what the Giaours call " a good nose for a deal " is not one of them.'

" Here I began to interrupt him with the usual compliments, and would have assured him that any man of ability had but to train himself for affairs to do as well as another, when he genially stopped me with a gesture and said :

" ' No, my dear Mahmoud ' (again the use of my name disturbed me), ' whatever else we are let us not be hypocrites. Let us frankly acknowledge our limitations. You, as I am now convinced, know how to sell and to buy, and have all the qualities for discovering the dearest and the cheapest markets. Much as I have desired to attain to the same faculties I have failed, and at my age (which, though it is not the 110 years reported, is at any rate well over sixty) it is too late to change. I will therefore make you what is called, I believe, in your world an offer.'

" (With what relief did those words fall on my ears ! I did not realize for the moment how greatly it was to his advantage to have begun by frightening your unhappy uncle and what an opportunity this had given him for negotiations !)

" ' I will make you a proposition. Think carefully over it, and at the end of a reasonable time give me your decision. I offer you two alternatives. The one is that you should continue your trade subject to the supervision of my agents, and that when you have reached a total of 1,000 pieces of gold you shall be impaled and the money confiscated. The other is that you shall continue to use your evident talents for the furtherance of this trade, but that I shall be regarded as a sleeping partner in the same, with half the takings. The choice lies with you. . . . Pray, pray take your time. Undue haste has spoilt many an excellent business contract, and I would not have you ruin your chances. Do not,' he continued, repressing my evident anxiety to accept his terms, ' do not let your judgment be prejudiced by any feeling of obligation. Think the alternatives over carefully and then let me know your conclusion. Take your time.'

" Restraining too great an evidence of haste, I told him that my mind was already made up and that I would be honoured to accept his second offer.

" ' I think, Mahmoud,' said he, rising, ' that you have acted with wisdom, though perhaps with a little precipitation. Let us, then, regard the matter as settled. Every evening my servants will call upon you for one-half of your takings, and they meanwhile will protect you in every way.'

" I prostrated myself once more, kissed the ground at his feet, and left the hut in a very different mood from that in which I had entered it.

" I remained in the camp for the matter of about a month. I extended my operations; and every evening the servants of the Holy One attended me and I handed over half of my takings. During the whole of that period my capital continued to increase prodigiously.

" But no good endures for ever. The time came when this even tenor was threatened in a very unexpected way.

" The Holy One was visited by certain ambassadors from the Grand Something or Other residing in the court of the Caliph, who informed him that his position was duly recognized by the authorities, and that they bore with them an Illuminated Charter confirming it. The temporal advantages of His Holiness's trade, however, were no less clearly evident to the Caliph than the religious ones, and His Holiness would therefore be good enough in future to hand over one-half of his receipts to the Imperial Treasury.

" Heaven knows with what bitterness the Holy Man agreed; which, having done, he sent for me again and told me that it was now necessary for him to ask me for three-fourths of my receipts. In vain did I point out to him that all great empires had fallen by the increase of taxation. He was adamant, and I therefore reluctantly agreed to the new arrangement; taking a solemn oath to observe it for at least one year. But I asked him whether at the expiration of that

time, in case I should find the new bargain more
than I could support, I might depart out of the city?
To this he agreed, and confirmed it with an oath
equally solemn.

" That night I put together all my accumulated
wealth (which now filled not less than four large bags
with gold and silver) and charging it upon the mule
of a peculiarly devout and therefore unobservant and
abstracted pilgrim, and drawing the innocent beast
away in the darkness by the bridle, I left the camp as
slowly and cautiously as I might.

" Emissaries were sent out to kill me within half an
hour of my departure. As I heard their approach I
turned my mule round towards the camp as though
I were arriving, and as they passed me, I said I was a
pilgrim who had lost his way in the night and asked
if I were on the right road for the shrine. This simple
ruse deceived them. They went their way and I was
alone once more. Still, their passage sufficiently
alarmed me. I gave up the road for a less frequented
path and wandered all that night through an unfamiliar
district, for my poor beast could go no faster than a
walking pace, so heavy were the bags of treasure which
he bore.

" By dawn I felt myself secure, and——"

But here the Old Gentleman heard the first intolerable note of the Muezzin and stopped short, motioning
to his nephews that they should leave him, which they
did with their customary humility, each wondering in
his heart whether he might not later feel a vocation to
the Religious Life.

المحلّة الجديدة

AL-MAHALLAT AL-JADIDA

That is:

"THE NEW QUARTER OF THE CITY"

CHAPTER XII

ENTITLED *AL-MAHALLAT AL-JADIDA*, OR THE NEW
QUARTER OF THE CITY

" **A** S I proceeded the next morning across the waste "
(continued Mahmoud to his nephews on
their next visit) " I turned over in my mind how best
to employ the considerable sum which my honest
mule bore so patiently upon his back. Here was a
year's sustenance for fifty labourers or more, and with
so much money a man earns more. For, as it is
written in the Holy Book, ' *The labourer is worthy
of his hire, but whatever is over is not for him.*' And
again, ' *Blessed are the poor.*'

" There are not wanting occasions for the employment of poorer men and the gathering of the fruits of
their labour into one's own pouch. But there is one
difficulty in all such matters, which is the point of
judgment.

" You will recollect (my dear nephews) how often
in the past a most careful investment of mine had gone
wrong, and how often a mere hazard, not even of my
own choosing, had brought me sudden fortune. How
in the matter of the sheep I was beaten almost to death
by the market-police, while in the matter of the horse
I had sold, three times over, an animal that had cost
me nothing and had fallen to me by the pure goodness
of God. How in the matter of the dates I had been left
penniless by a man of greater Business Sense, Foresight,

Organizing Ability, Eye for the Market, Knowledge of Men, and the rest of the virtues ; while in the Matter of the Holy Man I had—as my weary mule proved—done extremely well out of a quite unexpected accident. Even as this last example passed through my mind I remembered, for the first time, that the mule himself was a new accession of fortune, over and above the silver he carried. For I had not had the inconvenience of paying for him. He was a fine beast, and in spite of his fatigue still looked well bred. I estimated him at quite ten pieces of gold, and mentally added that sum on my tablets to the total value of my possessions.

" It was so musing that I found myself approaching a high tangle of reeds, through which a narrow path wound and was lost to view. On this path I engaged. The reeds on either side were so tall as to hide the farther landscape, and so closely set that one could see but a few yards into their mass.

" After perhaps an hour of such journeying my mule and I came out suddenly upon the firm bank of a broad and shallow river whose noise and coolness, swift current and clear stream were a delight after so many hours of arid travel. There did I sit me down. There did I unload and hobble my patient companion. There did we drink of the good water, and there did the mule eat plentifully of cool grass. But I made no meal, for the oat-cakes and cheese which I had taken from the Common Table of the Poor in the Pilgrims' camp were now exhausted.

" It was this circumstance which made me a little anxious for the day. I looked about me, stood up on the highest part of the bank, and then saw that the shore opposite had been artificially heightened to form a regular levee or embankment, beyond which the flat country was hidden. I determined to seek this point of advantage for a view. I reloaded my mule, carefully forded the stream in its various branches and climbed to the farther shore.

" At the summit of the embankment, which was evidently of recent construction, my effort was well rewarded, for I saw a sight that set at rest all anxiety for food and shelter.

" The embankment on which I stood swept round in a horseshoe shape—not everywhere finished, but everywhere traced out. It thus enclosed a peninsula, bounded by the river : a space of marshy ground full of stagnant pools and water-grasses. Three or four furlongs away, cutting across the whole neck of the horseshoe of swamp and stretching from the river to the river again, ran the well-built stone wall of a strong town, the flat roofs and low domes of which (it had no tower or minaret) made a ridge of snow-white against the intense blue of the sky. Far away beyond were distant mountains, purple in the heat.

" Scattered over the swamp itself and on the unfinished sections of the embankment were groups of labourers working with spades and barrows, and, overseeing them, near-by to me, a young man of energetic carriage, well dressed in a brown garment, rich, but suitable to his work and girded. He had no sandals, for they would have impeded him on such ground ; he bore an inlaid ebon staff with an ivory hand-grasp, and was occupied, when I first saw him, in shouting a new order to a distant group of diggers. His back was towards me. He had not seen my approach.

" As he turned, to proceed along the levee towards another group, he caught sight of my mule and myself and at once started to run, pouring out when he had reached us a mixed flood of greetings, warnings, and varied exclamations.

" 'We were to beware of the embankment ! It was but just raised and was not yet stable ! Was it not a fine work ? Half-completed, as we saw it, it had taken but three months. Did I notice how thoroughly it had cut off the river ? Had I not found it firm as I came up it from the bank ? Would I be pleased to go carefully lest the edge should be injured ? . . . and so on.'

" It was clear from such a salutation with what sort of man I had to deal. Here was an Enthusiast. It is a character of the utmost service to the Man of Affairs. He was of that sort which is labelled in our indexes as ' The Constructive Wild Man,' and happy is the Captain of Industry who chances upon such a one. He was perhaps thirty years of age, strong, short in stature, very dark in complexion, with steady but eager eyes, and such an expression of grasp, resolution, and immediate decision as should lead to a fortune, not perhaps for himself but at least for anyone who knew how to use him ; for he was as keen as a boy upon the matter occupying him, and therefore careless for the moment of all other things.

" I answered him with a mixture of sympathy, caution, and gravity, which I was glad to see impressed him. I praised his work vaguely but courteously enough. I asked the names of the river and the town, and also his own. All these he gave me ; and then asked me whether I would not share the midday meal he was about to take. I said I should be over-joyed to do so : and so I was, for I saw the prospect of refreshment at the charges of another, an opportunity, which remember—my dear nephews—is never to be neglected by men of clear commercial judgment.

" He led me, followed by the mule, to a shady place where a few trees stood on a drier part of the enclosed plain. There we found excellent meats, and there we reclined for above an hour, during the whole of which he did not cease to overwhelm me with description, praise, and prospect of the great enterprise in which he was wholly absorbed.

" This horseshoe bend, he told me, outside his native town, had never been utilized. It was flooded in the spring when the snow melted on the distant hills; the rest of the year it was a mixture of dry cracked mud and marsh, breeding fever, full of insects and ill-airs at evening. He had been left an orphan and was apprenticed to a maker of mill-wheels, such as were used in the stream above the city. One day the idea had occurred to him that such instruments could be used not only for the grinding of corn but for the raising of water from ditches and therefore for draining.

" With that his grand project had rushed into his mind. Why should not the marsh, which had so far been so serious a trouble, be turned to the profit of the city? An embankment would keep out floods, drains cut through the enclosed marsh would collect the water and dry the whole. These drains could be regularly pumped out by wheels which the outer stream would turn, and a large area of good land would be added to the crowded town. On this new buildings could be raised and gardens laid out, to the great profit of all the citizens. For the city was increasing in importance, people were flocking in, there was crowding and difficulty and high rents, yet no place over which to expand between the marsh and the hills.

" He had approached the council and headmen with this project. They had hesitated long. At last they had grudgingly advanced from the taxes a sum which he warned them was inadequate. Nevertheless he had set to work, and the results were now before me. The swamp was still swamp, the embankment not completed, of the drains not more than a sixth were dug, and the whole was a confusion of mud-heaps, apparent ruin and chaos, very unattractive to the eye and very unpromising, in its outward aspect at least, of any result. It had all the character of waste and folly—yet a sum of money, small in comparison with many private resources and insignificant in the budget of the town, would suffice to crown the whole and to replace the wretched prospect of unfinished labour by a noble plain of rich gardens and new houses. But the headmen of the city were now disgusted and would vote no more. Rather did they threaten him with penalties for his loss of public pence.

" I had, during this torrent of talk, interjected here and there a question and no more. I had spoken guardedly and yet with no disrespect for his enthusiasm. I had, as we say among the merchants ' sounded him.' I asked him in conclusion what sum he thought necessary for the completion of his enterprise. He named 300 gold pieces, about one-quarter of what lay concealed in my sacks upon the ground, which sacks (I had casually informed him) were filled with coarse grain from the hills.

" Upon hearing this sum given, a sum so well within my means, an interior light broke upon me. I did not pray for guidance, as is my custom in any business dealing of doubt. I was directly and immediately inspired. To this I owe the whole of my present position ; for it was the foundation of all that followed. I had suffered vicissitude. It is the lot of man. But henceforward my soul was to be filled with increasing and ever-increasing wealth until I should be able to call myself, as I do now, by far the richest man in all the Caliphate and perhaps in the world. This, my dear nephews, was the turning-point ! "

The old man's eyes were full of tears, his voice trembled ; never had the awestruck boys imagined that their uncle, in his greatness and serenity, could be so moved.

" Oh, my children ! " he continued in broken accents, " never forget in your own lives this master precept ; that of all those whom Allah presents to us for exploitation, none, none is so lucrative as the Creative Enthusiast ; the man who can make and produce and yet be managed ! the Genius devoid of Guile ! You may know him, that rare jewel, by his eyes."

The old man recovered himself with dignity, wiped his eyes on a piece of priceless embroidered silk from Samarcand, threw it out of the window, and, in his more usual tone, pursued the recital of his fortunes.

" The young man never dreamt that such a chance and dusty traveller as I, with my one mule, could help him. He had merely burst out with his story to me as he would have done to any human being that would hear him. I had the more advantage of him from his ignorance of my real wealth.

" I told him soberly at the end of his tale that it interested me greatly, that his idea was evidently sound, but that the stupidity, ignorance, and suspicion of town councillors were common not only to his city, but to all others—a thing which I, who had travelled widely, could judge. I assured him, out of a vast experience (which he accepted with the utmost simplicity), that he could hope for no more from such a source. I then fell into a sort of bemused condition, as though I were ruminating what could next be done.

" The young man, his hopes now turned into a new channel, and, after so brief an acquaintance (for such is the nature of these enthusiasts) already beginning to look to me for aid, watched my face most anxiously. I continued silent.

" At last he could bear it no longer. He asked me impetuously what I should advise—where could he turn ? What could be done ? It would be a tragedy— a murder—for his great scheme to fail merely because its obvious advantage could not be put before anyone who had the provision of 300 gold pieces necessary for paying the labourers till the plan was achieved. He sprang to his feet. He walked feverishly up and down. He betrayed all the symptoms of his case.

" I answered him with great deliberation and firmness. I said, first of all, that I had nothing. It was a pity, for I thoroughly understood his idea. I admired it. I believed in it. Indeed, it was obviously sound. If I had had the wherewithal (said I) I would at once have made the advance. If I had had even a portion I would have put that portion at his disposal if only to show my sincere appreciation of his genius. For it was the neglect of men like himself (I continued) that hindered the progress of the world. But so it was ! I had but my trade as an itinerant merchant in grain to support myself and a very large family which I had left at home in the hills. I had nothing laid by.

. . . However, my annual tour through this and neighbouring provinces brought me into contact (these were my very words) with many notables possessed of ample reserves. In this very town—now that he had told me its name—I remembered two or three correspondents with whom I had done business in the past, though I had never seen them. These I would approach. And if he would give me an appointment that evening after sunset I would tell him if I had been able to effect anything.

" He overwhelmed me with thanks, led me to an excellent house of call in the town, and, leaving me there with an appointed hour for our meeting in the evening, he returned to his labours with a lighter heart.

" I, for my part, retired to an inner room which I had hired, there disposed of my baggage (having seen to the stabling and feeding of my honest mule), and instantly fell upon my knees to thank Allah with all the fervour I could muster for His abounding grace. Indeed, my heart overflowed with gratitude when I considered the quite exceptional opportunity. I felt about this young man as does a caravan, when, after a weary march through the desert, there gleams a pure lake not half an hour away. How short a space of time now lay between this moment and the beginnings of splendid negotiations !

" Having so prayed with the deepest sincerity and humility, I first took out exactly *two* hundred pieces of gold from my sacks, tied them into a kerchief about my person, and then lay down upon a mat to sleep, first warning the servants of the place to wake me when the young man should return. I slept soundly for many hours.

" When they woke me it was already dark. I rose at once, lit the lamp, and received my young friend into the room. All was silent. We were alone under the one light of that subdued flame. The hour was propitious for what I had undertaken.

" I told him that I had spent the interval, since he left me, in seeking my wealthy correspondents and in making myself acquainted with their views upon the town's circumstances and upon the opportunities for investment. I said that I had briefly and very cautiously mentioned the works I saw going on in the swamp as I had approached their city, and that I had discovered at once, by their pitying contempt for his enterprise, that there was no chance at all of interesting them in its progress. They called it—as did all their fellow-citizens—a folly. They bitterly regretted the public money that had already been advanced. They would certainly advance no more. They talked freely of bringing him to trial for wasting the public revenue. As for any private investment of their own fortunes, I clearly saw that it was out of the question.

" Here I paused to let this information sink in, and was pleased to observe the growing dejection of his features. But before he could voice his despair— though he had expected as much—I relieved him by another strain. I told him I had raised a certain sum. Partly upon the security of my known stores of grain (of which I was carrying samples—pointing to the bags on the floor that contained my money), partly on my own personal security as an honest merchant, poor but of regular and punctual habit in payment, I had secured a loan which I had told them was for the general purpose of increasing my business, but which in point of fact I intended to put at his disposal—

such confidence had I in his scheme. I feared it would be insufficient, but it would be a beginning—later we might find further means.

"His honest, eager face changed as I spoke. It was delightful to feel that I could give so much joy, however brief, to so candid a soul. He had, however, a certain scruple. He said it was not his business, but he would rather there had been no ambiguity, and the money advanced for a purpose known to the lenders.

"I praised the nobility of such hesitation, but I pointed out that the risk was mine : that I had only spoken of 'a general purpose of increasing my business,' no false phrase ; that I was so certain of *our* success that the loan was at any rate secure. In any case, business (of which he had little acquaintance) was always conducted on such lines (I assured him) and my backers being also business men would be the last to split hairs on points of honour when I paid back their loan. This soothed him and he was now quite prepared for what followed.

"I asked him again what sum he required ? He told me he employed a hundred labourers, that their wages came to twenty gold pieces a week, and that he estimated fifteen weeks as the very least period in which the whole ground could be cleared and dried and set out. In all, he repeated, *three* hundred pieces of gold would be required : as he had said. I noted to myself privately once more that it was one-quarter of my hoard, and then, when he had completed his calculation, I thus addressed him :

"'It is as I feared! The sum I have obtained is hardly sufficient. I have raised but *two* hundred pieces of gold!' His face fell again. 'But that will take us pretty far,' I went on. 'We may with care *nearly* complete our work, and the rest it should be easy to find.'

" It has always surprised me how exact such men are in judgment and yet how little they use their talent to their own advantage. He was anxious. He was certain that beginning on too small a sum was dangerous. But I persuaded him ; for no more (said I) could possibly be obtained.

" What made all smooth was my proposal for Articles between us. These generously proposed that, though I had found the money, yet of any resultant profit we should take equal shares. ' I propose that your own salary during the work,' said I, ' should be small ; indeed, no more than your bare maintenance. For we have no margin, nay, less than we need. But if you are not agreeable, pray name your terms.' He could find no words for my generosity ! Of course he would live on the least possible sum and work to an extreme ! He had no right (said he) to claim a half ! It was achievement, not fortune, that he desired.

" I insisted. He gratefully yielded. We drew up the document in duplicate. He was especially gratified to find that I had left the whole direction to him. ' I know nothing of such things,' I said. ' I am only the Business Man. You are the Creator, the Artist : I am but the base mercantile instrument, and I shall be proud to share in your triumph.' As I said this I put into my eyes the expression of inspired admiration which we of the commercial world very properly assume when we are dealing with this kind of fodder.

" The next morning, in the cool, before the sun had power, our deeds were attested. I warned him to be utterly silent upon the source of his capital. I said I would be responsible for a rumour that a small saving of his own was engaged. He saw my point, and, though still scrupulous, consented. The work went forward.

" My next step I had already planned. I had privately set aside for it a fixed sum, the equal of what I had given my partner. I hired a pleasant little house and garden in the city, with a fountain of clear water in its shaded court. I purchased a stock of good clothes and even one or two not over-violent jewels—and I began to entertain.

" I bought—at a price which gave me pause—a really wonderful cook ; I learnt the games of hazard to which the wealthier of the place were devoted. The headmen of the various quarters of the city, the principal councillors and magistrates learned one from another of the excellence of my table and the interest of my play. I became their intimate. From time to time I spoke of my friendship with the Enthusiast and of my regret at his wasting his poor savings upon the dreadful mess outside the walls. They agreed—and all the while that fervid young man redoubled his ardour, himself worked side by side with his men, planned, urged them on, and effected prodigies of labour. Indeed, I feared for his health—a natural anxiety for one in my situation—but by the Mercy of Allah it remained perfect.

" He now, however, came to me more and more frequently and in a greater and greater anxiety. There were but fifty gold pieces remaining, but forty, but twenty ! . . . It was a matter of a few days ! . . . Already he had had to keep back wages, to devise half-shifts, even to discharge men ! . . . Could I not, oh ! could I not raise some further sum ? . . . As he had said, the work needed another month at least, and its present state was appalling, no visible security for a loan, all mud and confusion ! . . . I could only reply that I would do my best, but that I was not sanguine, and my long face increased his fears.

" Perturbed as he was he had the generosity to regret *my* loss in the unfortunate enterprise.

" I showed a strong indifference and told him that I was used to the rubs of this sad world and that my trust was in Allah !

" At last, as the day when his funds would be exhausted was at hand, I gave a feast of special importance to the treasurer and the chief magistrates of the city, and there led the talk on to the works still continuing. I heard the usual grumble that the sum originally advanced out of the taxes was sunk in a morass, that the young man had, apparently, funds of his own for continuing the nonsense and that yet the city could recover nothing from him. I approved a threat that, out of sheer annoyance, they might stop the whole thing and put him in gaol till he should pay, or at any rate suffer for, his unsettled debt to his fellow-townsmen.

" Then it was that I struck, for the hour was ripe ! I pleaded for him as a friend. I let them feel my influence, I waited for the suggestion—and I was not disappointed. The treasurer after a little solemn hesitation said to me : ' Sir, since you know this young fellow and seem to be in his councils, can you not discover what remains to him and perhaps make him reimburse the gold pieces he owes to our town-fund ? We should be beholden to you.' I answered that my intimacy with the Enthusiast hardly went so far, but that I would do my best. Only I begged them for the interval of a week.

" The day after the morrow of that feast the Young Man came to me in an excessive perturbation. The mud of his travail was still on his hands, and I was concerned to see him limping from the effect (as he told me) of a heavy barrow which had overset as he wheeled it and crushed his big toe. But he neglected the pain in his extreme mental distress and told me that, having paid that week's wages, his gold pieces were now reduced to *ten*. Even if he himself ate but dry bread in the next few days and sold his poor belongings he could not meet the next account, which was but seven days distant.

" I cast my eyes on the ground and delayed a while, the more to impress him. I then told him in grave and subdued tones that I had very bad news. I glanced up a moment to note the wildness in his eyes upon this blow, then cast them down again to the ground and continued : ' I have private advice—perhaps I should not have divulged it to you, for it was given in confidence, but my concern and affection for you have proved too strong—I have private advice that the council intend this very week to demand most formally the repayment of 100 pieces of gold which they say is due from you for advances long ago made, and failing payment to cast you into their dungeon.'

" The Young Man leapt suddenly to his feet, gave a loud shriek, and made to beat his head against the wall. It was with difficulty that I held his hands and restrained him.

" ' Oh ! Curse my birth ! ' he cried in a paroxysm of despair. ' And curse my generation ! My day has come ! ' He raved. He incoherently demanded miracles and alternately denied the Justice of Allah ! Grown more subdued but still distraught, he moaned of his affections. He told me—what I had hitherto not known and what interested me very little—that he had a little sister, orphaned as he was, who, if he were put away, would starve or become the prey of strangers. What could be done? What refuge discovered? Curse the day when his fatal dream had struck him! Curse his works! Curse the river! Curse the marsh! Curse the' city!'

"And so on—the usual reaction of enthusiasts. It was most distressing. I still held his writhing hands firmly till he was calm enough to hear me, and then said :

"'Listen to me. I have considered your case. I think I can rescue you. I have myself saved a little from my·trading operations of the last two months in this town. My credit also is somewhat extended. *I* will find what you need. For I respect genius and I do not judge by common standards——'

"I was proceeding when he burst out into extravagant gratitude; called me his benefactor, kissed my hand again and again, and irrelevantly alluded again to that little sister of'his who really had nothing to do with the case. I checked him and continued :

"'I will do more. You do not know your own value—I mean your own moral and intellectual worth— nor what admiration they excite in men who judge as I do that the rest is dross. Our enterprise is clearly lost '—he nodded his agreement. 'My investment you may say is gone : or, at any rate, I must take it for what it is worth as a thing half-derelict and gravely threatened by the authorities. But *you* shall not go under. *Your* high talents shall not be wasted so long as I have credit for commerce. . . . Come. Our original agreement is useless now. It is waste paper. Well, we'll tear it up.'

"'Oh, sir!' said he. 'And what of *you*? All

this trust in me and my work, all this fund of money laid out by you! All this kindness and support without which I——'

" ' Say no more,' I interrupted, ' my mind is made up. I have here a draft of my intention, which I hope will jump with yours.' So saying I pulled out duplicate papers on which were written very simple terms. The original (and now worthless) agreement for an imaginary and unobtainable profit was cancelled. I promised in the new draft to take over the wretched unfinished works (they were worth nothing), to indemnify the poor fellow against any public claims, and to guarantee him an ample salary for one year from the date of signing. I now added more. I bound myself, in the event of his death or prolonged imprisonment within this year, to pay to his heirs the sum of 100 pieces of gold. This, I pointed out to him, would provide for his little sister (of whom I had now heard enough), while to myself I excused the extravagance by considering his really robust health and the power of my protection to save him from incarceration.

" I would not have believed that a human being could feel so strongly. He fell at my feet, calling me his providence, his all, his bulwark and refuge. He said he did not know there was such goodness among men. I bade him not exaggerate. I reminded him how noble minds had in all ages loved to support the Arts, and cited Yussouf-abd-Arham, Sulim-ben-Achab, Muswuf, Wawoo, Mah and other worthies. At last our business was completed, the new deeds signed and attested by my servants, and the gallant fellow, for whose ingenuous character I still retain a profound respect, was put to sleep in happy exhaustion upon soft carpets in my guest-room. I. there left him to dream of his little sister and his mud-heaps, while I betook myself to a short casting-up of accounts followed by nightly prayers to the All-Merciful who guides His servant into pleasant places.

" Next morning I sent the Enthusiast back to his labours (with a little cash to carry on with) and very carefully thought out my plans.

" First, at the next dinner I gave, I told my guests (who were, as usual, among the chief men of the city) that I proposed a deal in corn with the factors of Tambulistan : the place did not, as a fact, exist, but the name was well chosen and attractive. They were distant (I said) but in correspondence with me ; and as they had a glut and I had news of a dearth in my own country I had taken the opportunity of a deal through third parties. I saw a profit of some 100 pieces of gold. Not more (said I). I was a modest man and only did business in a small way. My guests gallantly denied this and smiled in polite interest, but no more, till, a little later in the meal, I said that the transaction had been just a little heavy for me and that I had looked round for some one who would help in settlement and would share the profit. I told them this profit was fairly certain, that no ready cash was required more than I had myself provided, but that, as a bill or two would do no harm, I had obtained one from a friend at home. All this in the way of general talk.

" As might be expected, the Chief Magistrate of the town (my most honoured guest) approached me after dinner and told me privately that he would be happy to oblige. I told him there was no sort of necessity, I could draw what I would on my letters from home, or at any rate enough to meet the case. That if he *really* cared to share my little adventure I expected about ten per cent. profit on the sum engaged—but indeed it was too small for me to trouble him with it. I accepted his pledge of 100 pieces of gold—but I stoutly refused any paper. ' Your name is enough,' I said, ' I shall gratefully use it. My people will trust my word.'

" I gave out next morning that I was going into the hills to meet a messenger. I did indeed pass through the city gate and proceeded till I was well out of sight ; but as there was no sense in fatiguing myself I slept through the heat in a wood, watched through the warm night, and returned travel-stained in the evening of the second day.

" On the morning of the third day I met the Chief Magistrate in the Bazaar : I stopped him, chatted, and then and there paid him eleven pieces of gold. ' I met my messenger from Tambulistan ' (said I) ' we exchanged parcels, and I find I have netted just over the ten per cent. These eleven pieces are your proportion upon your kind investment of 100.' He protested of course that it had been no investment, merely a few friendly words of support ; but he took the money, and I could see that he was pleased. He was curiously pleased. Indeed, he was so pleased that, though a discreet man, he could not forbear mentioning the matter to his wife. Rich men love small windfalls.

" In a few hours, therefore, the Head Mufti, the Chief of the Guard, and two very important councillors had in their various ways touched casually upon the wheat trade during short conversations in which each had separately engaged me under the shades of the Bazaar. A little later, as I took the air by the riverside at evening, the principal Ascetic of the district, who had come in to buy his few lentils for the week, spoke to me briefly of the same matter. I gave each of them a different answer, alluding to various cargoes of wheat, caravans of wheat and tumbrils of wheat—all in technical terms ; to risks, to covering sums, to transfers from one district to another. In each case I refused anything but a pledge to stand in with a transaction somewhat beyond my unaided powers ; in each case I ridiculed the smallness of the little adventure ; in each case I paid, after the lapse of a few days, to one a single piece of gold as his profit, to another two, to another three. And each was very pleased.

" As the days went by I varied the procedure. Sometimes I regretted the unexpectedly small profit obtained. Once I deliberately announced a loss and sternly gathered reluctant contributions from my associates ; but immediately afterwards I did another fine stroke in imaginary wheat and paid a fat dividend to my friends—indeed, that particular affair cost me twenty-five pieces. But it was worth it. I got rid in less than a month of 200 pieces of gold in this fashion. It was a cruel trial, but proved, in the event, most fruitful. For though I would never advise in large investments, yet by this simple method my reputation for judgment in that which men most value—which is money—was assured.

" I had set 250 pieces aside for this experiment, and my total stock was running low when I steered my ship to port.

" First, out of my remainder, I brought to the city council fifty pieces of gold saying that I had with difficulty screwed them from my young friend, who was still digging away in the outskirts, but that he had faithfully promised the second fifty in two months' time. Next I created a sort of stupor in the now large circle of my friends by saying publicly and boldly that I was beginning to see something in this plan of draining the marsh. I reminded them that the Engineer had always been my friend, that I had always seen something in him, that in spite of his obvious lack of business sense I could not help admiring his talent in his own line.

" The place was by this time dried and levelled, the embankment was all fairly sloped and paved, the cuttings, heaps, and rubbish had disappeared. Then it was that I took a party of these my important friends out to view the place at evening from the city walls and quietly told them that it was mine.

" There it lay before them : a magnificent plain, reclaimed and ordered, firm land pegged out in rows and with neat placards of new streets, all named.

" You know, my dear nephews, the admiration excited in all men of affairs for one who has forestalled them. I rose in the estimation of my neighbours to a height beyond compare. They already had a most deep reverence for my keen perceptions in commerce which had been proved in so many little tips— insignificant in quantity, but, oh ! so universally accurate. Now, indeed, upon learning this great stroke (or, as they called it in the local language, ' Koo ') they were lost in surprise and respect.

" After sunset I counted my money. I had left precisely fifty pieces of gold : a close aim, a narrow edge of venture. But, as the proverb says, ' The bold hunter slays the lion, the timid is slain of the cub.'

" It was late in that same night that the Chief Magistrate knocked at my door with the greatest precaution, bearing a hooded lantern, and walking on tiptoe. He begged me as an old friend (but in a whisper) to sell him so much land in the new quarter as might suffice for a good house and garden. suitable for his son or even for himself. I told him that I would have no sordid dealings with so excellent a friend. I could not do less than *give* him such a site.

" I brought out a plan (on which the Engineer had already drawn out streets and public squares) and marked upon the main thoroughfare the plot I would assign to him. He departed with praise and blessings. Hardly had he gone when a yet more furtive step approached my door. It was the Mufti. He offered me a hundred pieces of gold for such a site. I generously gave him for *fifty* a larger one than he had ventured to beg. I marked it somewhat farther down the same main thoroughfare. He went away belauding my name and soul.

" It was near midnight when another footfall halted at my door : a councillor's. For fifty pieces he also had a site worth double, and in the same street. He had not gone an hour, it was the darkest of the night, when a much fainter shuffling of bare feet could be just perceived followed by a light trying of the latch. The door was opened a crack and the strong emaciated face of the Ascetic twisted round the edge and peered in. I beckoned him. He put his finger to his lips, cautiously secured the fastening of the lock—and then, bending forward, whispered in my ear. . . . I was a little surprised at the magnitude of his offer, but of course I accepted it at once. Such men have great influence with the faithful. He proposed to *let* his property or perhaps to hold for a rise. He would continue of course to live in his humble cell outside the city, in the wastes. He departed quickly and like a ghost. At dawn came yet another councillor, more bold than the rest, who made a plain business proposition for block fifty-three and was at once gratified.

" So for days the procession continued, each man coming singly and watching whether he were observed. Half the council had sites for little or nothing, and the other half had sites at rates really very reasonable.

" And all the while, to the mass of buyers who importuned me and clamoured about me, I said that only very limited sales could be made, and those of leases only, and even so not till a later date.

" Meanwhile the whole town council was converted. The councillors had quite lost their old aversion to the scheme. They earmarked enthusiastically and by a unanimous vote a special tax for the laying out of the new quarter, its planting with trees, the bringing of conduits to it so that fountains of sweet water might appear in private houses and in public places, and, though the levy was no light one, it was paid cheerfully enough by all the councillors, who were now curiously proud of their town's aggrandizement ; even among the mass of poor ratepayers there were no executions, but only one mild case of torture, and perhaps a dozen bastinadoes.

" The public money so spent was very well worth while. The improvement in my property was immense.; and when a fine road, bordered with trees, was laid down all along the embankment I obtained very heavy compensation from the city for the use of the ground and the cutting off of my approaches to the river.

" I, on my side, was not niggardly. I promised 100 gold pieces to the building of a new mosque in the centre of the place, on condition that ninety-nine others should do the same, and I started a hall of public recreation, the price of admission to which barely repaid the expenses of upkeep and cleaning, taxes, heat and light, interest on debentures (which I had myself very handsomely subscribed), service, literature, and secretarial expenses, decoration, approaches, annual depreciation, and at the most a profit of six to eight per cent. I also provided kitchens where the poorer citizens could purchase food at very little more than its value. These were of great service to the police, who had here a central place whence the movements of my less fortunate neighbours could be traced. I presented also public fountains with solid pewter mugs, attached to the stonework by strong chains lest they should be stolen, and I even went so far as to provide, free of all cost, public plans of the new quarter showing where unleased sites still remained and the terms on which they might be acquired.

" I made it a rule that any man building a house on my land should promise to give it up to me for nothing after twenty years ; but as many people were too poor to build their own houses I established a fund whence they could borrow the money at the ordinary rates of interest and the few dues, fees, deductions, etc., inevitable to such transactions. In every way did I develop and benefit this my creation of a new town.

" I had my reward in the profound respect and honour paid me by my fellow-citizens. These were convened by the Council at an appropriate date to decide what recognition should be made of my services. They finally agreed, after long discussion and many very eloquent discourses, upon an illuminated parchment, which was presented to me with the most flattering cheers and songs upon the public square of the new quarter, in a tent of purple silk specially voted for the occasion and later claimed as a perquisite by my butler.

" I replied in a suitable manner to the acclamations of the crowd and the kindly flattery of the councillors ; but I told them, at the end of my address, that I should feel ungrateful indeed if, upon such an occasion, a certain humble fellow-worker of mine were overlooked in the public rejoicings. Thereupon I extended my hand to the Enthusiast, that young Engineer of Parts whom I had so fortunately met some months before and whom I had arranged should be near the steps of my dais at the required moment. I handed him up. I smiled benignantly upon him as he blushed with happy shame and pleasure. I even set him at my side.

" ' It is all very well, my friends,' said I, as I concluded my little speech, ' to speak as you do of the foresight and business acumen, organizing power, and the rest of it, which—I hope justly—you ascribe to me when you tell me how, as with a magic wand, I raised all this new city from the marsh which preceded it. But what would such gifts be had they not been aided and supplemented by talents no less essential, such as those which we all admire in this young friend at my right ? He it is who has performed, sometimes in a very literal sense, the spade-work. His has been the hard, obscure, constant labour and vigilance, without which my own more conspicuous efforts would have been in vain ! '

" After a few subdued cheers from the assembly, most of whom had never heard of the young man, while the rest had forgotten him, all dispersed, and

I was free to seek repose in my own new and sumptuous house.

" I am glad to say that this public mention of my worthy young colleague was not all I did for him. As the agreed salary which I paid him by our contract would now soon expire, I arranged with the Council that he should have a permanent post as keeper of the public squares, at a wage more than double that of the gardeners, and be granted (on condition of good behaviour) a limited pension when he should reach his seventieth year, the same to be deducted in small weekly sums from his pay : which sums, as he was not yet thirty-two would accumulate to much more than was necessary and leave over and above his retiring stipend a balance for anything the Council might think useful. He was also lent, rent free, a small four-roomed house with a nice strip of front garden and a wooden shed at the side. His duties occupied him from a little before sunrise to the pleasant dusk of eve, with an hour off for meals and a fortnight's holiday in the autumn.

" Even his little sister was not forgotten. I obtained for her, from my friends among the religious authorities (notably the Mufti, who was most strenuous in her cause) the post of head cleaner at the new mosque. Her salary there was necessarily somewhat smaller than her brother's, nor had she any holidays, while her hours were a trifle longer. But, on the other hand, she had no responsibilities.

" Shortly after all this I determined to sell my holding in this new property and to betake myself to other mercantile adventures in further lands. I had been in this place more than a year. I had made very good friends. It was the scene of a success greater than any I had yet experienced. Nevertheless I felt I could remain there no longer. The field was too small for my expanding opportunities. There was nothing left to take.

"I announced, therefore, my intention to realize, and allowed a certain interval for a public decision upon the purchase of my land, and leases, and other interests.

"A curious discussion arose. One party, composed mainly of wealthy but intelligent young men, of university professors and of jail-birds, were insistent that the Town Council should buy all my land and the city possess it for the future ; for it was obviously wrong (they agreed) that improvements in land and houses should go to private individuals. The other party, which was made up almost entirely of builders and auctioneers, furiously opposed this scheme which (they said) struck at the roots of all morals and family life. *These* stoutly maintained that, in the natural scheme of Providence, all should be parcelled out among the highest bidders.

"For my part I was, like the great mass of the taxpayers, indifferent to either argument. All that interested me was the obvious fact that in the competition between these two groups on the Council the value of my property necessarily rose.

"At last the first party prevailed, the city bought me out (really a most interesting social experiment !), and I received the sum of two million pieces of gold."

"Two million pieces !" shouted the astonished little nephews in chorus.

"My children," said the old man with a kindly smile, "to you, coming as you do from such a home as that of your father, my dear brother, the sum must seem fabulous, though to me to-day it sounds moderate enough. Nevertheless, you are right. From that moment I count the great change in my life and the confirmation of that Divine Mercy which had always watched me hitherto, as I now know, but which henceforward was gloriously present in every act of my life.

" Before the day when I first saw that river and that town, first met the enthusiastic young Engineer, first formed my decisive plan, I had been a man subject to grave anxieties and sufferings ; now precariously affluent, now starving ; now again doubtfully possessed of some fleeting money. Then came the marvellous year I have just recited. Since then I have enjoyed the results of so much persistence and skill. I have gathered and enjoyed without cease the fruits of great and increasing wealth."

" Oh, uncle, what are these ? "

" They are," said the good old merchant in grave and reverent tones, " the honour of neighbours, the devotion of friends, the admiration of all mankind, a permanent self-respect, and—what is more important than them all—the Strong Peace of the Soul."

The intolerable howl of the Muezzin checked his nephews' reply, and they, their happy eyes shining as though they themselves were the recipients of these seven figures went home in a dream of gold.

الفلوس المصنوع من القرطاس

AL-FULÚS AL-MASNÚ MIN AL-QIRTÁS

That is:

"THE MONEY MADE OF PAPER"

CHAPTER XIII

ON the appointed day of the next week the little
boys were glad to observe that the number
of public executions had fallen so far below the average
that their uncle's entertainment of them could begin
quite half an hour before the usual time. They were
most eager to discover what further good fortune had
befallen him by the Mercy of Allah.

The amiable old man opened his mouth and spoke :

" Two million gold pieces is a respectable sum of
money. It weighs about thirty tons . . . yes," he
calculated rapidly on his bejewelled fingers, " about
thirty tons. The city could just produce it after
scouring the country for miles around, searching all
the more modest houses and melting down sundry
antique lamps, wedding rings, sacred shrines and
other gewgaws.

" The complete withdrawal of so much metal left
them a little embarrassed for coin in everyday affairs,
but really that was not my business. I packed a
hundred strong iron chests with the bullion, reserving
a few thousands in a leather bag, set them in carts,
added to my retinue a hundred armed men, marked
my cases plainly in large white letters ' SAND CONSIGNED
TO THE SULTAN,' and had all made ready to set out :
but whither ?

" Until a man's wealth has grown so great that he can command the whole state, he is always in some peril. He is envied and a target for vile taxes—nay for confiscation. . . . I had not forgotten the dreadful lesson of the island ! I pondered on what I had read of various regions, and had rejected each in turn as dangerous, when I heard by chance a man saying to his neighbour (with whom he was quarrelling), ' Remember ! This is not the country of Dirak where there is one law for the rich and another for the poor.' As you may well believe I deeply considered these random words, and within an hour I was giving an excellent meal to a Learned Man who taught in the University, famous for his knowledge of foreign constitutions. I spoke of the Franks, of the Maghreb, of Rome. On all he was most interesting and full : he spoke also with contempt of certain wild tribes in the hills who have a strange custom of choosing a retired Chief annually from among the less wealthy members, under the barbarous error that modest means conduce to honesty and sharpen judgment.

" ' As in Dirak,' said I casually.

" ' In Dirak ? ' he exclaimed astonished. ' Why ! Who can have told you such tales ? Dirak is the best administered, the most flourishing and the strongest of all states ! '

" ' No doubt,' I answered, ' but what has that to do with it ? '

" ' Why,' said he, in sudden anger (for this kind of learned man is commonly half-mad) ' it has everything to do with it ! Such advantages can only come from the secure rule of the rich. . . . A fool could see that ! '

" I soothed him by immediate agreement, professed

my admiration at his vast store of knowledge and
pumped him all that afternoon on Dirak.

" It seemed that in this admirable region the Rich
rule unquestioned to the immense profit of the State.
The Sultan is kept on a strict allowance that he may
be the puppet of the great merchants, bankers and
landholders who are the masters of the Commonwealth
and him.   The middle classes are allowed a livelihood
but no possessions, and are proud of their small incomes,
which usually put them above the artizans ; while
the populace are content to swarm in hovels under-
ground, to work hard all day and all the year round
for a little food and to revere and acclaim the rich
with frenzied cheers upon all public occasions.   Laws
and proclamations are purchased, and their administration is in the hands of the rich, of whom a
select few sit upon the bench and condemn a fixed
number of the populace, and a few of the middle classes,
to imprisonment every year by way of discipline and
example.   No man possessing more than a hundred
thousand gold pieces worth of land or stock can be
punished, and if a poor man tell any unpleasing thing
of such a one he is beaten till he admits his falsehood
or, if he prove obstinate, slowly starved to death.

" It is a model State.   All is in perfect order.
The palaces of the rulers are the most magnificent
in the world : all public office is faithfully and punctually performed.   It is the envy of every neighbour,
the pride and delight of every citizen however mean ;
for—what is the basis of the whole affair—every man
in Dirak is esteemed by the extent of his possessions
alone ; writing and music and work in metals and
painted tiles are esteemed for the pretty things they
are : holiness is revered indeed, but confined to the

well-to-do ; and a man's virtue, judgment and wit are rightly gauged by his property.

" My many adventures had somewhat blunted me to new sensations. But I confess (my dear nephews) that as I heard this tale an ecstasy filled my soul. I masked my emotions and simply said, ' An interesting place ! '

" ' It is reached by a plain road from here,' volunteered the Learned Man, ' though at the expense of a long journey : for it takes a caravan quite a month to reach the capital of Dirak from this place. You go up the river to its source in the hills, a week's travel to the east ; then the well marked road leads you over a pass to a most singular cup or natural cauldron, with a flat, highly cultivated floor, formerly the bed of a lake and surrounded on all sides by precipitous limestone cliffs, down which the road descends by artificial cuttings in their surface. This strangely isolated spot, famous for its gardens and simple happiness, is called with its chief village Skandir, and strangers are there most hospitably entertained.

" ' The only issue thence, on the far side, is by a narrow gorge leading through the mountains, beyond which again are vast plains of grassy lands, the grazing place of nomads : well watered and provisioned at reasonable distances by simple but well furnished villages. The great road goes through all these, still eastward.

" ' These prairies get drier and drier as they rise eastward until, for the last day of your progress, at the wells of Ayn-ayoum you must take a supply of water, for the next twenty-four hours are desert. You reach a crest of the slow ascent and see below you from the summit of the road some half a day's going across the plain below, the magnificent capital of Dirak.

" ' This noble city, whose name is Mawazan, was founded by the enormously wealthy——'

" ' Yes ! Yes ! ' I interrupted in a bored tone—for I now knew all I wanted to know, ' some day I must go there. A very amusing journey no doubt. But meanwhile business is business and I must start very early for the north to-morrow morning to look after some purchases I have made in grains ; and I must not waste any more of your time.'

" The learned are slow to take a hint, so I locked my arm in his after a friendly fashion and led him genially to the door, where he tried (unsuccessfully) to detain me for further remarks on yet another country famous for its enormous bats.

" When I had got well rid of him—it was already dark—I beat up my quarters without delay, aligned my caravan, added to the inscription on my iron treasure chests the words ' of Dirak ' (so that the labels now ran ' SAND FOR THE SULTAN OF DIRAK), marshalled my armed troop and set out in the night by the northern road.   But, long before daybreak, I ordered a deflection to the right, struck the great road along the river and so proceeded eastward into the hills.

" It was as the Learned Man had said : a week's marching to the sources of the stream led to the pass, and we saw below us at evening a splendid spectacle : that small oval plain of Skandir all girded with enormous precipices, a garden of fruit trees and grain with great prosperous villages in its midst, and the road picking its way by cuttings in the living rock down to the valley floor, and thence making straight for the main town.

" We reached it under a new moon in the second

hour of darkness. Its hospitality had not been exaggerated. The good peasants received us with every kindness and I was lodged in a most comfortable house, my chests and grain in the courtyard and my numerous retinue under lesser roofs around.

" Next day—as luck would have it—a wretched accident befel me ! I was taking the air at the door of my house, preparatory to ordering the start of my caravan, when I heard the ring of metal on the flat stones of the street. A child running past had dropped a small silver coin. I marked the gleaming spot as the child ran on unheeding, and naturally rushed to put my foot on it before it should be noticed by any other, intending to stoop gracefully at my leisure and pick it up when the coast was clear. But the Evil One, who is ever on the watch to undo the servants of the Most High caused me, in my eagerness, to slip upon a greasy piece of mud and I fell heavily upon the stones with a crash. My leg was broken !

" In the agony I suffered I quite forgot the silver coin (the void still aches) ; I know not who acquired it. I cannot bear to think that it was trampled in and lost to the world.

" At any rate, I was carried to my couch half fainting, the bone was set with excruciating pain, and I lay for many days unable to rise and eating my heart out at the added expense of my large company which was dipping deeply into my store of loose coin.

" My main treasure, stored in the hundred iron boxes, I dared not touch ; for the Chief of Skandir (who daily visited my sick-room) told me that he had affixed seals to the sand consigned to the Sultan of Dirak, his powerful neighbour, and taken it for safe keeping into his castle.

" The physician assured me that even when I might venture out on crutches it would be fatal, in view of certain complications which had arisen, if I were to think of travel.

" So there I was, imprisoned in this charming valley, with no chance of commerce, my spare cash dangerously dwindling, and a most expensive three weeks' journey ahead of me before I could reach my beloved Dirak !

" What was I to do ?

" My dear nephews, you will hear many harsh things said of those who prosper as I have done.   They are vilified through a base envy and the most monstrous tales are told of them.   But they are under the protection of Heaven, and that Guiding Power supplements their humble vows.   None can deny their ready response to Inspiration.   Hear what I did.

" First I purchased out of my remaining free gold a fine house that happened to be empty.   Next I had painted on its front in beautiful and varied colours ' MAHMOUD'S BANK.'   Next I told the Chief what advantage I designed for him and his during my enforced stay, by way of repaying him for their exceptional kindness.   Next I sent out written letters to all the wealthier men (and women, my dear nephews, *and women*), saying that I had begun operations in the buying and selling of market produce and that any capital entrusted to me would earn, for every hundred pieces, one piece a week, paid punctually at a certain hour.   To give colour to my scheme I sent my quickest-witted servant (amply rewarded) to watch the markets in the valley, to buy up fruit and grain at magnificent prices and to sell elsewhere as best he could.

" ' Never mind,' said I to him, benevolently, ' at

what loss you sell.   I desire to do these honest people
a service.'

"The volume of my commerce grew (at a heavy
charge !) and even the timid thought there might be
something in it.   I started the ball rolling by getting
my confidant to deposit a hundred pieces of gold, which
I had privily furnished.   At the end of the week I
duly gave him back one hundred and one in the
presence of many; and the story went abroad.

"Soon the Chief, his uncle and his mother-in-law
deposited and were as regularly paid one per cent
a week.   The thing began to buzz—but I watched
narrowly my dwindling hoard : it was a close thing !
. . . When I had progressed in this fashion for what
I considered a sufficient time, I judged it opportune to
initiate my new Policy of An Expansion of Exchange
through Instruments of Credit."

"Dear uncle——" interrupted the eldest nephew.

"Yes, yes," said the merchant, impatiently, " I
know that the term is new to you, but you will shortly
learn its meaning.   When I had occasion to buy articles
for my private consumption or to make an exceptionally
heavy purchase of my wholesale wares, I would frequently affect embarrassment, and approaching the
vendor I would beg him to accept, in lieu of immediate
payment in cash, a note which I had signed promising
payment in gold at sight, ' For,' said I to him, ' in the
rapid turnover of my business it is but a matter of a
few hours for me to be again in possession of a considerable sum of ready money.'

"I went to work at first with caution.   I never by
any chance issued a single note for more than ten
pieces, and whenever any one of these notes was presented for payment, even though that event should

take place within an hour of my issuing it, I promptly
honoured it from the reserve of metal which I had
kept back for the furtherance of my plan. I was careful to make these notes identical, to stamp them all in
the same place with my metal seal, and in every way
to make them, so far as I could, a sort of currency,
which, as you may imagine, they promptly became.
When a man carrying one of these instruments might
find himself called upon to pay, at some distance from
my place of business, he would at first tentatively
offer my note (perhaps at a small discount) to his
creditor. But as my integrity was by this time a
proverb (and never forget, dear boys, that integrity
is the soul of business) the Notes were more and more
readily accepted as time proceeded.

"The convenience of carrying such paper compared
with the heavy weight of metal they might represent,
the ease of negotiation, and so forth, rapidly increased
their circulation ; and in a short time I was able to
calculate with assurance what the experts in this
amiable science term ' the Rate of Circulation ' which
my notes had attained. I found that, roughly
speaking, for every five pieces to which I had thus
pledged myself upon paper two were sufficient to meet
the claims of those who presented them at any one
moment. And this proportion is known to this day
in that happy valley as ' the Proportion of Metallic
Reserve ' which must lie behind any Issue of Notes—
but I hear that since my departure they have got
badly muddled.

"Oh ! dear, dear ! " said the eldest nephew. " I am
getting muddled myself, Uncle."

"Don't listen to him ! " said his brothers in
chorus.

" Yes ! my children," answered the old man vividly,
" it is indeed a difficult subject. Only a few experts
really understand it . . . and I am one . . . anyhow,
you all see that I could now make new money as I chose
out of nothing ? "

" Oh ! yes, uncle ! " they all agreed, including
the eldest. " We quite see that ! "

" Well," said their revered relative in a subdued
tone, " that is a great advantage." But to proceed.

" After some weeks of these practices I found myself
the master of the fruit and grain markets, to which
I added certain adjuncts naturally suggested by it,
such as catering for public meals, the erection of
mosques, the undertaking of marriages, funerals, and
divorces, the display of fireworks, and the charging
of fixed fees for the telling of fortunes. This last soon
became a very flourishing branch of my business.
I employed in it at the customary wage a number of
expert soothsayers, and these, with the rest of my staff,
amounted to perhaps a quarter of the inhabitants ; nor
were they the least contented or the least prosperous
of the population.

" In a word, my dear nephews, when my operations
were concluded I found myself in possession of 200,000
pieces of gold, while my notes, which were everywhere
received throughout the State, stood for 300,000 more.
A simple calculation," said the worthy old man,
smiling, " will show you that my total new fortune
was now no less than half a million pieces, when
signs of economic exhaustion in the public and the
complete healing of my leg reluctantly decided me
that the time had come to seek fresh fields of effort
and other undeveloped lands."

As the merchant now puffed at his pipe in silence

the fifth nephew begged leave to ask him two questions which had perplexed his youthful mind.

" Ask away, my little fellow," said his uncle, kindly, " and I will attempt to explain any difficulty you have in simple terms suited to your age."

" Well, uncle," said the fifth nephew, humbly, " I cannot in the first place see how the 300,000 pieces of which you speak, and which as you say were represented by notes alone, constituted any real wealth."

" My dear little chap," answered his uncle, leaning forward to pat him upon the head, " you will have the intelligence to perceive that wherever such a note existed people thought of it as ten golden pieces, did they not ? "

" Ye-s-s," answered his nephew, feeling that he was getting cornered.

" Very well," continued the old man, merrily, " this attitude of mind being common to the whole community, and all having come to regard these pieces of paper as so much money, I had but to receive them in payment of my debts and then to buy with them the gold of others.   Thus all the gold entered my possession.   Eh ?   On my departure the outstanding notes were presented to the firm, I hear, and there was then no gold to meet them with.   A sad state of affairs !   Many clamoured and all sorts of trouble arose.   But by that time I was far away."

The little chap still looked puzzled.   " But, uncle," he said, " when the people presented the notes after you had gone, they may have thought they had wealth, but they hadn't any, had they ? "

" I don't know," said the old man, after a pause. " It is a most difficult point in the discussion of

currency. . . . I, at any rate, had been bold in the
story I told, and got hold of their gold."

" But the wealth wasn't *there*, uncle," persisted the
little boy. " It wasn't there at all ! "

The merchant with a benign air replied : " The
science of political economy is abstruse enough for
the most aged and experienced, and it will be impossible
for me to explain to you at length so intricate a point.
Let it suffice for you that so far as *I* was concerned the
wealth *was* there, it was there in fifty large leather bags.
. . . You had, I think," he added in a severer tone,
" a second question to propound ? "

" Yes," said his nephew with a slight sigh, " dear
uncle, it was this : Why under such favourable
circumstances did you think it necessary to leave
so early, seeing that your new trade was going so
well ? "

" That," said old Mahmoud in a tone of relief, " is
much more easy to answer. My leg was healed. The
resources of Skandir were limited. Signs were apparent
that the worthy populace, though unable to unravel
the precise nature of their entanglement, were already
very seriously hampered by my operations. Though
I was able to prove by statistics that prosperity had
increased by leaps and bounds, and though the Chief,
who was now my partner, kindly printed pamphlets
at the public expense to prove the same, numbers who
had formerly been well fed were now reduced to a few
handfuls of raw grain, the jails were crammed, much
of the land was going out of cultivation, and what
between the ignorant passions which such periods of
transition arouse in the vulgar, and the inability to get
more water out of a sponge when you have already
squeezed it thoroughly dry, I am sure that I was right

in the determination I then took to retire from this field of operations.

" Before leaving I offered my business for sale to the public in general. The shares, I am glad to say, were eagerly taken up. And as I gave a preference in allotment (another technical term) to those who paid in my own notes, I recovered all of these save an insignificant fraction, and was able to negotiate them again for gold in public exchange before my departure.

" Meanwhile the unscrupulous anxiety of the chaotic multitude to share in so prosperous a commercial undertaking as mine had been, permitted me to ask for my business more than four (but less than five) times the sum which I would myself have been content to pay for it.

" I loaded 300 more camels with valuables of various sorts, including nearly all the precious metals discoverable in the State ; I purchased a whole army of new slaves for the conduct of the caravan (paying for them in new notes issued upon the new company), and amid the plaudits and benedictions of a vast multitude, many of whom (I regret to say) were now in the last stages of destitution, I regretfully took my way through the gorge and bade farewell to the simple people of lovely and lonely Skandir to whom I owed so much."

*   *   *   *   *

" I proceeded from the people of the valley whom I had introduced to banking, and went out through the gorge into the rising prairies beyond the mountains. For at least four days' march beyond the valley my name was a household word to the villages through which I passed ; not only was I able to pay for all goods by a further Issue of Notes, but I would even reward any special considerations shown me by selling to the grateful inhabitants for cash such shares in my old Firm remaining at Skandir as I had retained to amuse me in my travel ; and these, I am happy to say, went rapidly to a premium. These shares passed at gradually lessening prices from hand to hand, and I subsequently learnt that in a few months they had become unsaleable. Those who suffered in the last purchases had only themselves to blame, and indeed did not think of blaming any other, while the first to sell at a high price still hold my name in reverent remembrance.

" When I had proceeded a few days further upon my travels I found that the enlightenment and civilization to which I had led the people of the valley was gradually dissipated, and within a fortnight I discovered myself amid the very brutish nomad population who absolutely refused to take paper in the place of cash, even when this form of payment was offered by my own body servants. On the other hand, the precious metals were so scarce amid that population that prices were extremely low, and I was able at a very small outlay in gold to feed the whole of my considerable concourse.

" Three weeks so passed in these monotonous grass lands among the nomad tribes, the road went forward to the east, rising all the way, and the soil grew drier and drier. We reached the wells of Ayn-Ayoub and filled our skins with water, we traversed the desert belt and camped near the summit : at daybreak we came to the escarpment and saw the wooded slopes falling away in cascading forests at our feet to where, far below, lay the splendid plain of Dirak and in its midst, far off and dark in outline against the burning

dawn, the battlements and mosques, the minarets
and tapering cypress points of its capital Misawan.

" What joy was mine to fall by gentle gradations
down the declivities of those noble woods into the
warm fields of the Fortunate State ! At every hour
of my advance new delights met my eye ! Great
Country Houses standing in magnificent parks with
carefully tended lawns all about, poor men who
saluted low as I passed and rich men here and there
who glanced a moment in haughty ease, fine horses
passing at the trot mounted by subservient grooms,
and, continually, posts bearing such notices as ' Any
one treading on this Lord's ground will be bowstrung.'
' No spitting.' ' One insolent word and to jail with
you ! ' : While at every few hundred yards an armed
man, before whom the poorer people cowered, would
frown at the slaves at the head of my column, and then,
seeing my finely mounted guard and my own immutable
face and shining garments coming up behind them,
would smile and bow and hint at a few small coins—
which I gave.

" In truth the Learned Man had not deceived me !
This land of Dirak was a Paradise !

" I rode into the city like a king (as I was—for my
wealth made me one in such a State) and took for the
night a lodging in an Immense Building, which called
itself a Caravanserai, but was, to the Caravanserais
of my experience, as the Sultan's Palace to a horse.

" There, in an apartment of alabaster and beaten
silver, I eat such viands as I had not thought to be
on this earth, while well-drilled slaves, trained by long
starvation to obedience, moved noiselessly in and out
or played soft music hidden behind a carven screen.

" Oh ! Dirak ! Dirak ! . . . but I must conclude.

. . . The matter was not long. With my gold I purchased my palace in the midst of this city of Misawan, entertained guests who asked nothing of my origin, bought (after a careful survey of prices) the excellent post of Chief Sweeper to his Majesty (which carried with it the conduct of The Treasury) and paid for a few laws which happened to suit my convenience, such as one to prevent street cries and another for the strangling of the red-headed poor : it is a colour of hair I cannot abide.

" From time to time I paid my respects to that puppet called the Sultan and bowed low in the Ceremonies of the Court.

" I had no occasion to hide my wealth since wealth was here immune and the criterion of honour. I displayed it openly. I boasted of its amount. I even exaggerated its total. I was, within two years, the Chief Man in the State.

" Yet (such is the heart of man !) I was not wholly satisfied. Of my vast fortune not a hundredth had been consumed. None the less I could not bear to let it lie idle. I was determined to do business once again !—By the Infinite Mercy of Allah the opportunity was vouchsafed.

" There lay on the confines of Dirak another State, called Har, very different. In this the Sultan was the wealthiest man in the community and a tyrant. Moreover it differed from Dirak in this important particular, that whereas in Dirak all office was obtained by purchase, in Har all office was obtained by inheritance, so that between the two lay the unending and violent quarrel between trickery and pride.

" One day—I had been the greatest man in Dirak for already two years more—the Sultan of Har, wickedly, insolently, and not having the fear of God before his eyes, demanded satisfaction of the Sultan of Dirak for a loss sustained at dice by his Grand Almoner's nephew at the hands of that Noble in Dirak called the Lord Persecutor of Games of Chance— which are, in Dirak, strictly forbidden by law.

" In vain did the Sultan of Dirak implore the aid of his Nobles : they assured him that none would dare attack his (and their) Omnipotent State.

" On the third day the Sultan of Dar crossed the frontier with one million, two hundred thousand and fifty-seven men, ninety-seven elephants, and two catapults. On the tenth he was but three days' march from Masawan.

" The unfortunate Sultan of Dirak, pressed by his enemy, was at his wits' end for the ready money wherewith to conduct the war. He had already so severely taxed his poor that they were upon the point of rebellion, while the rich were much rather prepared to make terms with the enemy or to fly than to support his whim of honour, patriotism and the rest.

" Musing upon the opportunity thus afforded, and recognizing in it once more that overshadowing Mercy which had so marvellously aided my every step in life, I came into the street upon a horse and in my noblest garments. I was careful to throw largesse to the crowd, at an expense which I had previously noted in a little book (your father has, my dear nephews, trained you, I hope, to keep accounts ?), and riding up to the Palace I announced to the guard that I had come with important news for the Sultan and his Council. After certain formalities (which cost me, I regret to say, no less than fifteen dinars more than I had allowed for) I was shown into the presence of

the Vizier, who begged me to despatch my business
hurriedly as the Sultan was expecting at any moment
news of an important action. I said with courtesy
and firmness that my time was my own, that perhaps
I had been mistaken in the news conveyed to me, but
that the financial operations I was prepared to undertake would demand a certain leisure before they could
be completed.

" At the words ' financial operations ' the Vizier's
manner wholly changed ; he was profuse in apologies,
admitting a little shamefacedly that he had taken me
for a soldier, a priest, a poet, or something of that
sort, and that if he had had the least idea of my intent
he would never have kept me waiting as he had unfortunately done. He proceeded in a hurried and conventional tone to discuss the weather, the latest scandal,
and other matters of the sort, until at my own time I
proposed to introduce the important subject.

" This I did with becoming dignity. I informed him
with the utmost reluctance that the enemy had already
approached me for financial assistance. I would not
be so hypocritical (I said) as to pretend that I had
refused them, or indeed that I had any sentimental
preference for one side or the other. As I thus expressed myself the Vizier constantly and gravely
nodded, as who should say that he esteemed no man
so much as one who showed himself indifferent to the
feelings of the vulgar. I next asked of what sum the
Government was in immediate need, and on hearing
that it amounted to about a quarter of my total capital
I put on a very grave look and said that I feared the
immediate provision of so large an amount was hardly
possible, in view of the poverty and embarrassment
of his unhappy country.

" When I rose as though to leave, the Vizier, in a state of the utmost excitement, implored me to reconsider so sudden a decision. He was prepared (he swore) to take but an instalment of the whole. Ready money was absolutely necessary. And if, with my profound knowledge of finance, I could devise some way of escape for his master, the most substantial proofs of gratitude would be afforded me.

" Upon hearing this I professed to be plunged into profound thought for about a quarter of an hour, and ended by slowly laying before him as an original and masterly plan the following proposal :

" The poor (he had admitted) were taxed beyond the limits of endurance, and were even upon the point of revolt ; the rich were hiding their hoards, and many forms of portable wealth were leaving the country. Let him abandon these uncouth and rapacious methods of obtaining revenue, and ask the wealthier of the loving subjects of the Sovereign to *lend* him at interest what they would certainly refuse to pay him outright. In this way a smaller annual sum by far than was now raised to meet the exigencies of the war would suffice to meet the obligations of the Government. The capital so raised would be spent upon the campaign ; the charge imposed upon the people would, it is true, be perpetual ; but it would be so much smaller than the existing taxation as to be everywhere welcomed.

" The Vizier sadly responded that though he would be very happy to undertake such a course he feared that the wealthy inhabitants would never lend (knowing, as they did, the embarrassment of the Government) save upon ruinous terms.

" I had been waiting for this confession, and I at

once suggested that I could act as go-between. I would, said I, stand guarantor. My great wealth would at once restore opinion, the loan would certainly be taken up, and I should only make the nominal charge of five gold pieces every year for each hundred I had thus guaranteed.

" The Vizier was so astounded at my generosity that he almost fell backward, but recovering himself, he poured forth the most extravagant thanks, which were hardly marred by the look I detected in his eye, a look certainly betraying the belief that such an offer from a commercial man could hardly be made in good faith. To reassure him I adopted what is known in the financial world as the Seventh, or Frankly Simple, tone. I told him without reserve the total of my wealth (which I put at a fifth of its real amount) and promised to bring it in cash to offices which he should permit me to establish in the city.

" Entering the next day with a million pieces of gold charged upon a train of very heavily laden camels, I set up my bank in the most crowded portion of the Bazaar, published news of my intention to support the Government, inviting the public inspection of the metal so lent, and at the same time proposing that any who desired regular interest of four pieces guaranteed by myself annually upon every hundred should come forward to take the loan off my hands. The hoards of gold still remaining in the country reappeared as though by magic—so much more delightful is it to lend voluntarily at interest than to pay away under torture for ever—and at last there applied at my office for the favour of extending a loan ten times as many citizens as the situation required.

" My terms with the Government were simple,

and, I am sure, moderate. All that I asked was that the tax collectors should in future pay their receipts into my chest, from which I pledged myself to hand over to the Government whatever surplus there might be after I had paid to the lenders their annual interest, four pieces, and kept for myself a fifth piece, which formed my tiny and not unearned commission.

" In this way I rapidly repaid myself and also took one piece on every hundred *others* had subscribed. The learned men of the place, who had never before imagined so simple and practical a plan, treated me with almost supernatural reverence. I was consulted upon every operation of war, my guarantee was eagerly sought for in other financial ventures, and I was able, I am glad to say, to secure other commissions without touching a penny of my treasure—I had but to hold it forth as a proof of good faith.

" The enemy was repelled. But victory was not won. The war dragged on for a year and there was no decision. Gold grew scarce, and again the Government was in despair.

" I easily relieved them. ' Write,' I said, ' promises on paper to be repaid in gold.' They did as I advised —paying me (at my request) a trifle of half a million for the advice. I handled the affair—on a merely nominal profit. I punctually met for another year every note that was paid in. But too many were presented, for the war seemed unending and entered a third year.

" Then did I conceive yet another stupendous thing. ' Bid them,' said I to the Sultan, ' take the notes as money. Cease to repay. Write, not " I will on delivery of this paper pay a piece of gold," but, " this *is* a piece of gold." '

" He did as I told him. The next day the Vizier came to me with the story of an insolent fellow to whom fifty such notes had been offered as payment for a camel for the war and who had sent back, not a camel, but another piece of paper on which was written ' This *is* a camel.'

" ' Cut off his head ! ' said I.

" It was done, and the warning sufficed. The paper was taken and the war proceeded.

" It was I that prepared the notes, and on each batch I exacted my necessary commission, my little commission, my due.

" It was not in my nature, dear nephews, however, in those days of hard and honest work, to lie idle. When I had put the Sultan on his legs it occurred to me that the *enemy's Government* was also very probably in similar straits. I therefore visited the enemy's capital by a roundabout route, and concluded with the Vizier of that opulent but agitated State a similar bargain.

" The war thus replenished at its sources raged with redoubled ardour, for ten more years, and. . . ."

" But, uncle," said the fourth nephew, who was an athlete and somewhat stupid, and who had heard of this double negotiation with round eyes, " surely they must have both been very angry with you ! "

The excellent Mahmoud raised his left hand in protest. " Dear lad ! " cried he, " how little you know the world ! Angry ? Why, each regarded me in the first place as a genius whose ways it was impossible to unravel, in the second place as a public necessity, in the third as a benefactor arrived at a miraculous moment ; and as for the fact that I was aiding both sides, I have only to tell you that among the people

of that region it is thought the proper part of all
financiers to act in this fashion. I should have been
treated with deserved contempt had I betrayed any
scruples upon so simple a matter. Nay, I am sure
that either party reposed the greater trust in me from
the fact that my operations were thus universal. . . .
But to proceed :

" The Mercy of Allah was never more apparent in
my career than in the way these two Sultans and their
subjects fought like raging dogs upon the proceeds of
those loans which the wealthy citizens upon either
side had provided, and upon the mountains of paper
which I spent half the day in signing.

" These loans increased ten, twenty, thirty-fold.
It was always I that guaranteed them ; I had not to
risk or expend one miserable dinar of my horde, and
yet yearly my commission came rolling in, in larger
and larger amounts, until at last the arduous but
glorious campaigns were terminated in the total
exhaustion of one of the two combatants (at this
distance of time I forget which), and his territory and
capital were laid under an enormous indemnity
(which I again financed without the tedium of myself
producing any actual metal of my own). As the
beaten State might have repudiated its obligations
I was careful to meet the patriotic clamours of the
victorious populace, and to see that the territory of
the vanquished should be annexed. You appreciate
the situation, my dear fellow ? " said the aged Mahmoud
conversationally to his eldest nephew.

" I think so, uncle," said the lad doubtfully, screwing
up his face.

" It is quite simple," said the wealthy old man,
clearing his throat. " The peoples of both States

(now happily united) were taxed to their utmost capacity; the one strong and united Government guaranteed a regular revenue; a proportion of this revenue was annually distributed as a *fixed* income to the wealthy few who had subscribed my loans; another portion, amounting by this time annually to considerably more than my original capital, was retained in my coffers; and the mechanism of this was the more simple from the fact that all the public revenues passed through my own hands as State Banker before any surplus was handed over to the Crown."

The old man ceased. His benevolent lips were murmuring a prayer.

At this moment the hideous call for prayer from the minaret would no longer be denied, and the seven boys, plunged in profound thought, retired slowly to the poverty-stricken home of the physician, their father. They found him tired out with having sat up all night at the sick-bed of a howling dervish, who in his last dying whisper (and that a hoarse one), had confessed his total inability to pay the customary fee.

اطمئنان النفس

ITMI'NÁN AL-NAFS

That is:
"THE PEACE OF THE SOUL"

CHAPTER XIV

ENTITLED *ITMI'NÂN AL-NAFS*, OR THE PEACE OF THE SOUL

" WE had arrived," said the excellent old merchant to his nephews when they were once more seated round him for the last of these entertaining relations. " We had arrived, my dear boys, in the story of my life, at my considerable increase of fortune through the financial aid I had given to two States, one of which after a long and exhaustive war had conquered and annexed the other.

" My position (if you recollect) at the close of this adventure was that without having spent any money of my own I was now receiving permanently and for ever a very large yearly revenue set aside from the taxes of both States.

" Not a man reaped or dug or carried heavy water jars under the hot sun, not a man groomed a horse or bent under the weight of a pack, not a man added brick to brick or mixed mortar, not a man did any useful act from one end of the State to the other, but some part of his toil was done for me, and this state of affairs was, as I have said, as fixed and permanent as human things can be.

" I was therefore what even financiers call well-to-do ; one way with another I was now worth perhaps twenty million pieces of gold : but that is but guess work, it may have been twenty-five.

" You might imagine that I would have been content from that day onwards to repose in my opulence.

" I might well have been tempted to do so, for to that opulence was added a singular and fervid popularity. I was alluded to in public and private as the man who had saved the State by his financial genius during the Great War. Even the conquered remembered me gratefully for the aid I had extended to them in their need ; while since I could not satisfy my personal desires without at least feeding a great host of dancers, bearers, artists, my kindness in affording employment was universally recognized ; moreover (since among these people wealth is a test of greatness) I was admitted to their Senate without the usual formality of a cash payment.

" The world was now indeed at my feet. But you must know," continued Mahmoud with something of sadness in his voice, " you must know, my dear, innocent lads, that wealth will not stop still. The mere administration of a great fortune tends to increase it, and when one has for years found one's occupation in the accumulation of money, it is difficult in middle age to abandon the rooted habit. Therefore, though I now had all that life could give me, I proceeded henceforward for many years to increase that substance with which the Mercy of Allah had provided me ; and I discovered at the outset of this new career that to be the financier I had become, and to have behind me the resources which I now possessed, made my further successes a matter not of hazard but of certitude. Shall I briefly tell you the various ways in which my efforts proceeded ? "

" Pray, pray do so," said his little nephews with

sparkling eyes, each imagining himself in the dazzling position of his wealthy relative.

" Very well," sighed Mahmoud.   " It will be of little use to any of you ; but if it does no more than confirm you in your religion what I have to tell you will not have been told in vain."

The merchant was silent for a moment, and then began the category of his financial proceedings :

" Neighbouring States which had heard of the powerful new methods I had introduced would approach me from time to time for financial assistance. To these I made the same invariable reply, that upon certain terms, which I myself would fix, I was content to ' float their loans ' ; that is, the rich men of their country (or of any other) should pay into my office the sums they were prepared to lend to such a State, and I would pay back a part, but not the whole, of the amount so accumulated to the State in question. The enormous service I rendered by allowing my office to be used for this transaction was everywhere recognized, and by such operations my fortunes proceeded to grow.

" It was at this moment in my career that I married my wife, your dear aunt, who generally resides, as you know, in that one of my country palaces called Dar-al-Beida on the banks of the Tigris some four days' journey from here. It is a delightful spot which I remember well though I have not seen it for years. . . . Some day, perhaps, I will visit it again, but not to sleep.

" Your dear aunt was, and is, my boys, a most remarkable woman : fit to compete with the master spirits of our time : yea ! even with my own.

" Her birth—I need not conceal it—was humble.

She was but a chance hireling in my offices, with the duty of sorting my papers and keeping indices of the same.

" Such was her interest in affairs that she was at the pains to take copies and tracings of many particularly private and important passages with her own hand, and keep these by her in a private place. I was struck beyond measure at such industry and preoccupation with business on the part of a woman (and one so poor !) I conceived an ardent desire to possess these specimens of her skill ; but—to my astonishment, and (at first) confusion—she humbly replied that a profound though secret affection which she had conceived for me forbade her to part with these precious souvenirs of myself. I was so absorbed in their pursuit that, rather than lose them, I married this Queen of Finance—recognizing in her an equal genius with my own. Our wedding was of the simplest. I took comfort from the considera-tion that it proved me superior to all the nobles of the court and indifferent to an alliance with their families.

" Immediately after the wedding my wife, your dear aunt, asked me for money wherewith to travel, a request I readily granted. She traversed for her pleasure I knew not what foreign lands, always, and gladly, furnished with the wherewithal from my cash box ; but on my returning later to Bagdad, my native place, she unexpectedly appeared at my door, and I was happy to build for her that country Palace of Dar-al-Beida to the charm of which I have alluded. Unfortunately its air suits me ill, while she (your dear aunt) suffocates in the atmosphere of Bagdad. It is often thus in old age. . . ."

Mahmoud mused and continued :

" But let us return to my further activities in that far land :

" I next designed a scheme whereby every form of human misfortune, fire, disease, paralysis, madness, and the rest, might be alleviated to the sufferer by the payment of regular sums of money upon the advent of the disaster ; weekly sums for his support if he were rendered infirm or ill, a lump sum to replace whatever he might have totally lost, and so forth. A short and easy survey of the average number of times in which such accidents took place permitted me to establish my system. I charged for 100 dinars worth of such insurance 110 dinars, and my benevolence was praised even more highly than my ingenuity.

" Men flocked in thousands, and at last in millions, to secure themselves from the uncertainty of human life by giving me of their free will more money in regular payments than I could by any accident be compelled to pay out to any one of them upon his reaching old age, his suffering from fire, or his contraction of an illness. Nay, death itself at last entered into this design, and having found that young men just of age live upon the average for forty years, I asked them to pay for their heirs annual sums calculated as though that period were thirty, and thus I continued to accumulate wealth from a perennial source."

" But why," began one of his nephews excitedly. . . .

" Why *what* ? " asked his uncle, severely.

" Why," said the poor lad, a little abashed by his uncle's tone, " why did they pay you more for a thing than it was worth ? "

Mahmoud stroked his long white beard and looked up sideways towards the highly decorated vault of the gorgeous apartment. He remained thus plunged in thought for perhaps thirty seconds, and when he broke the silence it was to say that he did not know. " But no matter——" he added hurriedly. " I paid for a law which compelled all slaves to insure and so was certain of a fixed revenue in this kind.

" And I had many other resources," he continued cheerily. " If those who had made many such regular payments to me to insure against death, old age, disease, and the rest, happened to fall into an embarrassed condition and to need a loan, I was always ready to advance them their own money again at interest, nor did I ever find them unwilling to subscribe the bond. Further I urged and tempted many to fall into arrears and so possessed myself of all they had paid in. The vast sums paid to me in these various fashions were sometimes too great for investment within the State, and I had to look further afield. But here again by the Mercy of Allah suggestions of the most lucrative sort perpetually occurred to my religious soul.

" Not infrequently I would lay out a million or two in the purchase of a great estate situated at some distance which, when I had acquired it, I would declare to be packed with gold, silver, diamonds, copper, salt, and china clay beneath the earth, and on its surface loaded with red pepper and other most precious fruits. I have no doubt these estates were often of a promising nature, though travellers have assured me that some were mere desert ; in one case, to my certain knowledge, the estate did not even exist. But it really mattered little whether I spoke truly or falsely with regard to such ventures, for my method of dealing with them made them, whether they were of trifling

value or of more, invariably profitable to many besides
myself and a blessing to the whole State."

" But, uncle," interjected another nephew, " how
could that be ? "

" You will easily see," said Mahmoud with a pitying
smile, " when you hear the sequel.   I was not so selfish
as to retain these properties in my own hands.   I
would offer them to the public for sale, and being in a
position to pay many poets, scribes, and public story
tellers who should make general the praises of the
estates in question, an active competition among
many thousands would arise to become part purchasers.
In the presence of this competition the price of a share,
or part property, would rise ; those who had bought
early would sell later to others at a profit, and these
to others again at a further profit still ; an active
buying and selling of these part properties in my
ventures thus became a fixed habit in the intelligent
people of the place, and those who were left ultimately
the possessors of the actual estates in question, whether
real or imaginary, were only the more foolish and
ignorant of the population.   Their agonized denounce-
ment of my judgment (as they wandered from one
to another attempting to dispose of their bad bargains)
was, of course, treated with contempt by the run of
able men who remembered the profits of the share
market at the inception of the business.   On this
account it was possible for me to continue indefinitely
to present for sale to the public every species of venture
which I might feel inclined to put before them : the
intelligent and successful were ever my applauders ;
the unfortunate and despised alone decried me.   And
these were, on account of my operations, so poor, and
therefore of so little significance in the State, that I

rarely thought it worth while to pay the authorities for their imprisonment or death.

" Within ten years there were no bounds to my possessions. It was currently said that I myself had no conception of their magnitude, and I admit this was true. From time to time I would pay enormous sums to endow a place of learning, to benefit the Ministers of my own Religion (and its antagonists), or to propagate by means of an army of public criers some insignificant opinion peculiar to myself or my wife, your dear aunt—whose strong views upon the wearing of green turbans by Hadjis and the illumination of the Koran in red ink are doubtless familiar to you.

" I would also put up vast buildings to house the aged indigent whose name began with an A, or others wherein could be set to useful labour the aged indigent who were blind of one eye.

" I erected, endowed and staffed an immense establishment, standing in its own park-like grounds, wherein was taught and proved the true doctrine that gold and silver are but dross and that learning is the sole good ; and yet others in which it was proved with equal certitude that learning, like *all* mundane things, is dust and only an exact knowledge of the Sacred Text worth having. But the Professors of this last science demanded double pay, urging (with sense, I thought) *first* that any fool could talk at large but that it took hard work to study manuscripts ; *second* that only half a dozen men knew the documents exhaustively and that if they were under-rated they would stand aside and wreck the enterprise with their savage critiques.

" Meanwhile I devised in my leisure time an amusing instrument of gain called ' The Cream Separator.' I paid my wretched Sultan and his Court for a law, to be imposed, compelling all men, under pain of torture, to reveal their revenues from farming or any other reputable trade, but taking no account of gambling and juggling as being unimportant and too difficult to follow. I next paid another sum to the writers and spouters and other starvelings to denounce all who objected. For less than double this sum I bought a new law which swept away all the surplus of the better farmers and other reputable men into a general fund and paid out their cruel loss, partly in little doles to the very poor, but partly also (for fair play's a jewel) in added stipends to the very rich with posts at Court : the Lord High Conjurer I especially favoured. Thus did I establish a firm friendship with the masses and with their governors and, I am glad to say, destroyed the middle sort who are a very dull, greasy, humdrum lot at the best, rightly detested by their betters as apes and by their inferiors as immediate masters.

" And on all this I took my little commission. . . .

" My children ! . . . My children ! . . ." ended the old man, his eyes now full of frigid tears, " I had attained the summit of Human Life. I had all . . . and there descended upon me what wealth—supreme wealth—alone can give : the Strong Peace of the Soul."

His tears now flowed freely, and his nephews were touched beyond measure to see such emotion in one so great.

" It is," he continued (with difficulty from his rising emotion), " it is wealth and wealth alone, wealth superior to all surrounding wealth, that can procure for man that equal vision of the world, that immense tolerance of evil, that unfailing hope for the morrow, and that profound content which furnish for the heart of man its resting place."

Here the millionaire frankly broke down. He covered his face in his hands and his sobs were echoed by those of his respectful nephews, with the exception of the third with whom they degenerated into hiccoughs.

Mahmoud raised his strong, old, tear-stained features, dried his eyes and asked them (since his tale was now done) whether they had any questions to ask.

After a long interval the eldest spoke :

" Oh ! My revered uncle," said he, in an awe-struck voice, " if I may make so bold . . . why did you leave this place of your power and return to Bagdad ? "

His uncle was silent for a space and then replied in slow and measured words :

" It was in this wise. A sort of moral distemper—a mysterious inward plague—struck the people among whom I dwelt. The poor, in spite of their increased doles, seemed to grow mysteriously disinclined for work. The rich—and especially those in power—fell (I know not why !) into habits of self-indulgence. The middle class, whom I had so justly destroyed, were filled in their ruin with a vile spite and rancour. As they still commanded some remaining power of expression by pen and voice they added to the great ill ease. One evening an awful thing happened. A large pebble—one may almost call it a stone—was flung through the open lattice of my banqueting-room and narrowly missed the Deputy Head Controller who stood behind the couch where I reclined at the head of my guests.

" It was a warning from Heaven. Next day I began with infinite precautions to realize. I knew that, for some hidden reason, the country was poisoned. Parcel by parcel, lot by lot, I disposed of my lands, my shares in enterprises, my documents of mortgage and loan. By messengers I transferred this wealth to purchases in the plains about Bagdad, my native place ; on the Tigris ; Bonds upon the Houses of Mosul and mills on the farm colonies of the Persian hills : in Promises to Pay signed by the Caliph and in the admitted obligations of the Lords of Bosra and the Euphrates.

" An Inner Voice said to me, ' Mahmoud, you have achieved the Peace of the Soul. Do not risk it longer here.' . . .

" When all my vast fortune was so transferred to Mesopotamia, I went down by a month's journey to the sea-coast, took ship, and sailed up the gulf for the home of my childhood. . . .

" I was but just in time ! Within a week of my departure an insolent message was received by the Sultan of my former habitation from the Robber King of the Hills demanding tribute. In vain did the unfortunate man plead his progress in the arts, his magnificent national debt, the high wages of his artisans and their happy leisure, the refinement and luxury of his nobles—not even their hot baths and their change of clothes three times a day could save them ! The cruel barbarian conqueror over-ran the whole place, sacked the capital, confiscated the land, annulled all deeds, imposed a fearful tribute, and had I left one copper coin in the country (which happily I had not), it would have been lost to me for ever.

" But by the time these dreadful things were taking place I was safe here in Bagdad—it was about the time the eldest of you was born. I purchased this site, built the Palace where you do me the honour of attending me (and also that of Dar-al-Beida for my wife,

your dear aunt, four days away) and have now lived
serenely into old age, praising and blessing God.

    *   *   *   *   *

" My dear nephews, I have no more to tell. You have
now heard how industry in itself is nothing if it is not
guided and sustained by Providence, but you have
doubtless also perceived that the best fortune which
Heaven " (here the old man bowed his head reverently)
" can bestow upon a mortal is useless indeed unless
he supplement its grace by his own energy and self-
discipline. I must warn you in closing that any efforts
of your own to tread in the path I have described
would very probably end in your suffering upon the
market place of the city that ignominous death which
furnishes in the public executions such entertainment
to the vulgar. If, indeed, you can pass the first stages
of your career without suffering anything more fatal
than the bastinado you might reach at last some such
great position as I occupy. Indeed," mused the kindly
old man, " Hareb, my junior partner, and Muktahr,
whom you have heard called ' The Camel King,' have
each been bastinadoed most severely in the past,
when their operations were upon a smaller scale. . . .
But we are content to forget such things.

" I have no more to tell you. Work as hard as you
possibly can, live soberly and most minutely by rule,
and so long as any dregs of strength remain to you
struggle to retain some small part of the product of
your labour for the support of yourselves and your
families. The rest will, in the natural course of things,
find its way into the hands of men like myself. . . .
And now depart with my benediction. But, stay,"
he said, as though a thought had struck him, " I
cannot let you go without a little present for each."

So saying, the kindly old man went to a cupboard of beautiful inlaid work, and drawing from it seven dried figs in the last stages of aridity and emaciation, he presented one to each of his nephews, who received the gift with transports of gratitude and affection.

Just as they were about to take their leave the youngest boy (a child, it will be remembered, of but tender years), approached his uncle with a beautiful mixture of humility and love, and bringing out a paper which he had secreted in the folds of his tunic, begged the merchant to sign his name in it and date it too, as a souvenir of these delightful mornings.

" With all my heart, my little fellow," said Mahmoud, patting him upon the head and reflecting that such good deeds cost nothing and are their own reward.

This done, the boys departed.

* * * * *

Next morning, on Mahmoud sending a slave to his cashier for the sum required to pay a band of Kurdish Torturers whom he desired to hire for his debtors' prison, he was annoyed to receive the reply that there was no cash immediately available, a large draft signed by him having been presented that very morning and duly honoured. As the sum was considerable, and as the payment had been made but a few moments before, the cashier begged his master to wait for half an hour or so until more metal could be procured from a neighbouring deposit.

It was in vain that Mahmoud searched his memory for the signature of any such instrument. He was puzzled and suspected a forgery. At last he determined that the paper should be sent for and put before him. There, sure enough, was his signature ; but the sum of 20,000 dinars therein mentioned was in another and most childish hand.   Then did it suddenly break upon the great Captain of Industry that the tiny child, his youngest nephew, who had asked for his autograph as a souvenir, was not wholly unworthy of the blood which he had collaterally inherited. . . . He wrote to the boy's father and secured the little fellow's services as office-boy at nothing-a-week.   He watched his developing talent, and was not disappointed.   Long before the lad was full grown he had got every clerk of the great business house into his debt and had successfully transferred to his own secret hiding-place the savings of the porter, the carrier and the aged widow who cleaned the place of a morning.   By his seventeenth year he had brought off a deal in fugitive slaves, taking equal amounts from the culprits for hiding and from the masters for betraying them.   By his eighteenth he had control of a public bath where clients were watched by spies and thus furnished a source of ample revenue.   Before he was of age he had astonished and delighted his now more than octogenarian uncle by selling him, under a false name and through a man of straw, a ship due to arrive at Bosra, but, as a fact, sunk off Bushire five days before.

In every way he showed himself worthy of his uncle's confirmed reliance on his commercial prowess. When the lad came of age, the Venerable Mahmoud gave a feast of unexampled splendour which foreshadowed his intentions.

For, indeed, but a month later, the old man began to fail, and in a few weeks more was warned by his physicians of approaching death.   He summoned scribes to his bed, dictated in a firm voice his Will,

wherein (after reciting provision already made—
under heavy pressure—for his wife) he left to the
youngest nephew the whole of his wealth, saying
with his last breath, " Allah! Creator and Lord!
Lest the Talent should fall into unworthy hands!"